The Lost Coast

AMY ROSE CAPETTA

CANDLEWICK PRESS

Copyright © 2019 by Amy Rose Capetta

First edition 2019

Library of Congress Catalog Card Number 2018962036
ISBN 978-1-5362-0096-6

19 20 21 22 23 24 LSC 10 9 8 7 6 5 4 3 2 1

Printed in Crawfordsville, IN, U.S.A.

This book was typeset in Warnock Pro Light.

Candlewick Press
99 Dover Street
Somerville, Massachusetts 02144

visit us at www.candlewick.com

For the weirdos

The first time I saw a redwood, I had a brand-new feeling—like discovering a color you've never seen before, or smelling snow for the first time if you were raised in a world without cold. Mom and I were driving up Highway 101 in a mostly good mood. We'd called Dad from the airport, and he hadn't sounded tragic, even though I knew he missed me. And I'd seen a dozen rainbow flags between San Francisco and this stretch of wildness. Every single one felt like a welcome sign.

I checked the GPS and saw that we had less than an hour to Tempest. And then I saw the trees and my breath was gone, my thoughts were gone, my heart tapped out a tight new rhythm.

Mom pulled over at the first opportunity without either of us talking about whether or not we should. I grabbed my phone but dropped it before I could take a picture. I already knew it would be disappointing compared to the real thing. My neck tilted and I drank in the trees. Green splashing against reddish brown. Trunks stretching and stretching until they made homes in the sky. I was staring at a thousand years, maybe two, pressed into a shape I'd always thought I understood. Back in Michigan, *tree* meant something I could run around in a single breath. Something I could take in with one glance. On the drive up to Tempest, these redwoods broke the rules.

A tree could be so alive it felt like a challenge. It could turn sunlight into long knives and stab them right through you.

"What do you think?" Mom asked, turning to me. The light brought out every drop of red in her brown hair. My hair was that color, too. But the smile Mom gave me was only hers, and I knew it too well — a thin wire of worry. She was wondering if she'd done the right thing. Even though I was the one who had looked at a map and picked Tempest. I was the one who had begged for a new life, my tears salted with guilt.

I turned from her smile, which knew all about those tears, back to the trees, which didn't know me at all. I studied cracked patterns running up the trunks like arteries. Bark the rusted red of old hearts.

"I love them," I said.

But it wasn't as simple as that. This love begged, too. It wanted me to step closer, to learn how solid the trees felt under my fingertips, but I got the sense that if I did, they would pull me deeper into the woods, and I would never be heard from again.

PART ONE

DAWN

Danny
NOW

I'm halfway up a redwood tree, wearing a dress as thin and dark as a shadow, a boy breathing hard to keep up.

"I think I liked the idea of climbing better when we were on the ground," he says.

His name is Sebastian. He's another transplant to Tempest. Besides that, what I know about him is as flimsy as the name tags they made us wear at new-student orientation. He has sprigs of dark hair. He's a nervous dancer.

"Don't you want to see the sun rise?" I call down.

It's the same question I asked a bunch of people I barely knew, when the house party thrown by some popular senior burned out, melted wax and crisped wick. Sebastian was the only one who actually listened to what I was asking. Who said *sure*. Which, I realize as I haul my stomach over a branch and pull myself to my feet, is not really the same thing as *yes*.

"Sure," he says again. "Remind me why we're doing this?"

The easy answer comes out. "We're Californians now! We can't just eat more avocados and talk . . . really . . . really . . . slowly . . . and act like we fit in." I know that I sound like I'm joking, but the truth is I feel every difference between this place and the one where I grew up. The food is better. The Mexican food is *infinitely* better. People smile at strangers. But there's a difference that I don't know how to talk about, something in the air that must have a chemical interaction with my blood. It makes me feel strange, so I want to do a strange thing to match. Like climbing a tree that touches the bottom edge of the sky. "This is a time-honored rite of passage that I just made up."

That answer peels back, and I can see the one underneath it. I don't want to go home yet. Mom won't stop asking if I hate the rental cottage, hate how temporary it feels, how it smells like burned dust and the brass beds scream when you turn over at night. I actually think the rental cottage is kind of cozy. I just didn't want to loosen my grip on the night.

I just needed to breathe in the woods.

I look between my bare feet and find Sebastian's face below me, all misery, like I've put him in a redwood prison and the only good part is looking up my skirt but he's pretty sure he has to feel guilty about that.

"I don't care, you know," I say.

"That we're both about to die falling from a tree?"

"That you know what color my underwear is."

I think it's red. I didn't pay that much attention when I put it on, but it suddenly feels relevant.

I grab the branch above me, my face pressing into the shaggy bark. It's softer than I'd imagined, and the limbs of the tree are strong, fanning out in spokes. When I reach a gap, my heart goes glossy with fear. I press off with my feet, and I am touching nothing but air until my hand cuffs the next branch and a scream drops back into my lungs, unused.

I'm not braver than Sebastian; I just want to get to the top more than he does. There is something waiting for me up there, and I won't be able to name it until I see it.

Now that I've gotten past the rough, patchy middle, the tight spin of branches near the top makes the rest easy. It's like climbing a spiral staircase into the dawn.

"Quick," I say. "We're missing it."

The treetops give way, leaving a jagged view. The gray sky is just black rubbed thin. A pale, secret shade of pink glows where the sky and the world touch.

I stop where I am and sit, my back settling against the trunk. Sebastian pulls himself up and stands right in front of me, his thighs barring the sunrise. "Sit down please," I say, and he does. Now his face is in my way, but before I can complain, the sunrise turns his hair into glory, softening each dark strand with coral and rose.

"You know what's weird?" I ask, my eyes catching on a break in the treetops, a pothole between us and the sunrise, right over the town we came from. "Being new feels a little bit like we don't exist. Like somebody in Tempest has to notice that we're here before we can really be here."

He looks down at his fingernails, which are nervously picking apart a small piece of the tree. "Maybe we can notice each other," he mumbles.

That wasn't really my point. But he looks so hopeful that I can't tell him the other half of my thought. It's too unwelcome. Too *Danny,* and I'm going to be different here. Somebody who eats avocados and talks slowly enough that people listen.

But not saying it doesn't stop me from thinking it.

We could die tonight, and it would be as easy as crumpling a name tag.

I pull my phone from the pocket in my dress. The screen's glare cuts against the soft burn of the sunrise.

"You're texting?" Sebastian asks, a whine trickling into his voice. It's not as cute as his nervous dancing, or even his half-hearted tree climbing.

"My mom likes to know I'm alive," I say. I don't owe him the rest of the story, even though it itches on my tongue.

Sebastian nods and keeps nodding until it's clear that he's working himself up to something. "Do you want to hang out? Sometime?"

I take a quick breath. He's right — what we're doing at the moment isn't *hanging out*. Nobody climbs to the top of a tree on a date. There are rituals. Rules. Tonight doesn't have ropes around it, so it's outside of everything real, a fact that leaves a sour memory-taste in my mouth.

Lip gloss, cigarettes.

"Danny?" Sebastian asks, his confidence draining as quickly as the dark. "What do you think?"

I don't know how to answer. It has nothing to do with how lovely and kissable Sebastian is. Even after all the girls I've been with, I sometimes find myself wanting to kiss a boy, and that makes it harder for a lot of people — I won't declare myself and stick to one side of a fence. I don't know how to explain that I don't even *see* the fence.

Sebastian does this nervous look-away, and his long,

exposed throat begs for my attention. This is when I should let my fingers drift toward his skin. When I would normally lean into the moment, touch my lips to his. Wind nudges me forward, urging me to do it. Yellow deepens to gold and pours in thick and heavy, and he's goddamn glowing. The moment is here.

This is where a kiss would fit.

But I can't. There is a weight making me too heavy to move. A hand pinning me in place. I'm not supposed to kiss this boy, and I don't know why. But I trust the pressure that is telling me *no*.

"Hanging out is a good plan, Sebastian," I say, voice deeper than usual, long patches of silence seeping between the words. *Almost* Californian. "Let's talk about it when we get back on solid ground. Of course, this tree is my natural habitat now."

Sebastian smiles, and I think I've saved us from death by awkwardness, but a new sound nudges me off balance. At first I assume it's the trees. Sometimes they are monumentally silent, but when the wind picks up, they creak like doors learning to open.

This sound is different, though. Fainter and farther down. *Shushshushshush* — a rain of steps.

I look past branches that took an hour to climb and would probably take about three seconds to fall past. Sebastian gives me a seasick grimace. I can finally feel the danger of what we've done together. I reach for the nearest thing that I can brace myself against, and it turns out to be Sebastian's thigh.

Below us, I see a sweatshirt hood but can't tell anything about the person beneath it, not that I'd be able to recognize someone from Tempest by the top of their head. I twist around to follow their path through the woods, but I've already lost them.

"Were you expecting someone else?" Sebastian asks with a laugh that skitters away from him.

The climb down feels longer than the one that took us up. The ground is much harder than the spongy redwood bark. I wiggle my feet back into my shoes. They're damp. My feet are damp. Everything is covered in a grainy coating of bark, like the trees have been shedding their skin.

Sebastian offers to walk me home, but I say that I'm headed in the other direction, which is true, and that my mom needs me back right away, which is also true and probably has been for hours. Sebastian gives me a last wobble of a stare and starts to walk away. Immediately, relief settles over me like the first of the tree-filtered sunlight.

I walk softly. Trees creak. Doors open.

The Grays
NOW

The mother tree is covered in mosses and ferns and saplings so bright green that it feels like defiance. The downed redwood would be beautiful on its own, but the four figures gathered around it turn it into the center of a scene painted in lace and jeans and silver jewelry, nervous breath and soft skin.

June ragdolls with her back against the trunk, legs stretched out, toes pointing. Flexing. Lelia nuzzles June's shoulder, drawing swirls that might be shells or galaxies on June's thigh with a wisp of a paintbrush, adding silver highlights to her warm brown skin, switching without a missed brushstroke to her own peachy-white ankle.

Their softness matches the morning, while Hawthorn stands at a spiky angle to it, pacing through the clearing, worrying a smoky quartz crystal in one hand. She touches the frames of her silver full-moon glasses as she stares into the stone's heart. Then she crouches and slides one finger through a swirl of pine needles. It looks like she's switching between books, unable to find the story she wants to read.

Rush stands on one end of the mother tree, bare feet nesting in moss. She turns the tree into a ship, her body a figurehead, as carved as any sea-girl who parts the waves, with swirls of dark hair reaching to the backs of her thighs. She keeps her body still and lets her voice do the roving, chasing down a song. Notes slip away from her, and she lets them go. The right ones will stick. The right ones will stay.

She sings toward the sea, because of Imogen.

This is more or less a normal dawn for the Grays, the splitting open of a new day. But without Imogen, it feels hollow and rotted inside.

Until they see another girl wafting through the forest.

Hawthorn stops moving. June and Lelia stop whispering paint over each other's skin and secrets in each other's ears. Rush stops singing.

They trade looks.

The Grays have mastered the art of looking at each other. Everything they do is heavy with meaning, like they're slipping stones in each other's pockets to keep their bodies from floating away in a riptide.

Hawthorn steps toward the new girl, but Rush surprises them all by being the first to speak. "You're here."

Rush is careful with her words, winces when the rest of the Grays talk too much. She has good reasons, but they love when her voice scratches against their ears, like it's found an itch they forgot about.

The new girl stares at Rush like maybe she feels that way, too. She has brown hair blessed with red, cut to different lengths, one side short enough to tuck behind her ear, the other hugging her jawline. She wears a short dress, dark blue as the glint on a raven's feathers. Her skin is pale in a way that says *elsewhere,* a white girl from a place where they don't value sun. The Grays notice everything about this girl that can be noticed by staring.

They drink her in.

"I didn't mean to interrupt." Her voice is jumpy, like it's used to leaping away from trouble. "I'm Danny. I don't know if we know each other. I've met a lot of people in the last two weeks. Were you at Mackenzie's party? I don't think I saw you. That's where I came from. I heard someone over here and I . . ."

"Found us," Hawthorn says. She steps forward again. When there's a single sunbeam between them, she reaches out and snares Danny's wrist, turns her hand up to the fresh stream of light. Hawthorn is trying to read this girl, to find where the truth bit into her palm and left marks. "Don't worry," she says with a victory smirk. "You're exactly where you're supposed to be."

Danny laughs, and it should be a nervous sound, but it's not. Rush can hear the music inside it. Hawthorn wants to put it in one of her mother's glass jars, the ones that line the barn in every size and shape and color, waiting for needing fingers to pry them open. The Grays want everything about this girl. They've been waiting for her.

Haven and Imogen
SIX WEEKS AGO

Haven knew that her sister was planning something big.

She always got pouncy right before a spell, like she might give you an enormous hug for no reason, or she might jump down your throat for doing something *wrong*. Her definition of wrong was always different from Mom and Dad's. So no matter what Haven did, she was always wrong.

Haven had the house to herself on the night Imogen took her backpack and went for the woods. Mom and Dad were on a trip to the Bay Area to get "real sushi" and spend the night with the friends they actually liked, the ones who thought living in Tempest was a bad joke.

Haven watched videos of a band she didn't really like on her phone so she'd be able to talk about them on Monday morning. If her friends quizzed her, she was ready. She did her homework and triple-checked the answers so nobody could say she wasn't trying hard enough. Then she erased a few of the answers so Imogen couldn't claim she was trying *too* hard. Right before Haven got into bed, she made a list of all the things she wished she had done instead and burned it with a single match.

Imogen wandered in around two in the morning — pretty normal when Mom and Dad were gone. Haven woke up for a few hazy seconds and then fell back asleep. It was when she got up in the morning and found her sister with two dark but misty pieces of sea glass where her eyes used to be that things got interesting.

The Grays
SIX WEEKS AGO

The day after Imogen went missing, they waited like nervous little kids. They showed up to their classes and jobs,
but inside, June was seven years old, hiding under the dining-
room table next to a cherry-dark stain. Hawthorn was six, in
the farthest corner of the hayloft, where the walls pinched
down to a point. Rush was even younger, the taste of the word
four as bitter as greens straight from the garden, so young that
when she saw monsters, she didn't bother asking if they were
real. Lelia was older — fourteen — sitting at her mother's side,
holding her fingers below the white-tipped nails, afraid of the
moment she let go.

On the second day, Imogen hadn't come back. The Grays
stood outside her bedroom window, which had gone as
empty-dark as she had.

The next four days, they were a fever, rushing through the
town. They visited each other on their breaks, biking along thin
margins of mountain road. Rush drove her unfortunate car
all over Tempest. They talked to Imogen's parents, her sister.

They tried to visit the hermit, but he wasn't around — he'd probably gone on one of his backpacking trips to Mount Tam or Mirror Lake. They picked at the story of what happened before Imogen disappeared, because that story was a scab, and even though it hurt, they worried the edges, needing to see the bloody scrape beneath.

On the sixth day, they knew Imogen wasn't coming back without their help.

On the sixth day, they took to the woods.

Hawthorn told them to wear candle-flame colors. Clothes that swayed and beckoned and would call someone else like them closer. June showed up in a flimsy moth-white dress cut barely to the tops of her thighs, silver sparkling at her neck and wrists, everywhere her heart sang against her skin. One side of her thick dark hair was freshly shorn, and she kept touching it, remembering how Imogen had freehanded the razor over her scalp and then kissed the velvet patch when she was done. Lelia arrived on June's arm, an unbreakable link. She was wearing boys' dress shorts and nothing else. The rest of the Grays were so used to it that they didn't blink. They did stop to compliment Lelia's makeup, the rings of smoke around each eye that summoned gold from her green irises. Rush wore a yellow tank top and ancient jean shorts, the blue rubbed to bone-white strings. She didn't feel like she'd been able to find the right outfit, but she couldn't borrow from the rest of the Grays — they wore smaller sizes than she did. Only June had a few things that might fit her, and June's style was very specific, spilling with ultra-femme flowers and prints. Rush had done the best she could with her limited wardrobe.

Then she wrote the last twelve things Imogen had said to her on her body, in places the other Grays couldn't see.

Hawthorn gathered the Grays at the center of the clearing, around the mother tree. The tiger lily shade of her dress blazed against her dark skin, and everyone told her how good she looked. She decided not to mention that she'd borrowed the dress from Ora's wash line. Sometimes Hawthorn felt as if all the best parts of her were borrowed from her mom, and it messed with her head.

It was getting dark, and the Grays gathered in a circle like it was the most natural thing to do.

"If we want Imogen back, we'll need someone with a special ability," Hawthorn said. "Scrying is too vague." What she meant was that she'd been scrying for days, scrying until her mind folded over with pain and her eye muscles refused.

"Did you try the trees?" Rush asked.

Hawthorn nodded. She only scried patterns in the redwoods when nothing else worked. She didn't want to take too much from their store of years and wisdom. But the bark had been stubborn. All it gave her was what she already knew — the shape of a girl, twisted, trapped.

"I even tried tea leaves," Hawthorn said. The rest looked at each other in a way that meant *So it's really that bad.* Hawthorn always said tea leaves were for old aunties and complete hacks.

"How can she be gone?" Rush asked. "We should be able to find her."

Imogen had always burned in a way that was impossible to ignore. While the rest of the Grays learned the language of the world around them one word at a time, Imogen had been born fluent, raw magic spilling from her fingers, slipped into the long pauses between her smiles. Imogen could set a blue stone at a girl's feet and she would find herself unable to stay away from the water. When Imogen went to the beach and sat with her knees gathered, no matter what the tide was supposed to be that day, the waves would reach for her.

Imogen was powerful.

More important, Imogen was *theirs*.

"Maybe there's someone at school who could help . . ." June said, breathless currents carrying her away from reality fast. The other Grays knew the truth about June. She was cursed with hope.

"If there was anyone else like us at school, we'd know it by now," Hawthorn said.

"What if we're ripping this new girl out of her life, though?" June asked with a shiver. "That feels wrong."

"The spell is for someone who *wants* to come," Hawthorn said. They knew the rules of using magic. *No harm* was the first. Stealing a queer girl from a happy life might not have been a cut or a bruise, but it was definitely *harm*. "We need to cast wide. We don't know how far away she is."

"What if we get, like, seventy of them?" June asked. "A whole army of new Grays?"

"She isn't a Gray," Hawthorn said, her eyes as sharp as June's athame, which June had brought, of course, the dark blade waiting in its engraved sheath inside her flowered canvas backpack. "We have the perfect number already. We just need Imogen back." Hawthorn looked up at the trees, which turned pure black at night, as though they'd been gulping the darkness. "Let's start climbing."

"You know that's not happening," Lelia said. "I don't do *up*."

June was the one who'd gotten hurt, but Lelia was the one who had decided that meant no more climbing. The fear that everyone assumed June would feel had skipped over her like a stone and landed in Lelia's heart.

"I'll do it," June said, even though today was a six on the scale of one to barely walking. The pain in her leg had the cold, heartless glitter of snow. Hawthorn held out her hands and helped June to the lowest branch of a tree.

Lelia looked up into the ragged dark, where the tops of the trees sawed into the moon-blue sky. "Nope. Sorry."

"We all need to do it or it doesn't work," Hawthorn said.

"Whoever this girl is, we need to bring her *here*," Rush said. "It makes sense for one person to draw the spell back down. Lelia can ground us."

Lelia tried to kiss Rush on the cheek, but Rush retreated quickly. The last person who had kissed her in any way — in every way — was Imogen. Rush needed to keep that feeling intact for as long as she could.

Rush and Hawthorn and June climbed, while Lelia stayed on the ground, looking up at them, spinning in circles.

"Pretty," June said as Hawthorn tossed her a ribbon.

"Rainbow silk?" Lelia called up. "Really?"

"Spells are made of symbols," Hawthorn said. "Symbols. Aren't. Subtle."

June tried to toss the ribbon to Rush, but it fell short, rippling toward the ground. When June looked down, her right leg tingled — her nervous system sounding a warning. "On second thought, we could have done this without the climbing."

"Too easy," Hawthorn said. "Don't forget the second rule."

Lelia threw the ribbon up to Rush as they silently filled in the rule. *The greater the risk, the stronger the magic.* The Grays tossed and tossed the silk around the grove, asking a question with their bodies. Asking for a girl. Beckoning her closer.

Calling out in a language only she would hear.

Danny

NOW

I sit down, right where I was standing. I cross my legs, hiking wet canvas sneakers up until they imprint on my thighs.

The girls watch me.

My breath is rough, scattering memories.

The feeling that California was the answer to a question no one had asked. The way I spread the candy-pastel map of the United States and picked Tempest in twenty seconds, without blinking. The trees, the trees, the trees. How they pulled me away from everything that made sense.

I look up and find four faces waiting. Their names were embedded in the story they just told, and now I dig them out. June, Lelia, Hawthorn, Rush. Those words dissolve, and I'm left with just two.

"The Grays," I say. "Part of me thinks you must be playing a shitty trick, and the other part of me already knows that first part is wrong."

The girl with ripples of long dark hair — Rush — shifts between me and the rest of the group. She puts her hands on my shoulders. These girls, with their touching. I only touch people when there's kissing involved. Anything else is off-limits. One of the unspoken rules. "Are you okay?" she asks.

My brain clicks through answers. "Yes. No."

"You can hold both things at the same time," Rush says. I watch her lips as she speaks — they're expertly lined and painted this black-cherry color that I can almost taste. Her face is the perfect heart-shaped kind that pinches to the delicate point of her chin. Her hands and her body are round and soft-looking, but her voice has a sandy roughness to it. When she sang, her voice was different. Smoother. The difference between polished crystal and raw. "You won't burst if you try to hold more truth," she tells me. "We're not riverbanks, right?"

"Umm, okay. True." This is starting to feel like a test I haven't studied for, like the dream where I show up to take the SAT and all of the questions are in ancient Greek or the pages are blank but everyone else has the normal test and is busy filling it in.

"You brought me here because your friend is missing?" I ask. Just to be clear.

The Grays nod. But they're not a matching set even when they're doing the same thing. There are the obvious differences: the sizes and shapes of their bodies, from wisp-tiny Lelia to broad-shouldered June; Hawthorn, who is all dramatic angles, and Rush, who is big and made of bold curves. I think Rush and Lelia are both white, Lelia with a perfectly baked California tan and Rush on the pale side. Hawthorn is Black, and June — maybe Pacific Islander?

And then there are their reactions to what I just said. June blinks at me, waiting and eager. Lelia's fidgeting, her arms over her bare chest. Rush is clearly upset. Hawthorn studies her toenails in a way that tells me she wants this part to be over. Each one has a different feeling painted over her prettiness. They're all beautiful, in ways that go all over the place, four different paths through the woods.

And they leave a space, no matter where they're standing or sitting, for the girl who's not there.

"You think I . . . can do something? To get her back?"

"What kind of abilities do you have?" June asks, kneeling in front of me, then wincing like it was a bad idea.

If they pulled me away from Michigan and replanted me here, I owe them. I grab around, wanting to offer them talents. "I have the ability to make most people in a small town uncomfortable. I'm good at surprising my parents . . . in a bad way. I disappear sometimes." I pause before the last one, but I can't see a reason to hold it back. "Also, I kiss a lot of people. Mostly girls."

June puts her hand up for a high five. I've never gotten this reaction before. Anger, yes. Silence filled with nervous blinking, yes. People trying way too hard to prove they're okay with it, so hard they pretty much prove the opposite, *yes.*

I tap my hand against hers.

"That's great for you," Lelia says, brushing down the white tank top that she must have brought with her, even though it seems to have appeared from nowhere. "But I don't see how it's going to bring Imogen back."

"Danny is here for a reason," Hawthorn says.

I'm looking for a response — for a reason — when the trees start creaking. At first it's a relief, because I don't have to say anything. Then all at once the morning is filled with the hard press of wind and the *groan, crack, wrench* of trees. That sound of doors being flung open, fast and hard, and I'm not sure I want to know what's on the other side.

"This will pass," Hawthorn says, but the wind doesn't agree with her. It rages and stomps.

Lelia shakes her head. "Blowing up the coast instead of down, too cold," she mutters. The girls bind themselves to each other with nervous stares. Hawthorn reaches out her arms, and Lelia and Rush hold on to her. June sits back, stretching out her leg, breathing hard and leaning against Lelia.

I stand up. Alone.

The wind demands that I sit down. It grabs my dress in its fists. It snarls my hair, bludgeons my skin.

"Danny," June says, her voice half-eaten by a gust. "Where are you going?"

"Stay with us," Hawthorn calls. Not an invitation. An order.

But I'm walking too fast for their words to snare me. I fight against the wind, throw my whole body into resisting it. It dies, and I stumble. The woods go back to normal so suddenly that I wonder if the wind was invented.

The silence of the early morning makes itself whole again, like cracked ice freezing over smooth or bones knitting clean. The trees, no longer wavering, reach up tall and straight. Fog stands around them like trapped breath.

So much fog that I am close before I see.

Lying there is a boy.

He is pinned to the ground, a sharp branch through his

chest. It must have been taken by the wind, falling hard, fast. I walk closer, in a brain-fog as thick as the one swirling around me. I keep moving until the details are too much, and my feet put a stop to it. There is bark shattered at the edges of the branch where it pierced him, blood weighing down the fabric of his T-shirt.

"Sebastian." His name comes out quick and broken. I want to be wrong. But those are his smile muscles gone slack. His long neck, thrown back, sunshine touching it softly, the way I almost did.

The way I *didn't*. Because I felt something bad coming, stepping on our heels.

The Grays catch up, leaving a space between themselves and Sebastian. They rake in breath, grab for each other's hands.

"How . . . ?" I ask, one word standing in for a hundred variations on the same question. *How did this happen? Where did that branch come from? How could this be possible, when I was up a tree with him less than an hour ago?*

"That wind did it," Lelia says. "And that wind was *not* normal."

Hawthorn tugs sharply at Lelia's wrist, and Lelia shuts up.

"What is that branch?" I ask.

"Widowmaker," Rush whispers.

I walk the rest of the way over to Sebastian, slowly. I kneel next to him. I don't look too closely at his chest. Instead, I focus on his eyes, as if they might snap open at any second. I lean over his lips, waiting for a breath to bring my hope back to life.

The Students of
Tempest High School
NOW

Nobody really knew the boy who got impaled, so nobody can get their hands around the fact that he's dead. Instead, everyone spends Monday morning unsettled in their auditorium seats. The principal gives a short, dumb speech. "We are all devastated by the loss of a student who should have been with us today." The sentences are empty boxes where details about the boy should go. It's like burying a casket without a body in it, which the students of Tempest know something about.

"Sebastian DeAureli will be missed," the principal promises. But most of the students never met Sebastian. He was like them, but he wasn't one of them.

Both those facts are unnerving.

The bell rings, the recorded sound fuzzy. The students get up, most of them gathering armloads of books for their classes and going about their normal day as if that will save them from having to think about a dead classmate. Some skip classes to smoke smudgy-sweet pot and make out in the scruff of woods past the soccer field. For others, gossip is the only cure.

One girl leans toward another at their lockers in the concrete shade and says, "The weird girls found him."

"Of course they did." The second girl vines her body against her boyfriend's side.

"Nobody could make a redwood tree lose a branch and hit that kid," the boyfriend says, trying to sound reasonable.

The first girl closes her locker with a metallic snap. "Yeah. But." They all know that something strange happened in the woods; they just don't know how to talk about it. Silence spreads like blood, warm and sticky, until everyone turns away from the dying conversation.

Danny
TWO YEARS AGO

It started in darkness, long nights with my eyes pressed closed. I whispered that I belonged here, alone in my narrow bed in our narrow town.

I told myself out loud, so I would believe it.

On the worst nights, I would get out of bed and walk the hallway to the kitchen, and sometimes open the back door and take a few steps outside. My feet told me all about the differences between worn carpet, chilled tile, living earth. I looked out into the darkness of the backyard, and it matched the darkness in my head. When I went back to bed, my legs twitched and my thoughts writhed and I had to sleep with ten blankets on top of my chest to hold me down.

Mom called my dad and said that I was turning into someone who couldn't bear to stay still, like him. They went on a few dates right after college, but it never turned into love and marriage. It dead-ended in me.

Dad was always traveling for work, and I remember Mom laughing like my night-wandering was a practical joke he'd played on us, leaving his genes to ripen inside of me and grow into dark, restless flower.

To anyone outside of our family, it started in October of sophomore year. I had a feeling about where I was supposed to eat lunch one day, and it pulled me toward the picnic tables in the courtyard, where sunshine tumbled down. I walked out of the cafeteria with my saran-wrapped sandwich and found Mia Livesy sitting on the last inch of a bench like the rest of it was crowded with people, only she was alone.

And crying.

Mia and I weren't really friends, but she looked at me sometimes like maybe she wanted to be, so I sat down and put my hand on her shoulder. Just perched it there, ready to take flight at the smallest sign that she didn't want me.

Then it was salt in my mouth, skin under my hands where Mia's skirt and her shirt didn't quite meet.

It was done as abruptly as it started, and Mia sank back into crying, deeper this time. Her tears fell into cupped hands, and when I tried to catch them instead, Mia told me in a ship-wrecked voice, "Get away from me. *Go.*"

I ran on numb feet.

I hadn't been the solution to Mia Livesy's crying. I had been the reason. Or at least part of it.

That night, I slept for the first time in months, all the way through the night, and woke up with my fingertips perched on my lips. There had been a smile there. The memory of it was as warm as ten blankets.

If I was going to keep doing this, there had to be rules, and the first one wrote itself: no crying girls.

Danny
NOW

I give the Grays space after the morning assembly, but I feel every inch of it. I walk by myself, thinking about how today might have gone if the widowmaker had stabbed empty ground. Would Sebastian have played it cool as soon as we were in public? Would he be walking in step with me right now, trying to touch my hand?

My new locker is at the very end of one of these open-air hallways. I dump my books, distracted by the pine-and-dirt taste of the air, the way it comes and goes as it pleases. Who designs these California high schools? Do they actually trust the students not to wander away between classes?

Why?

A girl steps into the frame of the far end of the hall. Her features look like they're specifically angled to catch the light. She's wearing a white T-shirt and a black jean miniskirt, and somehow it doesn't look standard or boring on her, like she's doing it to blend in, more like she's turning herself into a canvas to splash paint on later. Her arms are covered with bracelets and her fingers are stacked with a rainbow of rings. I name carnelian and rose quartz, amethyst and clear quartz before I run dry. The thing that I notice first, last, and a few times in between is her hair. It curls in a way that leaves air between each loose, lazy spiral. It's a red a bottle could never conjure, a red that jealous girls would kill to get.

I walk right up to her, because sometimes I can do bold, even when there's a pretty girl involved. *Especially* when there's a pretty girl involved.

"Hey," I say, grabbing for the books that seem like they're about to spill out of her hands. "I'm Danny. Made in Michigan, but I'm really glad to be . . . not there." I wince at how slick that wasn't. It feels like getting stuck halfway down a waterslide. "Are you new?"

The girl stares. Except she's not looking at me, not really, more like the patch of air in my general vicinity. When I try to catch her dark-brown eyes, I can't. But it's more than that. Their surface is frosted over. Like fog in the woods.

Or two shards of brown sea glass.

"Are you okay?" I ask. "Is this about Sebastian? I can walk you to the counselor's office." The vice principal gave me directions during orientation in a pointed way, like she knew about my history.

It occurs to me now that she probably does.

The girl's misty eyes roam, never settling, and I'm fighting the urge to back away slowly. Something about her feels strange, but that must be in my head, which hasn't calmed down since I found Sebastian.

"At least let me walk you to your next class," I say. I'm trying to stay grounded after what happened in the woods, and flirting with this girl is as good a lifeline as anything I can imagine. But it leads me right back to the last person I was flirting with.

The dead one.

The bell rang a while ago. We're the only ones left in the hall. I grab the girl's books, because now I've promised to help, but I've also promised Mom I won't ditch class under any circumstances.

"What's your next class?" I ask.

The girl doesn't say a thing.

I check her notebooks. Western History. Geometry Two. Beneath the class title, I see a name carved into the hard plastic, an imprint that she's worked in, one point at a time, no lines to connect them.

Imogen Lilly.

I drop her books, and they hit the concrete with a hard slap. When I scrape them up again, the girl doesn't move to help, doesn't ask me what's wrong with me or roll her sea-glass eyes. She's still looking at the hole where I used to be.

I slide her books back into her empty arms and run.

The Ravens
THE PAST TEN YEARS

The birds fly over the knot of people and their possessions called Tempest. They pick at it. They collect, gather, sort.

Known, unknown.

Shiny, dull.

Good, bad.

Help, hurt.

Lelia has eyes green as late-spring grass. Yellow hair with colorful strings in it. Watches the birds, neck back, chin poking the air. Pins a name to each one of them. The birds like being noticed. It gives a shine to the sliced black marbles of their eyes.

They bring presents.

Buttons first: a round red cranberry, a beveled jade, a wart of gold plastic. They drop the buttons where they know Lelia will walk. They follow with slick wingbeats. They cut the sky above Tempest with their bodies and scream when it heals over.

Lelia loves the buttons. Sews them onto a favorite jacket, wears it everywhere. They bring more. Scraps of people's lives. Paper and ribbons. Metal and porcelain.

Lelia gives back what she can. Not the pretties in the glass house. Nothing in that house ever comes outside, except for Lelia. So Lelia feeds them stories, and they stuff themselves full on the misery of what it means to be so human, so young. They might not be able to pick apart the words, but they know the song of sorrow. It is sharp in the throat.

They fly in and out of years.

Lelia. The birds.

And then, after years of walking alone, Lelia collects friends. Brings them to the birds like presents.

Shiny, shiny, shiny.

There is one in particular. Copper from above. Dark flash in her eyes. Water glitters when she walks near, turns to diamond. She talks to the birds as if they speak the same language. She keeps watch over her flock.

They fly in and out of years together.

The birds. The witches.

Danny

NOW

The Grays are waiting for me around the corner. Lelia and June stand back to back so they're holding each other's weight. Hawthorn looks down at her knuckles, working a bit of sharply scented balm into her skin, and Rush is staring at me like she never stopped. There's hope and fear in it. There's something bigger, older, deeper than whatever she thinks about me.

I spin around. Imogen must have gone back the way she came, because she's already gone.

I'm officially cutting class now, six periods into what should be a brand-new school year. A shiny new Danny.

"You told me she was *missing,*" I say.

"She is missing," June says. "We haven't seen Imogen in six weeks. She's been like . . . that."

Whatever *that* is, it's big and not easy to break through. Still, I want to yell at June, at all of the Grays. They brought me here because their friend won't talk or look them in the eye? She could be depressed. In some kind of medically recognized fugue state. She could be so pissed at the world that she doesn't want to connect to it anymore. There are options. Things that could explain this.

Words that can be used to put a box around whatever is wrong.

But I know from experience that boxes aren't always big enough. And I don't want to treat the Grays the way people treated me for so long. I want to believe them, the way nobody bothered to believe me.

"I'll help you," I say. "If I can." It sounds really nice, but in a way it's the most selfish thing I've ever said, because I want to be close to the Grays. Something about them pulls me in, holds me in place.

Their responses come in a tangled heap.

"*Thank you*," June breathes.

"It took you long enough," Lelia says.

Rush stares and stares, underlining the importance of what everyone else is saying with her hard gaze.

Hawthorn asks, "What can you *do*?"

The Grays
NOW

They pull Danny into the woods. There are no old-growth trees right near the high school, but there are still redwoods, scruffy upstart ones, punching their way up, fighting to own a patch of sky.

Lelia gives Hawthorn a highly refined *This won't work* glare.

"It's good enough for now," Hawthorn says.

But the real problem isn't the lack of proper trees. It's the lack of time. The Grays have never had to find someone's magic in a hurry. It's always been a careful process, searching out a path to a place no one's ever been. But here's something they know: the longer Imogen's gone, the less likely it is that they'll get her back. And then there's Sebastian, killed by a wind that Lelia insists was unnatural. Killed on the day that Danny showed up.

One girl unreachable, one girl finally here, one boy dead.

The gossip at school wasn't completely stupid this time. The Grays see the same pattern as everybody else. They just read it differently.

"How are you doing?" June asks, patting Danny's shoulder. Danny pulls away like June's fingertips are live flames. "Sebastian dying can't be easy, especially since you knew him."

"A tiny bit," Danny says, working her backpack straps off her shoulders and dropping the bag to the ground.

"Time isn't the only way to know someone," Rush says, the wind tugging at her hair, the words trickling into her heart.

Imogen had been in their lives since middle school, but if you measured it that way, it sounded like any other friendship. Like it was just a matter of having someone to sit with at lunch or go to the movies with on the weekend. Loving Imogen made everything brighter and deeper, like staring down into the sea and finding a world layered with strangeness and beauty. Losing her turned the world shallow.

The girls sit down in a circle. "So . . . how do we do this?" Danny asks.

Hawthorn takes the lead, and the Grays take it for granted that she will. "Normally I would say that you should start with whatever sort of working calls to you, try a bunch of different types until you build your own. I guess I should get this out of the way. There's a reason we're called the Grays and not the Wicca Club of Tempest High School." Hawthorn rushes through her explanation, pausing only to summon more breath. "It's not like we make everything up ourselves. But the craft is a braid of traditions, and a lot of those are tied to the places they came from. The way I see it, you can't swap out one for the other and expect it not to matter. Every place has its own rules, and Tempest is *highly* specific." Hawthorn lays her palms against the dirt, like she wants the ground to give her strength, like she might even ask it to speak.

"All right," Danny says. "So what happens next?"

But the Grays don't know, because Imogen would be the one to answer that question if she were here. She was good at schemes. Always leaping to meet new challenges and take the universe's dares.

"We thought you would come knowing your abilities," Lelia says.

"Be nice," June says.

"Not in my repertoire," Lelia shoots back. "And that's why you love me."

June rolls her eyes, although the Grays know that she really does love Lelia for her bristle, her bravado, her absolute lack of fucks.

Danny nods back and forth between Lelia and June. "Are you two . . . together?"

"Grays don't date each other," Hawthorn says, and Rush stops breathing.

"I don't date *anyone*," Lelia adds.

"I have an idea." June scrambles out of the circle and goes to her flowery backpack, which she dropped at the base of a tree. She tugs the zipper, shoves aside a few schoolbooks, pulls out a knife as long as her forearm, grips it by the redwood handle, and rushes back to the circle. The weight and darkness of the knife draw everyone's eyes. The sharpness forces Danny's breath into a new shape.

"Whoa," she says. "I don't go in for blood rituals."

Lelia smirks. "If we want to bond with you, there are better ways."

Danny's eyes flick wide.

"It's official," Lelia says. "I like messing with her."

"Okay, so this knife is special," June says, tugging Danny back to the point, literally and figuratively. "It's not meant to cut anything except air. I have a smaller knife for spell bits. String, candlewicks, that kind of stuff. This is for rituals."

"And there's a ritual to find what my magic is?" Danny looks like she wants to believe them.

She looks like she doesn't believe them at all.

"It's not really like that," Hawthorn says, slipping off her beaded sandals, connecting the soles of her feet to the sun-freckled ground. The other Grays follow, until everyone is shoeless but Danny. She stubs toe to heel, pushes off her dark-blue Keds. Hawthorn pushes her glasses up into her hair, lodging them in her curls, because the kind of sight they help her with is not the kind she needs right now. "You can prob-ably do a lot of things — cast spells, read the world differently from other people. But you're here for a reason. There's some-thing you can do that . . ."

"We can't," Rush finishes.

June nods, because Rush said the thing that they were all thinking. The unbearable thing. It means they can't bring Imogen back without trusting someone who doesn't know her the way they do.

June inches closer to Danny, who doesn't back away but clenches along invisible lines all down her body. "I'm going to make a few signs over you, to see if I can open up your intu-ition," June says. "I don't want to tell you what your magic is. I want to show it to you and then have *you* tell *us*."

"So . . . you're going to slice into my psyche?" Danny asks with what the Grays are starting to think of as her trademark smile. It's a nervous, flimsy thing, bright and fluttering, a kite somebody lost their hold on.

June swings the knife back and forth slowly, inches from Danny's face.

Danny's smile dulls.

And then it's gone.

Danny
THE PAST TWO YEARS

In the supposedly haunted bathroom stall during the winter dance, hooking up with Hallie Carpenter, whispers of a ghost keeping everyone away while we gasped each other's breath, worked our hands into the impossible spaces between tight dresses and skin.

Jenna DeWalt running her pen up and down my leg for an excruciating, perfect forty minutes while we watched a movie about the French Revolution in World History. I waited for her after school, wordless. We went back to Jenna's house and put on another movie, a romantic comedy, no beheadings. The lights on, then off. Jenna hovering over me, then pressed under me. The sound of bored straight people falling in love breaking around us like waves.

A friend of a friend from another school who heard I would kiss any girl who needed kissing. Ginger-mint breath and brown hair pinned up, with a few wisps at her neck. We sealed ourselves together in her car, pretending that no one could find us in the overlook near the state park, like the windows weren't just glass.

My mom looked at me when I came home, that narrow-eyed tweezer look, like she could lift this truth out of my soul as easily as she used to take splinters out of my palms.

It would have been one thing to show up for dinner with a forever-girlfriend. Mom would have been able to go to the basement and find a box for that, even if it wasn't the first one she reached for.

This was different, so I kept it quiet. Which led to rule number two: no one who likes to talk more than they like to kiss.

Danny
NOW

I come back to June's face, smiling, expectant. She drops the knife to the ground between our knees.

Her eyes are a soft, mossy brown-green. Her smile does things to me. Not the ones I usually experience when being smiled at by a cute girl. These are softer, like the clouds stretched out beneath an airplane.

"What did you see?" she asks.

"Not magic," I say. "But I'm used to being a disappointment."

"Disappointment," Rush whispers. "Bitter and pulpy. It's like chewing on a Popsicle stick after the Popsicle's gone."

I have no idea what Rush is talking about, but I'm starting to gather, one soft-spoken comment at a time, that maybe her brain doesn't work like everyone else's. Which makes me want to pull her aside and ask her more. I'm not sure about my brain, but my body definitely seems to follow its own rules.

I don't think the rest of the Grays would appreciate being splintered, though. They seem like a package deal. So I give Rush a nod that I can feel all the way down my spine and say,

"Yeah. I don't want to turn into anybody's sour old Popsicle stick."

Hawthorn presses her lips together. "I think we should take her to the hermit."

"Yes!" June claps, a quick little burst. "Hermit time!"

I have visions of an old man with an extra helping of beard, possibly to make up for a distinct lack of teeth. A man who lives in the woods, communing with trees and animals because he's reached the limits of human bullshit.

I like him already.

"When the moon's risen, meet us at the mother tree," Hawthorn says. "The fallen one, where we met last time."

I grab my bag and shoulder the ridiculous weight of five textbooks. "And moonrise would be . . . around . . . ?"

Hawthorn sighs as she digs her toes back into her sandals. "Nine thirty."

It does not go unnoticed when the Grays tramp back to
eighth period straight from the woods, June Ocampo twirling a great big knife.

It started ironically at first, the way everybody calls
them *the weird girls,* because everyone is a little bit weird in
Northern California. To most of the students at Tempest
High, *normal* is about as great as *syphilis.*

But there's the way they named themselves the Grays,
like they can claim an entire color. The way they never show
at parties, but sometimes people catch them running naked
through the woods after midnight, shrieking. How June wears
lacy baby-doll dresses but also necklaces that look like tiny
bird skulls. And Hawthorn keeps that smelly leather notebook
tucked into the pockets of her homemade dresses. Plus, every
time Lelia Boyle catches someone calling them *the weird
girls,* she corrects them with a shout loud enough to rattle the
lockers in junior hall. "It's WEIRDOS." Then she smiles a
switchblade smile and brushes her shoulders, like she's proud
of herself for some reason.

And there's Imogen. She's the only one most of them like, or maybe not *like*, but feel drawn to. But something's wrong with Imogen, and nobody can figure out what. Wrong enough that they don't even want to make up stories about it.

The senior girls gossip about Sebastian instead, and watch the weirdos roll their eyes and close ranks. Lelia is the only one who responds, hooking her thumbs under the floral suspenders she wears with a black muscle T before she hisses. It becomes a game. Get Lelia Boyle to hiss at you. Ten points.

And then the cloud of Grays shifts, and they notice someone standing at the back of the group, one hand bolted to the other elbow, hiding her left eye behind the sweep of an uneven bob. The new girl has gotten swallowed up by the Grays.

Her look is equal parts girly and grunge, green tights with runs in them layered under a short black skirt. The obligatory flannel, though she's wearing it shrugged off her pale white shoulders to catch the sun. Anyone who's noticed her would say that she doesn't quite stand out and she doesn't quite fit in. Only a few of them even know her name.

Danny Something.

On any normal day, her arrival would have been important, but on *this* day, they lost track of her. Now she's standing in the middle of the Grays, looking like she took a wrong turn and ended up on a dark road she doesn't know the name of.

Danny
NOW

I take my time getting home, which is a challenge, since the *town* part of Tempest is so small. A single strip of Highway 101, so short that you can watch it taper into the trees in either direction. There's a huddle of storefronts, old-fashioned bells making a big deal every time a door opens.

I stop into the diner and study the menu. They're not beholden to one category of food — they serve everything from chorizo omelets to sandwiches that are mostly sprouts to garlic-drenched pasta. I order the pasta to go. I'm begging forgiveness for the class I skipped, something I hope Mom will never hear about. Balancing a Styrofoam tower in one hand, I cross 101 and walk the last quarter mile.

An old-school neon sign, faded by daylight, marks Tempest Gardens. The cottages are quiet at midafternoon. Most people staying here are tourists, packing up cars filled with kids and coolers, coming back around dusk with hiking gear and bodily odors to match.

Mom's car is, of course, missing. She hasn't said much about her new job at a medical facility an hour away, which means she probably hates it. That fact settles on me like summer dust. Thick, hot, uncomfortable.

I fling open the screen door to cottage nine, put down the food, and peel off my shirt to take a shower.

Then I realize that Rush is there. For one stupid second, I think it's for me. She wants to talk to me in that rough voice, or sing to me in the smooth one I heard in the woods.

I crash hard into the rocks of reality. She's wearing an apron over jeans, and intense blue rubber gloves. Rush is cleaning the room where I semi-live.

I grab my top off the floor and put it back on over the black bralette I've been wearing under everything, the one that promises lacy fun. I cross my arms. Defending my boobs from — what? The fact that Rush isn't looking at them? "How did you get here so fast?"

"Broom," she says.

She doesn't signal, in any way, that this is a joke.

"Oh."

Rush points out the window at the parking lot, edged by cabins with lace curtains, trees crowding in like bodyguards.

"I have a car," she says, and there it is, in its rust-nibbled glory. A piece of the bumper missing. A crack in the windshield spidering up from a corner. Duct tape on door handles. I can't see the spells that she uses to hold it together, but I can't imagine anything else would.

Rush crouches to clean one of the brass beds with some kind of solution. It smells like chemical death and stings my eyes even from a distance.

I don't know what to say, but I know it's my job to come up with something. Rush is the quiet one.

"Saving money for college?" I ask.

"One dirty bed at a time," she says quickly, a melody strung through the words. It almost distracts me from the awkward truth that she's cleaning the bed I sleep in. The bed I dream in. The bed I sweat and toss and do *other* things in, when I'm alone and I need to feel something good.

Words bully their way out of me. "It's funny to see you here after . . . you know . . ."

"The woods? The wind? The boy with a hole where his heart used to be?"

"The way you talk is different," I say. Rush looks up at me sharply, as if I've poked her in the side. I don't know how to tell her that *different* is the best compliment I can give. I definitely don't want her to think that I'm making fun of her, so I stumble even deeper into the pit of my own feelings. "I was going to say that I love it, but that sounded like way too much in my head, and people are always telling me I'm too much . . ."

"I have synesthesia," she says, attacking the long, skinny bones of the brass headboard. "Lexical-gustatory, which means I taste words. Not all of them. And when people talk fast enough, it doesn't really give my brain time to do it." She slows down on the last bar, scrubbing at a spot of dull black, but it looks like she's somewhere else entirely. A place where dirty beds don't exist. "Synesthesia," she says again, slowly. "I'm lucky that word tastes good. It's like cold, cold chocolate ice cream."

She starts cleaning really hard, and I'm feeling weird about the fact that I'm standing here doing nothing. "Do you need any help?"

She looks up at me. Dark hair. Shining blue eyes. Almost amused. "You want to help me clean your room."

"I want to help you find your lost friend, but I'm not sure I can do that. Please accept scrubbing instead."

"Imogen would call that a false equivalency," Rush says, and goes back to her little cart for more death spray.

"So . . . no."

Rush crouches again, but this time she doesn't clean. She sits back on her heels. "I need you to find her."

Not *we*. Rush has peeled herself apart from the rest of the Grays, if only for a moment.

I follow an instinct to the point of no return. "You and Imogen were a couple?"

Rush nods slowly. I remember Imogen all at once, the girl we're actually talking about. The one with the red hair and the winter skin and the hollow stare. She probably used to look at Rush as intensely as Rush is looking at me right now.

She probably used to do more than that.

"I need to finish in here," Rush says, like she's all up in my thoughts.

Is she?

This girl is a witch. Maybe that's what her magic is. Does she feel me wanting to step closer, to set my hand where her glove and her shirt don't quite meet? Soft fingers on soft skin. Standing close and quiet, a river of unspoken questions.

Part of me is frantic, afraid that she knows.

Part of me is buzzing with hope that she does.

I go outside the cabin and wait around the back on a decorative little bench that it's possible nobody has sat on for ten years. Every time I try to walk away, I loop right back, like I'm tying knots.

When I open the door an hour later, Rush is gone, and the furniture gleams.

Imogen and Rush
EIGHT MONTHS AGO

They were in love.

It was possible but not true for a long time. And then they were in Imogen's room one charcoal afternoon in the middle of winter. In Tempest, winter was a season of dark, endless water, the world outside lashed with rain.

It felt like summer had forgotten about them.

"We need to make our own heat," Imogen said. She pulled her body on top of Rush's and braced herself. A joke. Until it wasn't. Rush was as hot as coals from sitting so close for so long. They kissed with the quick burn of paper, and once it started, they couldn't stop. Rush and Imogen ate through hours like that, mouths and bodies pushing against each other in a constantly changing balance, the kind of kissing that Rush had always believed in with the same fervor that she believed in magic.

Their past shifted as they told it to each other, revealing itself in layers, a slow undressing. The times that they'd met each other's eyes and laughed when no one else knew what was funny. That afternoon when Imogen had heard Rush play the cello, once upon a time. All those nights they'd stayed up later than the rest of the Grays, Imogen getting Rush to split a cigarette with her, but only because she'd brought a jar of honey to cure Rush's throat after the smoke ripped it up.

Imogen kissed Rush's throat.

Rush said she was ready.

"For what?" Imogen asked.

"For . . . you."

"You can't be," Imogen said. "We just started."

"I think we started a long time ago," Rush said. "We just figured it out now."

But Imogen wanted to be careful, because Rush meant so much. Because she didn't want to rip at Rush's heart. Because there was no amount of honey you could pour on a wound like that.

"Okay," Rush said. "We'll wait."

Danny

NOW

Walking through the woods that night, I text Mom every five minutes.

I'm alive. I'm alive. I'm alive.

I told her that I was meeting up with people who could potentially become my friends. I didn't use the word *Grays*. She doesn't know, specifically, about Hawthorn and June and Lelia and Rush. What would I tell her? They think they're witches? *I* think they're witches, but I'm not sure? I might be a witch, too, but don't worry?

Nope. Nope. Nope.

I text the same words, like a heartbeat.

I'm alive.

Mom asks about my day even though we went over all this at dinner.

Did your teachers spring any tests on you?

I used to tell her the grades I got on every quiz. The feelings I had about every friend. People said we were so close.

Loved that garlic pasta! Yum!

Mom abuses exclamation points, trying to convince me that everything is good. But I can't seem to move my thumbs.

You are so thoughtful today!

She doesn't know how much it stings to be reminded that I'm not a thoughtful daughter *most* days. Besides, it isn't even true. Today I skipped a class. Today I stripped in front of someone, even if it was by accident.

I shove the phone into my pocket.

Walking deeper into the woods is surprisingly easy. The moon blasts hard enough to create its own sort of noon. I want to spread a picnic blanket and stretch my body out, basking in the silver that's been swapped for gold.

The mother tree sprawls at the center of a clearing. The mother tree is dead, technically, fallen and tipped sideways, but there's so much life taking root on its soft bark: silvered ferns and even tiny trees.

June and Lelia sit in the moon-shade, using tarot cards to play a game like it's a regular deck. I think Lelia's winning, but maybe she just likes to crow. Hawthorn is sitting cross-legged on the tree's long body. She has her face turned toward the sky. She's counting stars. Or renaming them. Trying to move them with her mind, maybe? Moonlight drips down her long throat, studs her natural hair like fairy lights.

Rush is standing at the end of the tree. I walk around to join her and find myself staring at a claw of roots, the place where the tree used to become part of the earth. It's taller than Rush, ringed by spikes of tortured, twisted wood, and rotting toward total darkness at the center.

Rush is singing into that darkness. A whisper song in a

minor key. A mourning. For Sebastian? Or Imogen? For whatever they had together? Is that gone, or does Rush want to get it back?

Is that why I'm here? To save their love story?

To save all of them from having to live without this girl?

I can feel Imogen like she's nearby, watching. Now that I've seen her at school, I can draw her face up when I close my eyes. I open them fast because I don't know how to save her.

My breath thickens in my throat. That must be how the rest of the Grays feel every second.

Rush and I are caught together, staring at the end of a ripped-up tree that has more presence, more pull, than Imogen did standing in the hallway. Even death has more life in it than her body does.

Rush sings, and I wait for her to stop.

She sings and I don't ever want her to stop.

My arm brushes against hers. She shiver-jumps. When she looks at me and smiles, the beckoning darkness of the tree roots is overpowered. Some people have smiles like explosions. Rush has one like a flower, soft and uncurling. "You came."

"Yeah," I say. "I'm all yours."

There is a moment where it's just the two of us before Hawthorn slides her bare legs down the mother tree and the rest of her follows, thudding to the ground. "Come on," she says. "The hermit isn't far."

"But I was winning!" Lelia cries, throwing down the Queen of Cups.

"Imogen's gone," Hawthorn says in a *Do I really have to remind you* tone. "Nobody's winning."

The Trees
NOW

There is magic in the woods tonight.

The trees feel it.

The trees feel everything.

This is how redwoods survive. Yes, their bark is unrotting. True, they block the sunlight so other trees can't choke their view. But that's not enough to weather centuries. The trees know every whisper, every footfall, every prick of wind. They keep a catalog of beauties: the lemony tang of bark, the glossy red of heartwood, the long glide of forever, and the dart of a season. They know what happens in sunlight and darkness, and what slides through the spaces between.

Magic is moving fast tonight.

Some of it is trapped in human bodies.

The trees do not bother with human names, so much learning and forgetting. Humans might as well be fireflies. They live a breath longer. They love a spark brighter. Blink, and they'll be gone. But there are other things in the woods.

Things that linger, that settle, that *stay*.

The trees know *those* names.

Death is one.

Danny
NOW

We tramp through the woods, following some path I can't see. The tops of the trees are half a mile above us, but for some reason I feel claustrophobic. "So how is seeing some old guy in the woods supposed to help?"

"What makes you think the hermit is old?" Lelia asks.

"What makes you think he's a guy?" Hawthorn says, hot on her heels.

"Well, he *is* a guy. But it's best not to make assumptions," June says. "For instance, Lelia is nonbinary."

I stare for a second, my brain frozen.

"Don't worry—she gave me blanket permission to tell people," June adds.

Lelia presses her cheek against June's shoulder as they walk, which is pretty impressive friendship choreography. "I kind of hate having to tell people," Lelia admits, "but I do want them to know, so June is helping me out."

"Right," I say. I know a little bit about nonbinary genders, but where I grew up, people have barely wrapped their minds around *gay*. I've been waiting to meet anyone who can handle more, and here they are, and I'm the one who can't keep up. "Uh, what are your pronouns?"

"*She* is fine, at least for now," Lelia says with a shrug. "And while we're here, I'm not allo either."

I silently thank the internet for teaching me that allosexual is one end of yet another spectrum, with asexual at the other.

"You're ace?" I ask.

"Gray ace," she says with another shrug.

"She's a double gray." June beams.

The whole thing seems so ordinary and everyday to them. These new maybe-friends of mine can't feel that they're an earthquake, rattling everything into new places, breaking the ground open.

"I'm a girl," June says. "Of the girly variety. And I like girl-types."

"She's pretty proud of that triple crown," Lelia says, the kind of teasing that's pure sweetness.

"I prefer the term *femme as fuck*," June says, practically shouting it. "And I'm proud of anyone who isn't afraid of who they are," she says at a slightly more normal volume. "It's not an easy thing."

Of course, as soon as I think California is an earthly paradise made of rainbows, the Grays tell me it's not that simple. Still, I can't help but say, "It might not be easy anywhere, but it's different here. I can feel it." Like seismic activity. "What about you?" I ask Hawthorn.

She turns back to me, hair bobbing as she steps. "Ora gave me endless speeches about how you shouldn't be too eager to label and box people."

"Ora?" I ask.

"Hawthorn's mom," June pitches in.

"Really?" I figured from the way Hawthorn was talking that Ora was her older sister. And I've never met anyone who uses their parents' first names. Is that a California thing, too? Or just a Hawthorn thing?

"Ora is my mother, and she is very, very real," Hawthorn says. "She thinks if you get really attached to a single word for someone, that's not good, because how can a whole person fit inside one word? And then maybe they find one that fits better, or they use more than one, or they never find one that fits — that's the natural flow of things. But I happen to think that words are important, too. I mean, Ora calls herself a witch, right?" I didn't know this about Hawthorn's mom, and it makes me want to ask a mess of questions, but I nod and wait, because Hawthorn doesn't seem finished. "Yeah, so . . . here are my words: I'm a bisexual Black witch with a pretty strong lean toward masculine folks."

"They can be ridiculously cute," I admit.

I find myself back in the tree with Sebastian, except the tree is swaying, creaking, groaning, the winds too high.

"Rush, I think it's your turn," I say, trying to steady my voice.

She looks down at her feet, matching one word to each step, intent on the rhythm, in her own little Rush world. "Fat. Queer. White." Then a skipped step, and she finishes the list off with "Cello player."

"So, what word fits in a way that makes you happy at this very moment?" June asks me. "Lesbian? Bi? Pan? Queer?"

I grab for that word — and not just because Rush said it. It feels right to me. Less limiting in who I am, who I'm with. No solid lines around the definition. A way of saying *different* that doesn't have an apology folded in. "Yeah. Queer."

I couldn't imagine saying that in front of anyone before the Grays. Not even Mom. A lack of homophobia is so far ahead of the game where we're from. I wince, remembering how upset she was when she found out I'd been kissing girls and hadn't told her, like she'd fallen down on the parental job. I didn't know how to explain that it was about more than who I was kissing. It was about *me*, everything about me. And my mom might be okay with *gay*, but *queer* would make her cringe.

I'm shaking with the power of it.

I take out my phone and send a quick text.

I'm alive.

Hawthorn brings us to a stop.

We've reached a tree that's no taller but much wider than the ones around it. That's not the real reason it stands out, though. The tree looks like it's been burned from the inside, hollowing out a space that reaches about three times as tall as I am. It probably looks like an adorable hollow during the day, but at night it's a dark scream.

"*That's* where the hermit lives?" I ask. "They let him do that to a tree?"

"It's been that way for at least a hundred years," Lelia says, making her way around the trunk. "When the pioneer types first got here, they needed a place for their animals, to keep them safe, so like any good conquerors, they found something ancient and beautiful and set it on fire to solve their problems."

"Why didn't that kill the tree?" I ask.

"Because redwoods are badasses," Lelia says.

"They wear their hearts on the outside," Rush adds, running her blue-polished fingertips down the bark like rain.

"What Rush means is that everything about a redwood that's alive is in the first few inner inches of xylem and phloem and all that stuff you probably don't remember from biology class," Lelia says.

"Lelia is our resident tree expert," June says, her round cheeks glowing with pride.

"Wait until you see a redwood with a faerie ring around it," Lelia says. "It starts with this upward growth from the roots — it looks like a dark cloud of twigs and branches — and it creates a full circle around the trunk of a tree. People used to think you could walk through a faerie ring and end up in some kind of enchanted world. You should go in one sometime, Danny. It's terrifying, by which I mean the best."

"Lelia knows everything about plants and animals, anything in the natural world," June says, still in best friend bragging mode, which makes me weirdly jealous. I don't think anyone has ever talked about me that way.

"No humans or domesticated creatures," Lelia adds. "I'm sorry, puppies are cute, but they are *not* magic."

There's that word again. "I know we're on some epic hunt for what I can do, but . . . what do all of *you* do?"

Hawthorn points at each of them in turn, starting with Lelia and June, then moving on to herself and Rush.

"Naturework, athame, scrying, song." As if those are as solid and possible as lesbian, bi, pan, queer.

I want a word like that.

I want a word that's *mine*.

"What about Imogen?" I ask. "What could she do?"

"Everything," Rush says.

"Whatever she wanted," Hawthorn says.

Two different answers, and both impale me with jealousy. Whatever power these Grays think I have, it can't be as big as that.

"Imogen has an affinity for water," Lelia says.

"Wait, I thought *you* did naturework."

"Overlap is allowed," Hawthorn says, suppressing an eye roll. "This isn't a sports team; we're not taking positions."

Lelia pulls out a joint and lights it with the metallic snap of a Zippo. This is quickly becoming a normal sight — people here seem to smoke as much as they drank back in Michigan. After a quick inhale, Lelia hands the small bony joint off to Rush and lets out the smoke. "I mostly look for portents in nature, and pieces to use in spells. Rocks, herbs, flowers, bark. Imogen was . . . *is* a water witch," Lelia says, fielding a frustrated head shake from June. It's way too soon for past tense. "Water is in a lot of things, specifically people. I mean, humans are basically waterbeds with feelings."

"Imogen has a lot of sway with people," June confirms as she passes to me.

I take the joint and slip the wet paper between my lips, invite the burn into my lungs. I've only done this a few times;

I'm not an expert. The smoke tastes like someone lit Mom's spice cabinet on fire, and I let it out with a cough. "I'm sure Imogen's sway over people had nothing to do with her being this really gorgeous, pale redhead who makes being a witch look cool instead of something that sends people running for the nearest torch."

I hold the joint out to Hawthorn, my arm extended. The pinprick of red glows fiercely, like it's trying to burn a hole through the world. The smoke travels from my lungs to my brain, where it clouds my worries, giving them weight.

I shouldn't have said that.

The Grays want me to find Imogen, not have opinions.

Hawthorn waves off the joint, and I pass it back to Lelia, starting another round.

"Ora said something like that once," Hawthorn says, pulling her arms tight across her chest even though it's barely cold out. Of course, cold is all a matter of perspective, and mine was forged in zero-degree winters. "When my mother met Imogen, she said, 'That girl might have magic in her heart, but never forget how much of her power is handed right to her by other people.'"

Rush takes the joint, but she doesn't smoke. I realize that she's just been staring at it, quietly, and passing. "Yeah," she finally says. "People love Imogen."

"The hermit has his own kind of power, not really magic," Hawthorn says. "It's this way of looking at people and seeing what they're hiding from themselves."

"Is he going to come out here or . . . ?"

June nods me toward the tree. "He waits for people to come to him."

I walk through the opening. It's much cooler inside the tree, as if this place has its own weather. A blunt darkness fills the space, and it takes me a minute to get used to the subtle shades hidden inside of it. When I do, there is nothing but a bike, a set of dirty clothes, and a dampness that won't leave me alone.

I mogen baked things and brought them to his tree. Lemon bread. Hazelnut cookies. Chocolate praline. He got high on philosophy with June and more traditional substances with Lelia. Sometimes Hawthorn came back from his tree with mussed hair and a *Don't you dare ask* look.

Rush asked the hermit where *home* was, the word tasting of slightly burned toast. He gave a rambling backroad of an answer, from an abandoned degree in psychology at UC Santa Cruz to a hometown in Virginia. Rush hummed songs for him, ones that sounded like blue hills at twilight.

On a bright day when they were all in the woods together, he asked, "Do you folks want to see my party trick?"

The Grays looked at one another, silently debating. Imogen stepped forward, having been voted the spokesperson with a round of nods. "As long as that isn't a southern way of saying your penis."

The hermit laughed and grabbed June by the waist, spinning her around in an impromptu dance. "I can look you in the eye for ten seconds and tell you something about yourself that nobody else knows. Maybe that *you* don't even know."

"Me first," Lelia said, cutting in.

He steered her around the clearing, a smooth box step. "You don't hate everybody half as much as you used to."

Lelia scowled, but the hermit had already taken some of the sting out of it.

He turned back to June. He looked into her mossy-brown-green eyes, one finger beneath her chin. "You tell your parents that you believe in God, and you tell your friends you don't, but you haven't decided yet." June thumbed the hollow at her neck, where a small gold cross was supposed to live. Her very devout Filipino Catholic mother would worry if it wasn't there, which was why June put it back on every day before heading home. Her parents didn't seem to mind the Grays, or June's room filling up with crystals and herbs, as long as June joined them at church every Sunday. June lived in fear of the day when they noticed she wasn't really singing along with the hymns. She was too busy trying to figure out if the magic she felt when she was out in the woods with the Grays was the same as the magic her mother felt in that big, dark room filled with shuffling people and the smell of incense.

Hawthorn was running away from the hermit's tree, hell-bent on leaving before he got to her. "You are as lovely as twenty sunsets put together!" he yelled at her fast-retreating back.

She turned, dark eyebrows rising above the silver frames of her glasses. "You said it would be something people don't know."

"You're as sad as twenty birds in a tiny cage," he added.

"You said it would be something *I* don't know."

Hawthorn walked away before the hermit could really figure her out.

Rush was sitting on the ground, ankles crossed. She looked up at the hermit, letting him gaze down into her blue eyes as if he was trying to do a trick dive.

"You're a little bit in love," he said, the words dipped in apology.

"With who?" Imogen asked, but Rush didn't answer. *Couldn't* answer.

"Your turn," the hermit said to Imogen, shaking her off the subject.

Imogen met the hermit in the middle of the clearing. Instead of staring back at him, she looked at the trees. The ground. The tiny patterns in the skin on the backs of her hands, the ones you had to squint for, the ones that looked like shattered glass.

"You're afraid of your own shadow," the hermit said.

Danny
NOW

I don't think the hermit's coming," I say. But it's more than that. This place feels emptied out, scraped.

"We have to wait," Hawthorn says. "He's coming back."

"He should already *be* back," June says.

Lelia is looking around inside the tree, as if the hermit might be hiding somewhere. Everyone else stands outside, waiting uncomfortably as she kneels and checks the little pile of clothes, dampness gnawing its way up her jeans. She puts both palms flat against the ground. "I don't like this water."

"Why?" Hawthorn asks.

I can hear how hard she's working to keep her voice steady.

"It doesn't belong." Lelia lifts her fingers to her lips, licks them. "It's . . . it's salt water."

"Please don't mess with me right now," June whispers. "We saw a dead body the other night. This is not the right time, okay?"

"I'm not making anything up!" Lelia snaps. "I'm paying attention, being present. That's what witches are supposed to do, right?" She glances at Hawthorn for backup, but Hawthorn has turned away from the rest of us, her hands snagged in her hair, the muscles of her back clenched like she can't find a way to breathe out.

It occurs to me that maybe I shouldn't have gone back to the woods with the people who were there when Sebastian died. I don't know what's happening, but I know that the Grays are afraid.

I text my mom.

I'm alive.

She drops the exclamation points. She starts to question.

When will you be home?

Are you still with those friends?

And then the question marks fall off a cliff, and it's just

Come home soon

"I can't stay out here forever," I admit.

The Grays look at one another with a sort of tremble. I feel my guts tighten, as if their collective worry has reached into me and taken hold.

"All right," Hawthorn says. "We'll have to do this fast. We can't wait weeks or months for your power to show itself. There's a ritual," she tells me, and I already don't like it.

"The fog dance is a rite we came up with a long time ago. We've all done it," June reassures me.

"So what's the problem?" I ask, because they're all looking cagey.

Lelia steps up. She is, among other things, the bad-news bearer of the group. She doesn't seem to take any glee in it — it's more like it's a chore that she's the best at. She claps a hand on my shoulder. "There's a small chance that you'll get lost in the woods and you won't find your way out."

I think about the slippery spaces between redwoods, how they all start to look the same. The miles and miles of name-less streams and endless groves. "Don't they have rangers to keep people safe?"

"The Lost Coast covers hundreds of square miles," Lelia says. "Even with a few rangers, it's mostly non-human territory."

I think about what it would mean to get lost in a place like that. Freedom, at first. Then a slow trickle of fear.

Hawthorn slips a notebook out of her dress pocket. I didn't even know her dress *had* pockets. The leather looks so soft that it reminds me what leather really is: skin. There are stones sewn into the cover, worked into braided leather inlays.

"What's that?" I ask. "A . . . ?"

"Don't you dare say spellbook," Hawthorn says with a pen in her mouth. She's talking around it as she whips the cap off. "This is our chronicle." In handwriting as spiky as thorn-bushes, she writes *Danny's Fog Dance*.

"Spellbooks tell you how people have done magic in the past," June explains. "They're . . . pre-made. Magic is like love. You see how other people do it, you have the stories and instructions they leave behind, but then you have to figure out how *you* do it. It's not one-size-fits-all."

"We won't be far," Hawthorn says, scrawling as she speaks. "Just stay with the fog until it spits you out."

I don't ask what to do if something goes wrong, because I want to be braver than I am. I want to be whatever Imogen was to them before she got lost. The kind of person they'd go to any lengths to get back.

Rush is there at my side. I didn't even know she'd moved from her spot by the opening of the tree. "The fog can get a person lost," she says, "but sometimes lost is where you need to be for a while."

"Wandering off into nowhere is one of the few things I'm good at," I admit to her.

"You're not going *nowhere*," Hawthorn corrects. "You're heading toward a truth that you can't see when the normal world is clouding things. It can get in the way of you seeing your magic."

"I'm walking into a literal cloud to get unclouded?" I ask.

"One more thing," Hawthorn says, her words dripping with *I know you're going to hate this.* "It's a skyclad spell."

I look around at the rest of the group, inviting them to help me out. The Grays look at each other instead of me. Not a good sign. I pull out my phone. I'm getting a solitary bar of service, but it's just enough for me to look up this word. *Skyclad* means, literally enough, clad in nothing but sky.

As in naked.

"You're kidding," I say. "I thought this wasn't an elaborate hazing of the new girl, and you pull this?"

"It's important," Rush says.

"Necessary," Hawthorn amends. "Clothes are part of the everyday world. They're getting in your way."

"Don't worry." June points behind me at the open entrance of the tree. "There's a dressing room."

"An *un*dressing room," Lelia says with a snort.

Hawthorn cuts her off with a single slashing hand gesture.

The night pries at my worries, and I slip my shoes off, shake my short stubby ponytail out. The wind gives my hair a quick finger comb. If I was feeling a little bit stoned from Lelia's joint, the dull sweetness leaves as I step back into the maw of the enormous tree.

The world outside shrinks to a whisper.

The world inside grows and grows, until I hear every scratch of air against bark, and I feel the tree *lurch*.

I shrug out of my T-shirt and work my skirt down. I'm naked in the dark sway of this place, shaking hard. I can only remember shaking like this once. It's definitely how a first time feels.

I run out of the tree, into an empty forest under a star-pinned sky. The Grays are gone, but the parts of me that are usually hidden are still grateful for darkness. I don't feel that twitchy need to cover myself with my hands. I slow to a walk, the trees shifting my body taller, quietly reshaping me. Soon I'm stretching my arms high. Running again to test the bite of wind on my skin.

And then I see the fog seeping between the trees, breathing toward me, a low constant sigh.

It's around my ankles, pulling me in.

It's around my entire body, cloaking me.

I can't see myself anymore. The distraction of my skin is gone, and I'm melting away. Whatever I thought of as *Danny* is suspended in droplets. Still there but loose, different.

I don't know how I'm supposed to find my magic. Or how I'm supposed to use *that* to find Imogen. So I think about what I do know. The Grays, who connect me to her, a living tether, making it feel like she's here with me. As present as the sky. As everywhere as sky.

It feels the same as when I walked out of my classroom last year and made it to the highway. The floating certainty. The haze of need. But this time, there are no rules trying to hold me in place.

The Trees
NOW

A new magic is awake.

The trees feel it. The trees feel everything.

Some secrets stay close to the trunks of the redwoods. Others have been carried away. Like the bones. The bones are gone, and the trees fear that an important story left with them.

Too much has been hidden, and here is finding magic.

The trees reach with long branched fingers. The one who carries fresh magic looks up as they clamor and crowd. But she is too busy with her fog, wrapped in its clammy embrace, and they do not know how to reach her.

Words are not the way they speak. There are other languages, though. Weather, sky, soil. Wind and time.

They look for a new way to whisper. They pick another magic-girl, the one with a song always trapped in her throat.

And they make the forest play for her.

They curve wind, creak wood.

She opens her mouth and lets out three notes, stepping-stones from here to somewhere else. She sings them as though she is running her fingers over smooth bark, mindless and soft, over and over.

Danny
NOW

I walk through fog until my body dissolves and my feet are cloud. I spill toward Imogen. Her presence is strong, a pulse throbbing under skin.

But feeling her near and reaching her are two different things. I push forward, my breath straining and my heart going wild. I have no boundaries, only blood and magic racing, building, trying to reach her. And something larger than her.

I am close.

I am close.

And then . . .

I lose that sense of nearness, that delicious, infuriating *almost*.

The fog spits me out, just like Hawthorn said it would.

The Ravens
SIX WEEKS AGO

One day, copper-girl goes into the woods alone, and when she comes out, she is changed. Dull. Water sits flat as she walks by, does not whisper in eddies and curls. Her hair still shines red, but it is a flat shine.

The glow they seek comes from inside, burns through.

The birds fly over the woods in case copper has dropped something, hoping they might pluck a shiny soul from the ground and bring it back to her. They search and search, and one day they find a girl walking, a copper girl whose eyes flash dark.

The birds land and look at her, shifting on their pebbled legs.

Not the same girl.

She glares at the birds. Then she tries giving them a smile, buried bright, her shine covered with dark earth. The birds want to dig at her until they have the rest. They are hungry for shine.

They fly toward her. She screams at them.

The ravens consider leaving Tempest. One of their witch-flock has gone dull, the others are leaking sorrow. But when they circle the edges of town, they do not want to untie themselves. They are part of this knot. They cannot leave without letting the witches go.

The witches are known.

The witches are good.

The birds scream at one another.

Help. Help.

Danny
NOW

I'm looking around in circles. I lost her. It's like Imogen was swept away by the fog, while I was dumped out here.

Why?

The question breaks into pieces as the Grays run toward me, a tumble of skin in four different shades.

They're naked.

If there was any bit of fog left in my body, it clears as I stare at the Grays. I drink in curves and angles. I blush at unforgiving beauty. And then I wince away, like I've been staring too long at the sun.

I close my eyes, and in the darkness, I hear music. It takes me a second to realize that Rush is singing.

The same three notes, over and over.

June hops up and down, clapping her hands. "Danny followed the exact path we did the last time we were in the woods with Imogen. She came to the spot where we saw her before . . ."

Before they lost her.

This is where I lost Imogen, too, or at least the feeling of her. But not entirely. There's still a trace. I describe all of that, as best as I can, with words that feel like they can't possibly contain the whole truth.

Lelia is wearing her eternal frown, but Hawthorn pinches the stem of her silver glasses, which I guess she gets to wear even when she's skyclad. She looks at me like I'm something rare.

"You're a dowser," Hawthorn says.

It's a word I've heard before but never really paid attention to. "Don't they find water?"

Hawthorn takes a deep breath and looks set to give the definition, but Rush beats her to this one, words tripping to get out. "Dowsers have searching magic. They find what's hidden, precious, out of reach. A lot of the time that means water. Some look for oil or gemstones. Forgotten graves."

That last one sends a swarm of imaginary spiders over me.

June touches my arm lightly. "What's the thing *you've* been looking for?"

In Michigan, it was girls to kiss. Then I started going farther, searching harder. Looking for something that I've only caught in gasps: the first time I said *Tempest,* when I tipped my neck back to take in the redwoods, when the Grays stare at me like I am something they need. When Rush stares at me like I am something she needs, even if it's for all the wrong reasons.

The feeling of Imogen in the fog, so close.

"Dowser," I say.

And the word shakes.

And the world shifts.

PART TWO

DAYLIGHT

Imogen and June
EIGHTEEN MONTHS AGO

They were the climbers, always headed up, bark under their bare feet, a not-falling prayer on their lips.

June knew that she had to look carefully if she wanted to find the right trees. Most redwoods resisted the idea, their branches starting a third of the way up massively tall bodies. She and Imogen made a map of beginner climbs, trunks with low access and evenly spaced branches. Soon they were testing much larger trees. "Way out of our league," as Imogen liked to describe them. June loved that moment when her toes reached a branch they had no business reaching. Most days, that was enough. Most days, they didn't believe they were going to make it to the sky.

But every time June came back to the ground, it got harder to stay. She didn't really fit there. Not with her family, even though she loved them. Not with her girlfriend, who started their relationship with a flood of all-night kissing sessions before her interests narrowed to one thing: a move to San Francisco, where they could find a cramped apartment and live on the glory of takeout and parties. Not even with the

Grays, who seemed deeper into their magic than June was, wading around in power while she played with a very cool-looking but essentially useless black knife that she'd found at a tea-and-tarot shop in Santa Cruz and picked up like it was a missing piece of her body.

She tried to carve sigils with it, but that felt like passing notes to the universe and hoping it paid attention. June wanted magic to tease the universe apart, to show her the parts of it she didn't already know. She wanted to cut and see the muscle and blood, the slippery organs, the parts that most people wouldn't look at.

Maybe June insisted on looking deeper because she'd been sick when she was younger, the kind of sick that required long hospital stays. A rare West Coast case of Lyme disease had taken two things: the concept that June's immune system would fully recover, and her patience for everything but the most honest parts of life.

She broke up with her girlfriend and spent the next week wandering around the woods in a haze of disappointment — until one day Imogen led her to a spot with a riot of birds and squirrels high overhead. "There's a whole other reality up there," Imogen said, pointing at the thick weave of branches that closed above them, creating a sort of blanket, only letting through a mist of light. "In the tops of those trees. A canopy world."

"I want to see it," June said.

"Of course you do," Imogen said, like that had been the whole point.

June used a flowery headband to strap her athame to her thigh. It was too big to fit into a pocket, too dangerous to keep in hand.

Imogen understood why June was bringing the athame. She was the one who always said June had a strong, clear third eye. She encouraged June when she talked about the possibilities of that knife, when she carted it everywhere, waving it in a slow, careful dance. Imogen believed in June, in the deep parts of her that no one else saw.

The tree they had picked was the definition of impossible. It stretched so wide at the base that it made June's mouth fall open. It tapered and tapered almost to a vanishing point above their heads.

"Look," Imogen said, pointing to a sapling next to it with a crown that reached the lowest branches of the massive tree. The one June had started thinking of as *hers*.

June knew that if she waited too long, she would never let herself climb. She took a running start at the small tree, free-climbing hand over hand, her feet scrabbling at the bark, chips flying. The little tree swayed with her weight, bending as if she were leading a dance. And, just like when she was dancing with a pretty girl, the rest of the world blurred around June, leaving only what was directly in front of her in sweet, sharp focus.

She leaped, and for a single second, she was flying. But she met the massive tree too hard. Her right hand didn't find the hold she'd expected. Her fingers ripped bark, and it splintered into the white spaces under her nails. She got a single second of lift by pushing with her toes. Her legs glimmered with pain. She reached up for a branch, but she must have misread the distance. Nothing waited above.

While June was falling, her knife sliced the air, and her pinned-open eyes caught a glimpse of another place, a murk-and-mistlight place filled with dark towers made of fog where the trees should have been.

June met the ground. The only thing that existed was pain. It was loud and simple. Not like what she'd seen the moment before, a whisper of a place that she was already convincing herself didn't exist.

"It's okay," Imogen said, and at first June thought that Imogen was talking about her leg, which was *not* okay. But then Imogen was looking into June's eyes, her dark ones sparking with fever, and saying, "I saw it, too."

Danny
NOW

After the fog dance, I thought everything was going to change. When I wake up, the world is even more aggressively normal than before.

I glaze my eyes and make it through my classes with minimal trouble before it's time for my first shift at the after-school job I promised Mom I would get. My workplace, a little shack off the highway called Coffee Gods, is only two parking lots down from the school. The manager hands me a green half-apron. Last night, I was swimming naked through fog. Now I'm learning how to wrap day-old muffins and where to find the almond milk.

"Most of our customers drive up," says the manager, a girl who looks half a second older than I am. "If you get a walker, don't make them wait too long even if you have a line on the other side."

The other new hire, Courtney Something, nods as if the universe hinges on this information. As if planetary orbits will be interrupted and stars will fizzle out if we forget.

"Do you think you're all set?" the manager asks.

Courtney nods. I'm less sure. I've only been half listening. There is something buzzing in my head.

The feeling of milky air on bare feet, bare everything.

The slipping-away of Imogen.

That word.

Dowser.

Would my entire life have been easier if I'd known about that word? Would I have figured it out on my own, or would I have pushed through without it? The questions make me dizzy, like I'm standing on the cliff's edge of some other version of my life, looking down.

My phone buzzes. I reach for the open mouth of my bag.

"No phones," the manager says automatically.

"Yeah, that's not going to work," I say. "I have to check in."

"With your parole officer?" Courtney asks.

I can't tell if she's joking or if she actually thinks I'm a juvenile delinquent.

"My mom."

Mom is upset about the time I spent in the woods without checking in, the time lost to the fog. Last night, after I got in, I told her that my phone lost its charge faster than I thought it would. I reminded her that I hadn't come home late, and I'd stayed in Tempest the entire time.

Mom let out a hard exhale, like she was trying to chase the paranoia out of her chest. She told me she was overreacting.

I agreed.

Which officially makes me the worst daughter in California.

The manager tells me that I can check in with my mom, but all other texting will be punished. Who else would I text? I can't imagine the Grays using cell phones. They probably write letters to each other in old-timey script.

The manager leaves us to deal with the afternoon crowd. With only two people in the little shack, it's easier to move. Courtney spins around seamlessly in black yoga pants, packing fruit and ice into the blenders, while I scoop dark-brown grit into filters, the smell traveling straight past my nose, waking up my brain.

It wafts past the memory of last night and sticks on the sight of Sebastian, blood soaked through his T-shirt, eyes staring up at nothing when they should have been looking at me.

A glossy black car pulls to the window, and I take an order for two mango sunrise smoothies.

This is fine. This is doable.

Less than an hour later, I hear two motorcycles pull into the parking lot. When I look out through the walk-up order window, I see that they're the old-fashioned kind with a skeletal look to them, mostly metal with a kiss of chrome. One of the riders is welded out of sharp angles, the other full-blown curvy. Fingerless leather gloves grip handlebars. Two pairs of boots — one studded and leather-tasseled, one that would look more at home on a long hike — crunch into the gravel. The taller girl pulls off her helmet, revealing red cheeks stuck with blond hair.

"Lelia?" I ask.

"No," she says. "I'm Lelia's slightly-less-evil twin."

I wait for her to smirk, confirming that this is a joke.

"You have a motorcycle license?"

She rolls her rich green eyes. "And a dad who never grew out of collecting toys. Can we move on?"

My eyes slip to the other rider. *Rush*, I think, right before she pulls away her helmet in a one-handed motion, shaking out her long dark hair and proving me right.

"Our girl here does *not* have a motorcycle license," Lelia says as she throws her arm around Rush's shoulders. "She has something even better. A rebellious streak."

Rush burns bonfire red, but she doesn't deny it. I hadn't thought of her as the rebellious type. Or the blushing type.

"I thought you drive that old car," I say.

"The Deathmobile?" Lelia asks in a way that makes it perfectly clear the Grays have baptized it. "Yeah, we don't let her drive anyone around in that thing."

"There's nothing wrong with my car. But these *are* more fun," Rush admits. She gestures to the bikes.

"So. Uh. Can I get you something? A mango sunrise? Some muffins for your joyride? I've heard it's not a real joyride without muffins."

I wince. Courtney looks at me like there might be something medically wrong.

"We think you need a dowsing rod," Lelia announces. "To find Imogen."

I can't believe Lelia came right out and said that in public. But there's something satisfying about the way Courtney leaves us alone now that she thinks we're up to something witchy.

"A dowsing rod?" I ask. I have a vague idea of what that is. "You mean a big tuning fork to wave around?"

"Something like that," Rush says.

"It was Rush's idea," Lelia adds, like she can hear the surprise rattling around in my skull. "But I have somewhere we can go to get started with it. I guess I couldn't wait." She puts her fingerless gloves on the counter, hard, startling Courtney, and leans through the order window, sticking her head inside of Coffee Gods and looking around with a proprietary kind of stare, like she might buy the place later. Or rob it.

"Do you get off work soon?" Lelia asks.

I glance over at Courtney, who is dutifully combining frozen strawberries from several plastic containers. They *thud, thud, thud* as she gives me a tight-faced look.

I want a dowsing rod.

I do not want to lose this job, the last shred of Mom's trust, and possibly the whole new life I asked for.

"Not really," I say. "Two more hours."

Lelia and Rush nod at each other like this is what they expected. They're going to leave me here. I can feel a trapdoor plummet open in my heart. Maybe they won't bother to come back.

Lelia stomps to her motorcycle, showing me the back of her leather jacket, scratched with white letters: *The Witch Your Mother Warned You About.*

"I'll take one of those muffins," Rush says.

She inspects the list of baked goods by the order window, peeling off her own ancient leather jacket. No mottoes splashed across the back; instead it's got moon phases stitched in silver. Rush works her way out of a green flannel layer, tying the sleeves around her waist, a quick knot tugging at her white tank top. It becomes a very not-innocent version of hide-and-seek as I take in her plum-colored bra straps, the first dip of her breasts. The fabric rides up on one hip, exposing a spot above her jeans.

Stop running your eyes all over Imogen's girlfriend.

I'm supposed to bring Imogen back. I *know* Rush wants her back. This is every flavor of wrong.

Yet I can't unglue my attention from that spot on Rush's hip. I've waited forever to meet a girl who doesn't treat her body like a natural enemy. Someone who moves through the world like there's more than the troubled surface.

She looks up and catches me noticing her, which was inevitable, since I wasn't really hiding it. Her eyes gleam under thick dark brows as her lips pinch to a point. They're freshly glossed, and I can smell black-cherry sweetness.

"I . . . um. Do you know what flavor you want?"

Rush smiles at me, way too sudden. "The one that's good enough that every time I say the word *muffin* I taste it again."

Lelia snorts. She might not be watching, but she's definitely paying attention.

My fingers shake as I reach for the basket. It's nothing, just a baked good that I didn't even make. But I don't want to get this wrong. I don't want to get anything wrong with the Grays.

This is about the Grays.
This isn't about you and Rush.
There is no you and Rush.

My fingers run over saran-wrapped muffins, closing on an espresso chocolate chip. I think up and reject ten flirty comments. I've never held myself back like this before. Never slipped a leash on my feelings and *tugged* every time I wanted to get closer. When I unwrap the muffin, it releases the smell of butter and coffee, crumbs flying everywhere. I put it on a thin paper napkin and hand it to Rush.

She snatches a piece of the sugared top, opens her lips, and slides it onto her tongue. She chews for a second. With her eyes closed. Her long hair swishes as her mouth works over the bite. "Yep. That's the one."

Rush can't be flirting with me, so my mind opens every drawer and flings them upside down, looking for another explanation. Maybe Rush is desperate to feel every little thing, since Imogen can't feel anything.

Rush wraps the rest of her muffin in the napkin and sticks it in her jacket pocket, hands me cash. Then she and Lelia straddle the motorcycles, bringing them to life, throaty and restless. Rush hums, the high notes layering over the roar. She curves out of the parking lot, leaving music like a choppy wake.

I've heard those notes before: Rush sang them in the grove last night.

"Hey," I call after her. "What's that song?"

But Rush is too far away to hear me. I think about chasing her — slapping pavement with my Keds, running down the highway after a motorcycle. My impulse around Rush is to be reckless. But the last time I left the place I was supposed to be and ran toward the road, it didn't go well. Courtney frantically asks if I've started on the orders for drive-up customers. I blink and notice a line of five cars that has somehow built up. I ask Courtney to repeat the orders. I make a smoothie and watch my hands on the shivering blender like they might turn into birds and fly away.

Rush and Imogen
NOW

Rush thought about going back for Danny at the end of her shift, but there's something she has to try first. She waits for dark and then walks through the woods, keeping her eyes down on the silver laces that spike her old hiking boots. She pushes her hair back with each step. It's always trying to spill forward, to have its way. When she's playing her cello, it leans over the scrollwork as if it wants to tangle in the strings, to wind itself around her bow, nestle in the hollow spaces inside the instrument.

She wishes she could play tonight. Not the way her parents want and expect her to play. Not even the way her sister used to play. Her own Rush way, finding the notes and then setting them free, one by one. Listening as they turn faint and soft and disappear on the horizon.

But tonight is for singing.

There is Imogen's window in the distance. Outlined in a white frame, scribbled in with darkness.

Rush wants Imogen to see her, standing there in a white camisole that Imogen liked because of the way it breathed loose, gapping around Rush's curves, what Imogen called her *lavish girl glory*.

What was she wearing, the last time they . . . ?

Rush can't remember.

It feels like a tiny betrayal.

She thinks of Danny, with her quicksilver smile and her obvious staring, leaning over the counter at Coffee Gods.

Rush stays safe within the border of the woods. The Lillys would not like a visit from her now, or ever. They hate all of the Grays, but they hate her with a special force that parents reserve for secret relationships. Rush pictures Imogen's bedroom, and a small avalanche of memories and feelings come with it.

Imogen has to be in there, doesn't she? If she's blank, where else would she be?

Rush's mouth opens and sound leaves her, traveling over the yard. She doesn't add words, because the flavors can get muddled and bitter; they can bleed together in your mouth until you want to spit them out. Purely formed vowels leave only a linger of sweetness in the back of your throat.

This is a song Rush made herself. She's tried singing at school; she's tried at the mother tree, in all of Imogen's favorite places. Maybe home will be stronger. Maybe the bed where they—

Rush cuts herself off.

At first she wanted to keep the feeling of Imogen preserved. But that means pretending they were perfect together, that every kiss was as good as the first one. Now when she feels a sliver of the past it lodges under her skin.

Rush's voice wavers, and she tells herself to keep steady, to stay focused on the future.

Bring Imogen back.

Then they can sort things.

Then they can find *perfect*.

Notes climb from her body. They build a ladder to Imogen's window. They let themselves in.

Imogen stirs. She hasn't woken like this in weeks, and she feels sick with a combination of headache and prickly muscles. Something is dragging her away from her body, back where she came from. Something else is tugging her toward the window.

Her feet graze the floor, and the sense of *home* floods her. She's never liked this place, but it's worn its way into her body, her mind. Imogen knows every line of the dresser under her fingers. She can feel out the knots in the hardwood floor with her toes. When she gets to the window, she knows where the moon will drape shadows. There's a faraway shape in the woods, right past where the yard ends.

Rush sees Imogen at the window, and her breath catches. Then she sings even harder than before.

Maybe having Danny here is helping her, bringing Imogen closer somehow, and Rush's song can do the rest.

Lights go on downstairs.

Rush swears into the darkness. "Fuck, fuck, fuck." That word tastes like biting her own tongue.

More lights flick on, and a figure appears like a paper cutout in the back-porch light, long arms wrapped around a toothpick body. It could be Mrs. Lilly or Haven. Imogen said that the day Haven turned thirteen, she made a list of everything in the pantry and crossed off items, one by one, until she only allowed herself to eat rice and plain chicken and steamed vegetables. Mrs. Lilly poured approval over Haven's dinner plate every night, like it was something she could fill up on.

Rush hated that story. It reminded her of her own mother telling her that she needed to "watch herself" if she wanted to be picked for orchestra spots. Her father, grabbing cookies away from his daughter and then stacking them up three at a time because it "didn't matter" if he ate them.

"Is someone out there?" The voice is young, freshly cracked open.

Rush wishes she had a song for Imogen's sister, something to help her right now. At least Rush has the Grays.

Haven is completely alone.

Rush remembers what that feels like. Before Imogen found her in the cemetery, Rush's closest friend was a cello.

Rush takes a step forward, into the pale wash of the moon. She lets Haven see that it's her. Which is not very smart, considering how much Mr. and Mrs. Lilly hate her.

Haven stares at Rush like she's a bad thought come to life. "You're not supposed to come here anymore," she says, as weak as a shove from spindly arms. "Nobody wants you here."

Haven's words scratch Rush's heart, or maybe they open a scratch that was already there. Rush steps back into the protection of the woods. Imogen's window is empty, and Haven locks the back door.

Which means Danny is the only hope Rush has left.

I've made it through another shift at Coffee Gods. Almost. I keep looking at the time on the register, glowing at me like a promise. 4:15. I'm going to restock the fridge and then wipe down the espresso machine while Courtney takes the rest of the orders. She makes smoothies with precision, her fingers sharp on the buttons. I push carton after carton into the back of the fridge. I check the clock again. 4:17. There can only be so many minutes until this ends and I'm far away from almond milk.

Back home. Or at least in the cottage.

Safe.

No cutting class. No skipping out of work. No disappearing from the places I'm supposed to be. No flirting with girls I'm not supposed to like. When I make it through a day, I tell Mom, and she smiles like I should get a gold star for not ruining my own life.

The sound of the blender falls away, and Courtney's back turns to stone.

"Could you *please stop*?" she asks. "Or at least learn a song that has more than three notes?"

I didn't realize I was humming. But there they are, warm on my lips, the notes that Rush sang in the woods on Monday night. And then again, as she rode away from me.

Have I been humming all day? Through classes, passing periods? While I was pulling every shirt out of my suitcase this morning, trying to decide which one was good enough for the inevitable moment when I saw the Grays?

I try to push the notes down, but they don't want to stay put. They keep working their way out of me, rising and rushing past my defenses. I am all soft breath and slippery notes. I can't stop.

"Sorry," I mutter to Courtney.

But I'm not really. I just know that's what I'm supposed to say.

That's how it worked back in Michigan. I told my parents I was sorry a thousand times, but I was sorry for making them worry about me. Not for what I was actually doing.

"Aaaaand your friends are back," Courtney says.

Crouched in front of the refrigerator, I drop a container of lemonade. I have to wipe the sticky spill before I can make it to the window. I hope for Rush in a motorcycle jacket. I hope for all of the Grays, arm in arm, storming the shack and breaking me out.

I don't get either of those fantasies.

The Grays are gathered in the corner of the parking lot, a closed circle, their backs to the world.

"Hey," I call out, but they don't look my way.

"Burn," Courtney says, punching the pulse button on the blender.

"Why don't you finish up here, and I'll see you tomorrow?" I hate the pleading in my voice. I want to leap over the half-door and never look back. But I need this job. I need Mom to know that I'm trying.

Courtney eyes the Grays. They've broken out of their circle and they're laughing at something. June spins, arms tilting wildly. "Tell them to stay away from me, okay?" Courtney says. "I heard what that one girl did for Ana Viramontes, and I don't want them doing any of their . . . you know."

"Magic?" I ask, and watch her flinch.

My smile comes out, strong as black coffee.

As I leave, I look back at blondish Courtney with her endless supply of identical yoga pants and her T-shirts that probably cost fifty dollars each, plus the makeup that's supposed to make her look ten years older. The whole effect is one of intense blending in. High-school camouflage. I wonder what happened to make her that way.

But I don't wonder for too long, because the Grays are waiting.

"Let's go," Lelia cries across the parking lot. When I get closer, she threads her arm through mine, drawing me into the circle. "I have something I want to show you."

"Can I get there and home in an hour?" I ask.

I can see the Grays wanting to push back against my pre-sunset curfew. I can feel their nervy, collective need.

They want Imogen back. My mom's rules are not a priority.

"I get it," June offers. "My parents are protective."

"So is Ora," Hawthorn declares, as she toes the parking lot gravel. "She's protecting me from being a boring, non-magical girl who can't take care of herself."

"My parents used to be hard on me," Rush says, her arms tight around her middle. She looks tired, her eyes underlined in old makeup.

"Used to be?" I ask as we start walking, Lelia at the head of the party. "Past tense? Is there a spell I can use on Mom so she trusts me again?" *Even though I maybe don't deserve it,* I add in my head.

A stray ray of sun blinds me as we pass between the shadows of the buildings. I've agreed to this field trip without actually saying it. We walk behind the line of shops, revealing the backside of Tempest. There are dumpsters and shady-looking back doors and rust-laden staircases.

"Magic isn't an emotional Band-Aid," Hawthorn says. "Anything you do comes back to you threefold."

"So if I mess with someone's trust, I'll end up with three untrustworthy assholes in my life?" I ask.

Hawthorn's hand dives into the pocket of her patchwork dress, and she comes up with a piece of citrine. "That's a little simplistic, but yeah."

Lelia shouts back, "Believe me, no matter how intense your mom is, she can't be as harsh as the Lillys."

I've never really thought about Imogen's family before.

In my head, the Grays *are* her family.

We round the corner of the mechanic's shop and emerge next to a mural dedicated to the glory of Northern California, mostly surfers and redwoods and grape farming. It's cheesy, but the colors are perfectly chosen, soft yellows and shadow green and the slap of Pacific blue. In front of the mural is a small group of the largest birds I've ever seen.

Ravens.

They're something I've heard about but never actually seen. I am staring right at them, and I don't believe they exist. I'd always assumed they would be larger versions of crows. But it's more than that. They are deeply, darkly black, weighty and huge, their glossy sides overstuffed, as if they've been swallowing shadows. Or secrets.

Lelia crouches down to their level. The ravens' eyes fix on us, and I almost run. "They've been vocal lately," Lelia says. "I figured as long as they keep showing up, they might as well help us with your dowsing rod."

"Wow," I say, because I've got nothing else. Just air that needs to come out of my lungs. Wonder that needs to spill out of my mouth.

"Pretty amazing, right?" Lelia asks, clearly liking my reaction. She stands and sets an arm around my shoulders. We've never stood this close before, and I get a whiff of nutty suntan lotion and aggressively minty mints.

Rush watches the birds in a way that makes it clear she's got us at the edge of her vision.

"Ravens are the best finders in these woods," Lelia says, pounding my shoulder. "They've been bringing me stuff since I was eleven. Having one of their feathers will add serious power to a dowsing rod."

"You're not actually going to . . . pluck one of those birds, are you?" I ask.

"Are you fucking kidding me?" Lelia runs at the ravens screeching, but it's a joyful sound. She truly doesn't care what anyone — at least any human — thinks of her. I do wonder if she's trying to impress the ravens, though. They take off, shredding the air with sound.

When I look back at the ground, they've left a dark snowfall of feathers. Lelia swoops to pick one up, kisses it three times, and twirls it as she hands it to me. "What do you think?" she asks.

The raven feather is as long as my forearm. I run a finger along the soft edge, as downy as the endlessly kissable spot at the back of a girl's neck. I poke one finger with the slanted tip of the feather, almost expecting it to draw blood.

I look up. The ravens are part of the sky again. And I'm part of whatever is happening down here. The feather is mine because the ravens gave it to me, because Lelia thought I should have it, because there is magic inside of me, waiting to be used.

It feels like a part of myself that I tried to put in a box is tumbling over and pouring out. Now that the need for a dowsing rod is awake in my heart, I won't be able to rest until I have the whole thing.

I kiss Lelia three times, swiftly, the way she kissed the feather. *Thank you, thank you, thank you.* My lips land on her cheek the first two times, and then she turns her face to me and I catch her tart pink lips.

Danny
ONE YEAR AGO

At the beginning of junior year, a day came when I woke up feeling — not wrong, but raw. Like all of the colors in the world had been sharpened to a painful brightness, and the air had the convincing weight of a hand, tugging on my skin.

During fourth-period study hall, I sneaked into the control booth for lights and sound in the auditorium to make out with Hallie Carpenter. She was supposed to be wearing drunk goggles in health class, and instead I was spinning her endlessly in one of those chairs that plummets when you find the lever.

She laughed when I told her I wanted to hang out.

"Not like a date," I said, which we both knew was impossible. Even if our town wasn't drenched in homophobia, Hallie had a boyfriend. She talked about him exactly once per make-out session, but I felt a complete blank where my jealousy was supposed to be. "Some night when you're not busy with Jason or homework or track or whatever, we should just . . . go somewhere." I was trying so hard to sound calm about this while the nerves screamed inside my skin.

"We *are* somewhere," Hallie said in a kiss-roughened voice. "Besides, where do you even want to go? The movie theater is a complete mess. They don't have *cup holders*. One night Jason and I were so bored, we went through the Wendy's drive-through for fries three times."

She kept talking about Jason and fast food, and I couldn't waste any more time, so I started kissing her, pressing with my whole weight like I was a blanket, like I was ten blankets, like I was enough to hold us both down.

Three periods later, the end of the day was in sight but impossible to touch. I was taking a test in reading comprehension, filling in endless little ovals, and I got up and walked out. The teacher was busy at her desk and she probably thought I would come right back. Maybe I mumbled something about needing the bathroom. If I said anything, I didn't remember it two seconds later. Another set of double doors, and then I was out of the building, headed over the front lawn and the insincerely green soccer field, to the crest of the highway. I stood at the edge of the road, not sticking out my thumb. I just stared at the pavement like it owed me something. A car stumbled to a stop.

The woman driving the car powered her window down. She looked old enough to solidly be called an adult, but other than that, I couldn't tell her age. Was she in her late twenties? Thirties? It wasn't cold, but she wore a wool jacket, the long sleeves rolled above her spiky wrists. "Where are you going?" she asked.

"I don't know," I said. That wasn't true, though. Something

inside of me knew. It just wasn't the part that made words. "As far as you can take me?"

She gave me a wincing smile, like that answer made sense to her, and she wasn't happy about it. Something in my brain told me that I was supposed to be afraid of anyone who would stop at the side of the road and pick up a girl hitchhiking in plain sight of the high school, and something else in my brain pounced on that thought and muffled it.

"I'm Jackie," she said, waiting for my name. When I said I was Danny, she nodded, like knowing that made what we were doing marginally okay.

She pushed a button, and the automatic locks clicked open.

I climbed in. Her car smelled like cigarettes and orange peels, though I couldn't see any stubbed-out ends or flaking rinds. We drove for at least five silent minutes before she looked at me, a few glances. Maybe she was trying to stay focused on the road. Or she didn't want to see too deep into whatever my trouble was.

"You shouldn't get in cars with strangers," she said. "You know that, right?"

We passed the turnoff for my house, a long, curved section of road just past the tiny regional airport. I must have looked at my neighborhood with a certain kind of need on my face.

"Do you want me to drop you off at home?" Jackie asked.

I thought about my house and the blankets waiting at the foot of my bed, the way I had to take three painkillers at a time to get my legs to stop slashing the sheets. "I want absolutely everything except that."

"Girl after my own heart," she said, pulling out a pack of cigarettes from a hidden overhead compartment. When she offered me one, I heard my mom's voice floating through my head, telling me about the importance of accepting hospitality.

I took the cigarette but refused the lighter, saying that I wanted to save it for later. Jackie nodded like I was wise beyond my years. We crossed the line out of town, and automatic locks inside of me clicked open.

I knew all the rules about not trusting people, and not getting murdered, and I rode with Jackie anyway. Every time I tried to talk, she shook her head, like I was breaking a pact. We traveled a pattern of midwestern squares as the sky choked on gray clouds. The only things along the side of the roads were gas stations and the low bodies of gray box stores and mountains made of people's trash. We made it to Indiana before Mom called and I picked up and told her the truth.

It didn't even occur to me to lie.

"What were you thinking?" Mom screamed through tears.

I didn't have an answer, not yet. That's what I'd been looking for, and I hadn't even gotten close.

Jackie dropped me off at the next gas station. It had a little fake restaurant inside, a cluster of dark tables and a smell stuck halfway between cleaning products and lunch meat. "Sorry," she said. "I don't think I can handle being yelled at by someone else's parents."

I had to wait for three hours, sending Mom a picture of myself in the gas station every five minutes.

I'm here.

I'm alive.

Dad called and asked what I'd been thinking, a harsh echo of Mom. He said I'd stuck one foot in my own grave. But even after Mom picked me up and I apologized a thousand times, I kept thinking about that woman's car, how sour it smelled, and how if we drove long enough, her tires would drink up all the black pavement in the world, and I would unfold myself from the passenger seat and end up somewhere else. The air would be breathable, and the faint scent of oranges would stick to me everywhere I went.

Danny
NOW

The next day, the Grays, minus Rush, all have third lunch, and Rush is willing to skip class. Imogen has first lunch, they assure me.

We pass the cafeteria because it's way too nice to sit inside voluntarily, and head for the courtyard. I follow Hawthorn and Lelia as they tramp over endless freshmen and sophomores to get to their favorite spot. The five of us keep our hands linked, even though it's hard to walk like that. We cut through a circle of popular kids, and red hair causes me to crank my neck, but this girl is too young to be Imogen, and her face isn't blank. There's a crease that should be a smile as she listens to other girls talk about their crushes.

Hawthorn tugs the chain of the Grays, and the feeling travels, a pulse that reaches me at the end. "So we have the hours between dawn and school, and the hours between school and when your mom gets home, but only the days you're not working?"

"And lunch and study halls," June says.

"No study halls," I mumble. "I don't have any in my schedule. Mom was worried they wouldn't keep track of my attendance."

"What about nights?" Hawthorn asks, sitting down abruptly. We fall around her, and lunch appears from bags. "Can you at least get weekends?" I shake my head. "Just Saturdays?"

"Only daylight hours," I say, "at least until I build up some good-daughter points again." I hate thinking of it that way, but it's true. Good behavior is currency to parents, and I don't have any to spend.

"This might become a problem at some point," Hawthorn says, tapping her lips.

"Why?" I ask.

June unfurls a black lace parasol and Lelia, the pale one, huddles in its circle of shade. Rush has become one with the grass. Hawthorn sits cross-legged, her long legs pulling her skirt into a tray for her lunch. She lines up each item neatly. Thin-skinned plums, carrots that haven't been babied, some kind of cookie that looks like it's mostly oats.

"Let's not worry about that right now," she says. "Dowsing rod first."

"After school?" I ask.

"Ora needs me today," Hawthorn says, not elaborating.

I wonder how long it will be before I feel like I can ask *why*. I might have gotten drunk on the sight of the Grays naked in the woods, but there are parts of them I still don't get to see.

"I can't make it either," June says, attacking a sandwich

with eager bites. "Babysitting. Do you have any brothers or sisters, Danny? I have six." She notices that I'm not eating and holds out half of her sandwich.

"Only child," I say, accepting the offering with a grateful nod and a few wolfish bites. The minifridge in cottage nine is woefully limited. "My parents were never really together, in a romantic sense."

"Really?" Hawthorn asks, changing the lineup so the carrots come after the oat cookie. "Mine either. My dad is one of Ora's best and gayest friends. I visit him in Hawaii sometimes. I'm Ora's only baby. She might believe in herbal remedies for everything else, but let me tell you. When it comes to birth control, it's seven forms on top of each other."

June nods so earnestly that I laugh. "I believe in a woman's right to be good at birth control. Catholic parents. *Six* siblings."

"Your parents get so busy, June," Lelia says, sniffing at a cup of coconut yogurt. She sets it aside and wipes her hands on her skinnier-than-thou black jeans.

"Ahhhh," June says, capping her ears with her hands. "That's it. I'm banning all sex talk. Forever."

"There's nothing wrong with sex," Hawthorn announces. "It's perfectly awesome for people who are into that sort of thing." She flicks a glance my way, and I realize that she made that little PSA for me. Because when we first met, I told the Grays that kissing is my favorite activity. Hawthorn remembered, and cared enough to make sure I didn't get accidentally slut shamed.

I'm with four magical Grays, and we're sitting here talking

about sex in broad, buttery daylight. I might not have anyone to date at the moment, but it's definitely better than the world I lived in before.

And then I look over at Rush, and she's ignoring her dark-green salad dotted with strawberries, looking up at the mountains like she can't handle us right now, and I wonder what we did wrong.

What invisible line we crossed.

Rush and Imogen
FIVE MONTHS AGO

They couldn't stop kissing. They kissed like it was their calling. They stayed in Imogen's bedroom for days, begging Imogen's parents for permission to have night after night of sleepovers.

Imogen's parents liked Rush best of the Grays. If she had opinions, they never heard about them. She was soft where the rest were loud. But they didn't know what she was hiding under all that soft. They didn't know the way their daughter sank her teeth into it, hard enough to leave watery blue marks.

Three nights of sleeping in Imogen's queen bed before something inspired her parents to force the lock and find them a stitch away from naked. Haven stood in the hallway, her eyes *wide wide wide*.

There were long, frosty speeches about being too young, setting a bad example.

They met in the woods instead, even when it was raining. Rush pressed Imogen against a tree, the waterlogged bark as deep brown as her eyes. No matter how long they stayed in the drowning woods, the water never touched them. It parted around their bodies, flowed around their tangled feet.

And then, one night when the ground was almost dry and the stars burned cloudless, Rush said she was ready. Really, really ready.

Imogen looked all over Rush's body. She could feel her magic rising. "I don't know if we should."

"You don't want to be with me?" Rush asked.

"I do," Imogen said.

"Then be with me."

"You say that like it's simple." Imogen's hand was stalled on Rush's thigh. She tried to move it down, but she kept stopping herself, and Rush definitely noticed. They had blown past the point of no return a long time ago. She was going to hurt Rush now, either by doing this or by *not* doing it.

She looked away from Rush's skin, scalded by the light of a full moon, and gave the woods a thorough stare.

"Nobody will find us here," Rush said. "Unless someone's following us . . ." Prickles broke out on her bare arms.

Imogen felt it on her own skin, a bed of nails.

Danny
NOW

I wait for Lelia and Rush at the end of the senior parking lot. They both have study hall last period, and Rush's car is missing from where she usually parks it, under the stand of eucalyptus trees. I sit in their fractured shade, breathing in their balmy smell, already counting down how long I have before I need to get home.

Two motorcycles slice into the parking lot. The few students left still walking to their cars all turn to watch.

Which, I'm sure, is exactly what Lelia wants.

But what does Rush want?

I stand up, and cat-eyed eucalyptus leaves skitter down from my lap. I must be giving Lelia a look, because she shrugs as she tugs off her helmet. "Sorry. But we're not going to have many more perfect days like this." The three of us look around, like we can see fall seeping in at the edges of Tempest.

I take Lelia's raven feather out from between the pages in my math notebook, where I've pressed it for safekeeping. I touch its treacherously soft edge and steal a glance at Rush. She's got on jeans with a million holes and, under her leather jacket, a lacy sleeveless shirt that turns her soft, round shoulders into a serious temptation. She's staring at me again, but this time she catches me staring back.

"Are you ready to work on the dowsing rod?" she asks, excited. Breathy, even.

She wants to help me find my magic, maybe she even wants me as one of the Grays. But it's all about getting her girlfriend back.

"Let's go downtown," I say, feeling a vague pull in that direction. "We should check out the wood shop. They might have something I can use for the dowsing rod."

We walk down the line of shops, a dark parade, leather and raven feathers, and I want the entire town to see us. I feel like I am telling Tempest where I belong. Not stuck in Coffee Gods with Courtney. Not in the high school, boxed into another set of classes. Not even in the cottage with Mom.

Lelia walks the white line of the highway, and I weave back and forth over it. A truck snakes into view and I jump back at the last second. Lelia laughs, rough and loud. Rush trails behind us, singing. A song that pulls from the deep greens of the mountains and grabs the sharp rays of sun and adds them to the percussion of our tramping feet. I don't know if she's singing because the day is so beautiful or if it *makes* the day so beautiful.

I wonder if that's what magic is. Being so bound up with things that you can't tell where they end and you start.

We open the door to the wood shop and the bells ring, a sharp cluster of sound. I stop. "Do that again," I say, and Lelia flaps the door like a wing.

The bells ring. It takes Rush a second, but then she's with me. Face turned up, eyes closed, taking in the sound. "Not quite the same," she says, and hums the notes that she did the other day.

I run out of the wood shop, down the single row of stores, opening doors, flinging them wide. Looking up into the crevices of doorways for bells and measuring their notes against memory.

I run up the last porch, pounding three steps. This storefront is the old-fashioned kind that stands out much larger than the actual store behind it. It's lined with wooden plaques that have been hand-marred by a knife. *Postcards. Gifts. Wood carvings. Bone carvings.* I pull the heavy wooden door.

Notes drift down like snow. Three notes, cold and cutting. I know that discord. The way they tangle.

"That's it!" Rush says, running up behind me.

"That's it," I say, a pitch darker and a second behind.

The Bones
NOW

The bones don't remember who they used to be when they were all together. When they were glued with muscle and sunk deep under flesh. Now they are kept together by a wisp of spirit. It follows the bones like a shadow.

It doesn't know where else to go.

"I hate this place," says a voice as hard as the rain that came with death, washing everything clean.

"Why?" Another voice. From another place. It has a different way of threading words.

"It's a tourist shop." The first voice again. "There are *tchotchkes* here. And some of them are distinctly racist."

The bones don't belong here in the stale, mealy air. They were brought wrapped up in something soft and left in a darkened corner. The person who carried them stayed silent. The cold silence of guilt. The frantic silence of trying to forget.

It was raining, raining.

At least it's dry in here.

"What are these?" the second voice asks, drawing close. There are soft hands. Searching fingers. Someone picks up the bones, one at a time. It feels wrong. Bones are not meant to be touched. They are meant to be buried. First in bodies. Then in dark earth. Or they can be burned, and then the spirit that clings to them like ragged skin will learn to fly.

"Those are *not* animal bones," the first one whispers. "Not even a little bit."

"Humans are animals," says a third voice, softer than the first two.

"Imogen, Sebastian, now this," says the first. "Do you think Imogen's in danger? *More* danger?"

The name *Imogen* means something. It feels like grabbing at the past and coming up with empty hands.

"We need to take these," says the third voice. It trembles, balanced on the edge of some great sadness, trying not to fall.

"We can't exactly carry them up to the cashier," the first says. All three voices are becoming clear. Each one distinct to the spirit that keeps watch over its bones. "What if the police get involved? We're the weirdos of Tempest, California, and we've already found one dead body this week. I'm not interested in playing witch hunt."

"So we take them," says the second one. "Nobody will miss them, not in this place."

The bones are picked up again, carried with fear and reverence, tucked under clothes and pressed close, not to be seen. They are only pieces of the story, broken and brittle.

The bones don't remember who they used to be.

It takes longer than anyone alive will admit, to grow into who they are, to feel it deeper than skin, to *know.*

It is easier than they believe to forget.

Danny
NOW

As we walk out of the shop, the bones make a sound that knocks against my nerves. Like dice that we rolled, dice that won't stop chattering and settle down long enough to tell us if we won or lost. We have the better part of a skeleton stuffed in our bags, in our pockets, under our clothes, next to our skin. Lelia put the skull in her messenger bag. We scramble all the way back to the high-school parking lot, where Rush and Lelia swing their legs over their motorcycles. I'm left standing in an empty parking space like an idiot.

"We need Hawthorn," Lelia says. "And possibly her mom."

"What does her mom have to do with anything?" I ask.

"Ora's an old-school witchy type. Plus she's got an entire coven at her back. She'll know what to do."

"June first," Rush says.

"Obviously," Lelia shoots back. She palms her helmet. And then she shouts at me. "Come on!"

"I'm going to come with you . . . how?" I ask, my mind stuck.

Rush slides forward on her seat. That slight shift of her body is an invitation to come closer.

"I don't have a helmet," I say.

"We have a dead body," Lelia whisper-shouts.

Once she's tossed that card, all I can do is climb onboard. My toes skim gravel as I wrap my hands around Rush's waist.

"Ready?" she asks.

Yesterday, I would have said yes without thinking. Today is different. Today Sebastian isn't the only dead person in Tempest. Two bodies since I arrived in town, and I found both of them. If there was any question left about whether I have finding magic, it's officially blown to bits.

"Just go," I say.

The motorcycle shocks to life. Trembles between my legs. Rush steers us out of the parking lot, onto the highway, and the wind undoes me. Hair whips my face. My clothes feel like they're flying off. Wind touches me everywhere, except the places that press against Rush.

The trees keep us company as we ride. They keep our secrets, and we never even have to ask. Maybe that's why the Grays love them so much. Maybe that's why girls like me are always in the woods.

June's house is on a downslope filled with split-level ranches. Kids who look like her — the same wide cheeks and black hair and visible happiness — run around one of the yards. They're yelling at each other in a mix of English and Spanish and a third language that I don't recognize, which might be Tagalog. The whole scene has such a normal, comfortable afternoon feeling that I almost forget why we're here.

Lelia knocks around in the bag with the skull inside and pulls out her phone. She sends a quick text, and June comes out a minute later, shouldering her flowered backpack. "You owe me twelve favors," she tells Lelia. "My parents wanted me to watch them all night. Lina came home early, which is basically a miracle." She flings herself on the bike and attaches herself to Lelia without any of the drama that I stirred up with Rush. June even has her own helmet, deep purple and glittering in the light. She sees something in our faces that makes her immediately ask, "What's wrong?"

There are no words for what we're doing. What we've done.

Our silence tells June the degree of trouble we're in.

We roar north and turn sharply, heading into the pitch and heave of the mountains. Soon we're skidding up unpaved streets. Lelia and Rush slow down, down, down, until we're crawling along a road with a few trailers lining it. And then we reach a farmhouse that stands both proud and ramshackle, painted a light blue that serves as a sky-like background for a thousand varieties of weeds and herbs and wildflowers.

I can picture them at home now. Lelia in one of those gorgeous glass-skinned houses that people in California seem to have instead of mansions. June in a nest of middle-class normalcy, brothers and sisters swirling around her. Hawthorn here, set among the brambles. The only ones I can't see in their natural settings are Rush and Imogen.

When I picture them, they're together, in one of the Tempest Gardens cottages, Rush's cleaning products forgotten, Imogen poised over her in a brass bed, Imogen's eyes not misty but perfectly clear. She dips low, red curls pooling as they kiss.

Rush brings the motorcycle to a stop just as I realize what I'm thinking about. I ease my arms off her waist. Slide away. Rush turns, still straddling the seat. "We'll have to save the dowsing rod for another day." She dismounts and heads into the knee-high weeds, singing to herself as she ruffles the flowers. The idea of Rush with a girl who is infinitely prettier and more powerful than I am should probably make me jealous, but mostly it makes me want to know more.

We leave the motorcycles on a dusty path and walk to one of the outbuildings. It takes me a second to realize that everyone else is following me. I know where Hawthorn's going to be, or maybe my feet know.

I've brought us to a little shed, open to the elements on one side. We gather along that side, waiting for Hawthorn to notice. It feels like the bones are obvious, like she should be able to *feel* them. But she just keeps working over an honest-to-goodness cauldron, wearing a rubber apron.

"What are you making?" I ask, stepping forward to look into the depths of the black pot, crusted with age.

"Lemon-thyme soap," she says, ladling the heated mixture into a cast-iron mold set on a sawhorse. "Ora sells it at the farmers' market."

"We have a problem," Lelia says, her words weighted with the proper amount of *We're in deep shit*. "Our dowser dug up something."

"Not literally," I add, because I want it to be clear to Hawthorn that I did not exhume these bones.

Lelia opens her messenger bag and holds out the skull. It's exactly what every replica of a skull looks like, except it's more solid and delicate at the exact same time. June gasps so hard that the butterflies in the weeds outside take off in a fluttering tide.

Hawthorn sinks to her knees, the apron she's wearing stiff underneath her, the backs of her legs bare. She's wearing ancient Chuck Taylors. I don't know why, but that lodges in my brain. Barefoot witches in the woods are one thing. Teenage girls who help their moms make soap after school should not have to deal with this.

Lelia says, "We thought maybe Ora could —"

"No," Hawthorn says, cutting her off.

"Hawthorn," Rush says. "If she could help . . ."

"Ora would think we're too young to handle it, okay?" Hawthorn says, stripping off her apron. "She'd want to bring in her whole coven. And some of them are really normal people in their daylight lives. Someone would call the police."

"We've already touched the bones," Lelia says. She looks to me and Rush. "All three of us." Guilt closes in on us like night falling. "We need to know who the fuck that is," Lelia says, nodding down at the skull.

"Right," Hawthorn says. "Let's go to the High Point."

June takes the skull and stares right into it, through its hollowed-out eyes. "This isn't like finding Sebastian," she says. "That looked like a coincidence. This looks like . . ."

"Like we're part of it," Rush says.

"Aren't we?" I ask.

The Grays close ranks, giving each other very important

stares, none of them willing to offer me one. I think about turning around and leaving Hawthorn's farm before another body turns up, but I know I'm a part of this, even if the Grays don't consider me part of them.

We head out into the simmering gold afternoon. Hawthorn leads us toward the High Point, whatever that is. I look ahead of me, at the line of retreating backs climbing toward a rise, boots and sneakers and sandals swishing through the long grass, hips swaying, hands gripping bones.

I don't believe that any of the Grays would kill someone. But I didn't believe in ravens yesterday, and I was staring right at them.

The Grays
NOW

Lelia sets to work, picking up the bones, putting them into some kind of order, giving them the shape of a body as best she can.

Danny dances back and forth, the kind of nervous ballet that makes Hawthorn want to brew some rose-hip tea and makes Lelia want to bash her own skull against a rock.

"What is it?" Lelia asks tightly.

"You seem to know a lot about human bones," Danny says. "But you said that your magic doesn't include people, right?"

Hawthorn holds up a palm. "Just because you're a dowser doesn't mean you're invited to dive around in our personal lives."

Danny cringes, a recoil that the Grays notice a little too late. They don't mean to keep pushing her away; they've just been a group for so long that it's bound to happen sometimes. Especially when Danny whips out something that sounds so much like an accusation.

"So there *is* a reason Lelia knows so much about this," Danny says, standing with her back to the ridge known as the

High Point. She looks less interested in the view than in glaring at the Grays.

"You should stop talking," June says, inserting herself between Danny and Lelia. June doesn't look like an imposing physical presence — until she does. She's bigger than all of the Grays except for Rush, with significant muscle under her soft skin and fluttering dress.

Lelia looks up from the slim, snappable bones of the rib cage, taking one more glimpse of Danny before she tells her. "I was obsessed with anatomy freshman year. It lasted exactly as long as my mom dying."

Danny shuts up.

The Grays were Lelia's friends before cancer did its evil, predictable thing. Lelia's not that much of a witch, and she knows it. She likes making little piles of stones and spending her spare time pressing and drying moss and petals, and hanging out with ravens instead of people, but that's not the same as having big-time magic. Being a Gray keeps her connected. To the world. To humans she doesn't hate.

Which is why she needs to figure out what's going on, what kind of trouble won't leave them alone. People are turning up dead, and she can almost smell how unnatural it is. Salt water in the woods. Bones in the tourist shop. This could eat up her friends the way cancer ate up her mother, ate up her life, made it impossible to be around people without them looking at her with a weird mix of pity and pure selfish fear, as if what happened to her might be something they can avoid if they don't stand too close.

Danny can't keep quiet. "I shouldn't have said . . ."

"No," Lelia says. "You shouldn't." She slides the last rib into place, forming a slender cage. "But you get points not for giving some mealy excuse." She looks up at Danny, the blush already scraped off her cheeks, the glow of her magic dimmed by so much death. "I can see how much it's bothering you."

"Saying the wrong thing?" Danny asks.

"Being the one who finds them."

"We need to ask the bones who they belonged to," Hawthorn says.

Heads swivel. Eyes pin. The Grays are all looking at Danny as she dances back and forth. Finding a lost name sounds like a job for their dowser. "You make that sound like a *thing*," she says, "that a person can just *do*."

"You have to come up with some kind of . . . correspondence," Hawthorn says. She hasn't started with the basics of magic since the Grays were first learning. It feels like taking a thousand steps backward and then working her way forward through thick mud. And then there's the fact that everything she taught the Grays was supposed to make their lives better, and now she feels like she's patching together survival tactics. "Every element in a spell stands in for something else. You're building a metaphor, then bringing it to life. Like, when Rush sings, every note has meaning. The mode she chooses . . ."

"That's like the key . . ." Rush adds, her voice a shimmering overlay.

"That means something, too," Hawthorn finishes.

"Your songs are *spells*?" Danny asks, staring at Rush with an amazed, hopeless intensity that the other Grays pick up on right away.

"What did you think they were?" Lelia asks. "Top forty witch radio?"

"Everything we do has intention," Hawthorn says. "Most magic doesn't change the world. It's about being *in* the world. Appreciating its gifts." The words sound rote, even to Hawthorn. She grew up believing them. But two dead people are not exactly what she would call *gifts*.

Danny is light on her feet, and watching her pour herself into the work is a bit of shine against black clouds. This girl is a silver lining come to life. Gray turned bright and beautiful.

She picks up bones and puts them back down. She hummingbirds around the skeleton. It took them long enough, but the Grays finally start paying attention to the girl in front of them.

This is how the Grays fall in love. This is how the Grays do everything.

In the weirdest possible way.

This is how they go down.

Together.

Danny
NOW

I can feel the Grays watching me, eyes at my back, but I can't think about them right now.

This is between me and the bones.

Here is the curved plate of a skull. Here is the ridge of a collarbone. Here is the tiny, impossible bone of a fingertip.

I look over each one until I've oriented myself. Like staring at the stars until they form constellations. Those stars are the bones of the universe. Dead and gone, but they still shine white, white, white.

"What happened to you?" I ask.

The bones are silent. Their secrets don't budge. This isn't how spells work, according to Hawthorn. I can't talk to a person who used to be there. It's like trying to walk in the front door of a house that doesn't have one anymore. I need to find another way in. I need to craft a bridge. I need to build a spell.

But I'm not a singer like Rush, and I can't read the world like Lelia. I don't have a dark knife like June or a lifetime of magical knowledge in my pockets like Hawthorn. I'm not Imogen with her bottomless well of power.

All I have is the ability to follow bizarre whims. To dance after people I barely know. To reach for what I need most and hope I don't come up holding air.

I touch the bones. Palm to the place where a palm goes.

I hold a hand that isn't there.

A fleshed-out feeling comes. I am in the woods, dancing with a girl. Her wide brown cheeks spotted with a blush.

My hand pressed to her hand.

June.

This is a memory.

I come back to the High Point, dizzy with what I've figured out, nervous at how much I still don't know. The Grays are a blur around me, moving to get a better view of what I'm doing, Hawthorn writing it all down in the chronicle. Her pen scratches and scratches at white paper.

I feel pressure, like a hand at my throat.

I need the Grays. I can't go back to a world without magic, a world without *them.*

I stand over the body. I touch my foot to the bones of feet. Some of the toe pieces, the little white stubs, are missing.

I get a glimpse of bare feet on dark earth.

I look down at the feet from above, an angle that means *mine.* They're planted wide and confident, settled into the dark space of a burned-out tree. They might feel like they're my feet, but they clearly belong to someone else. The toes are long and squared, the nails half-mooned with dirt.

I come back to myself again, the Grays all around me, murmuring. Rush sings a full-throated song. The same one she was singing the night I first saw her. Or maybe that was morning. It's all a dizzy blur.

I get on my knees at the foot of the skeleton and crawl my hands out, careful not to disturb the bones. The heels of my hands catch on prickly pine needles and imprint with sharp stones. I lower myself over the slender cage of ribs, the birdcage of bones. I hover, holding myself up.

My heartbeat triples.

I hear someone saying a name. It's blurry, under water. It must be raining. I smell the release of the woods, a deep green sigh unlocked by the rain.

"Neil." The voice is so washed out by the sound of water that it's almost not there at all. "I'm sorry."

Water rises past my feet, swallows my waist. This is not just rain. There are panels of darkness on both sides of my vision, and in the center, a view of the woods, a single long splinter of daylight and trees. I've seen this view before. I'm inside a redwood. And the space is flooding.

I try to leave, but I can't move.

And then I feel hands all over me, pulling me back into my own body. Lelia and Rush and Hawthorn and June.

I grab on to their names, hold them like lifelines.

They drag me away from a sharp, broken shard of the past. Their hands are warm and everywhere. My arms, my back, my legs. They give me a quick review, a reminder of what is me and what is not.

My eyes snap open, and I hack the air into pieces with coughing. Water comes out of my lungs.

The Grays step back.

I roll onto my knees and cough until there's nothing but salty strings of spit that I have to wipe away, my back caving as my lungs empty. I look up at the Grays, my body still twisted around someone else's pain.

"Who's Neil?" I ask. "And how did he drown in the woods?"

The Grays
ONE YEAR AGO

The first time the Grays met the hermit, he was still called Neil.

He was exactly the kind of tourist that seemed to be magnetized to Tempest. June noticed him first, biking down the highway, sweating enough to fill a small lake. He wore a bandanna, ragged shorts that looked like they'd been bitten by a wild animal at the bottoms, and the kind of backpack that probably cost four hundred dollars when it was new.

"Oh, look," June said, pointing as if she'd noticed an interesting cloud formation. "A boy."

Imogen turned, and the Grays followed the line of her eyes. Everything they lit on become important, even if it was only for that second. "Yours," Imogen said to Hawthorn, waving a hand and dismissing the whole thing.

The Grays lingered at the side of the highway. Tourists were busy cranking their necks to take in the view. Motorcycle packs flocked from the Bay Area like this was a natural migration route. The Grays had seen at least four since that morning, including a beautifully weathered all-lady group. They had talked about how that could be them in fifty years.

"No motorcycles," June had said with her nose scrunched.

"I'll get you a sidecar, baby," Lelia said, wrapping her arm around June's shoulder, melting her back into a happy state.

They talked about what their motorcycle gang should be named as they walked in a slow trickle toward the diner. Hawthorn and June were both set on Bel's Hells.

"Okay, but not enough people know that Bel is a Celtic god," Lelia said. "They won't know how good that is."

"*We'll* know," June argued.

Now that Imogen had stopped looking at the boy, he was just scenery. But he skidded to a halt right next to them and drawled in an unexpectedly southern way, "Hey, there. Can you point me to the nearest campground?"

"You can't really camp in the redwoods, except in a few special places," Lelia said. "They're protected." The Grays heard the rest of the sentence, the part that was too heavily implied to even bother saying: They're protected from tourists and fancy backpacks and people like *you*.

Imogen twisted her lips, considering something that the rest of them couldn't even see.

"Okay, so you don't have a campground," the boy said, singling her out. "But you know something I *can* do."

Imogen peaked her eyebrows. She wasn't used to people noticing as much as she did. "There was a hermit who lived in a burned-out tree for about a thousand years. But she died two months ago, and nobody's taken her place."

"Because it's sacred," Hawthorn hissed.

"Because it's filled with spiders," Lelia added.

"Same thing," Imogen said, using her midnight-colored nails to flutter away any other arguments before they even formed.

"Sounds perfect," the boy concluded with a smile.

Imogen took a Sharpie out of June's flowered backpack and drew a map on his arm. She gave the hermit's tree a nice, juicy *X*.

The boy nodded thanks at all of them, spending an extra second on Hawthorn. She frowned at him in a way that made him smile again, his dimples pricking their way into the hearts of the Grays, even if they weren't interested in *that way*. He told them, "You should come by. I'm staying for at least three days." And then he stayed forever.

As far as the Grays were concerned, they had made a hermit.

Danny
NOW

The Grays walk me back down to Hawthorn's farm. It looked wild an hour ago. Now it's a tame bed of flowers and a gently rotting old barn.

Hawthorn is strangely quiet. She disappears into the farmhouse and comes back a minute later with a set of keys dangling from her palm. A substantial chunk of smoky quartz on the end of the key chain catches the dying light.

She presses the stone into my palm. "Hold this. It should ground you."

I form a fist around the hard lines of unfinished crystal. The angles of the quartz press into my skin as hard as someone shoving their body against mine while we kiss, the pressure like a point on a map, telling me, *You are here, you are here, you are here.*

"What's happening?" I ask.

"The stone is . . ."

"No," I say, unwilling to turn this moment into another magic lesson. The Grays are holding something back, and I'm not going to let this stay unspoken. I clutch the smoky quartz harder, almost hoping that Hawthorn's mother rushes out of the barn, takes this mess right out of our hands.

But no one comes to save us.

"If Neil really did die in that tree, it wasn't a natural death," Hawthorn says, tugging at a tiny braid that runs through her curls.

"Do you think someone used magic to kill him?" I ask. There's no point in dancing around it.

Hawthorn shakes her head. "Witchcraft and murder *don't* cross paths," she said. "If for no other reason than the cost always comes back to the witch who cast the working. It would be easier to kill someone outright."

"And risk being caught?" I ask. "What if someone was upset enough, and they didn't care about the price?"

The sky glows, a flashburn that means the day will be over soon. The flare of life that comes right before death. I think about Sebastian in the tree, living at the very edge of his comfort zone. I was the thing that he reached for, right before death. And I barely noticed how important that moment was. I was trying so hard to find the Grays, even though I didn't know it yet.

Did someone want Sebastian dead? Neil, too? What about Imogen?

Hawthorn is sighing up a storm. "If someone really did want to kill people with magic, they would have to find a way to do it that diverges from every legitimate form of witchcraft. We *don't* make spells for this."

"It's against every law of nature," Rush whispers.

"But the laws of nature are breaking," Lelia says. "Or at least severely cracking."

"Neil is dead," June says. "*Our* Neil."

"At least his bones are buried now," Lelia says to Hawthorn. "And not in that creepy store." The Grays put the bones to rest in the woods near the High Point as I watched, still trembling and coughing up the last of my vision.

"Are you okay?" Rush asks, and I think it's for me—but she's talking to Hawthorn this time.

Lelia sets a hand to the back of Hawthorn's neck as she hangs her head low, working the muscles there, releasing a tightness that must have been building since we first found the water in the hermit's tree. "Get Danny home. We can't have her mom stopping us now."

Hawthorn drives me in her mother's truck, and this time I leave the silence between us untouched. It starts to rain quietly, unexpected drops cutting across the sky, as sunset glazes the town and the trees.

By the time we turn into the Tempest Gardens parking lot, the rain is already stopping, gone as quickly as it came. Hawthorn walks me toward the cottage, one hand on my back, her long fingers splayed from shoulder blade to shoulder blade.

She stops me a few feet from cottage nine. I assume that she'll knock on the door, deliver me home, but instead she pulls me around the side, into the mulch of the border garden. There's only one type of flower here, a Barbie-pink nasturtium. Hawthorn looks down at them as if this is all their fault.

I crumple a few under my feet as she tucks me into the space between the corner and the window.

"You're sure it was him?" Hawthorn asks. "I mean, absolutely sure?" Her voice is different than usual. It reminds me of the redwoods I've seen that have been hit by lightning, their tops stripped of bark, pale insides showing.

It takes me a second to find the truth, and then another second to be sure of it. "You and the hermit?"

Hawthorn shrugs.

"Do the rest of the Grays know?"

Is it terrible that I want to know all the things you don't tell each other?

"They do and they don't," she says. "I couldn't really talk about it with them." She looks down at her feet in their cloth sneakers. They're damp from standing in the border garden after the rain.

I see his feet in bare earth.

I feel something, a wisp of what the hermit felt for her. It's there, as warm as the last droplets of sunlight.

"The Grays didn't understand about Neil?" I ask. "Why?" I think about all of the restrictions we put on each other, all the ways we don't understand. I didn't want to believe that could happen here.

Hawthorn squirms, looking up at the sky. "Except for living in a tree, Neil was really . . . ordinary."

"Ohhh." *Ordinary* is the one of the few things the Grays wouldn't be able to get their otherwise open minds around. But I can't imagine Hawthorn ran into that particular quality a lot, growing up on Ora's farm. "Maybe that made him special to you. Maybe that's something about him you actually *liked*."

Hawthorn winces, as if I found a truth she was planning on keeping hidden from herself for a little while longer.

I give her one of my secrets in trade. "That boy we found? Sebastian? He was out in the woods because of me. We climbed a tree together. We almost kissed."

Hawthorn nods, like she hears all the parts I'm not saying.

She grabs me by the wrists, gently, and pulls me toward her, her lips softened by a lifetime of beeswax. I meet her with a matching sadness, slowness. The funeral kissing falls away quickly, and here is the heart of it. Her skin. My breath. She pulls me closer, sets her fingers lightly against my collarbone, delicate, because something's about to break. I'm kissing her like she's a boy I barely know. She's kissing me like I'm a boy she'll never get to love.

The door of cottage nine creaks wide.

I figure we'll rip apart from each other. I've had enough scares, enough interrupted moments and close calls to know how this works. But Hawthorn keeps her hold on my wrist, she keeps her body close to mine, and I don't let go.

"Danny," Mom says, peeking around the edge of the cottage. "Are you out here?" She has a pencil shot through her dark-brown hair, but it's falling everywhere. She gives us a very serious look, which summons the normal, confident Hawthorn up from the depths. Her scowl makes Mom smile. "I guess I should be happy that you're bringing them home now."

Them.

All the people I kiss.

Does she think I'm experimenting?

Starved for someone to be with?

A queer girl who has to kiss everyone she stumbles across, because that's part of the deal?

I don't want to ask, because the answer will probably break my heart. I don't want to tell her the truth about the Grays, because she'll never get her mind around it. She's willing to accept that she's got a messed-up teenage daughter. But would she believe that she has a magical one? There are parts of me — maybe the best parts — that she will never see, because they're too strange.

If the word *queer* would make her cringe, *witch* would send her running.

I flare with a blush. She probably thinks I'm embarrassed at being caught, but the truth is that this redness goes deeper, thrusting angry roots. Mom is willing to see only part of my story. She wants this to be easier to understand — wants *me* to be easier to understand. She turns around and waits for me in the doorway, fingers tapping on the frame, eyebrows up.

The Students of
Tempest High School
THE PAST SEVEN YEARS

If you pressed someone to talk about Imogen Lilly in middle school, they would probably say she was the girl with curly red hair and a strange absence of freckles, the girl who strayed to the edge of the woods during lunch and ate her sandwich in the shadows, the girl who looked up at the treetops instead of keeping her eyes on the ball during gym, no matter what sport they were supposed to be playing. She didn't belong to any clubs or cliques. She didn't talk to anyone.

Mostly, she whispered to herself.

And then high school came like a whirlwind, and she was right at the center of it, unruffled by the storms that slapped everyone else out of their personalities and left them naked and shivering.

Imogen arrived at Tempest High with her own style, solid opinions on every possible topic, and a smile that could burn through fog. Everyone noticed her long black skirts, tiny black shorts, shirts with no bra underneath, messy red braids, and wide-brimmed black hats that would have looked stupid on anybody else but on her, somehow, looked *right*.

One day Erin Wong was crying in the bathroom stall that was pretty much reserved for girls who were upset or getting sick. Imogen kicked in the door, put an arm right around Erin's shoulders, and said, "What did he do?" not in a sweet, caring whisper-tone — more like her voice was a knife and could reach all the way across the school, cutting whoever had hurt this girl.

Erin cried harder. When she finally calmed down, Imogen was sitting on the tiles with her, pulling things out of her scaly black bag.

The next day, Erin was wearing a tiny bottle of water around her neck and smiling. By the end of the school year, half the girls in the sophomore class had bottles that didn't quite match but all carried a few precious drops of water in them.

When the boys asked, the girls shrugged mysteriously and said it was a new style. Nobody gave Imogen away. The boys still smiled as she walked toward them, their faces — and sometimes other parts of their anatomy — perking as they passed her in the hall.

They all wanted her, in different ways, even if they didn't know why, even if they couldn't name the lack that she was supposed to be filling. The students treated her like a drug dealer or a minor goddess or both. And everyone put up with the Grays, a gang of shadows that followed her around wherever she went.

Mom can't be too pissed about catching me with Hawthorn, because she lets me eat the leftover lo mein from the Chinese restaurant in Arcata, the one that she stops at on her way home from work when she doesn't want to cook.

I haven't actually broken a rule, so she doesn't puncture the silence with anything except small talk.

What do you want for lunch tomorrow?

Should we schedule a call with your father this weekend?

Are all the girls at your school that pretty?

I answer.

Anything.

Sure.

No.

There are plenty of *technically* pretty girls at school, even openly not-straight ones. But the Grays are special. After them, anyone else would pale in comparison. I realize, with a cold stone in my stomach, that I haven't even considered kissing any other person at Tempest High.

If I told Mom that, she would probably give me a hug and extra lo mein and call it *progress.*

But what if it means that I need the Grays too much? What if it means that they have all the power and I have nothing?

I do my homework, and when it's filled in enough that I won't get in trouble tomorrow, I change into drawstring shorts and a T-shirt, climb into bed early.

I turn from one side of the bed to the other, mash my face into the feather-soft mattress like that will somehow cut off the oxygen to my fear. But the way it felt to take Neil's final breaths sinks roots. It sends tendrils outward. Starts to grow.

Two boys killed in the redwoods.

One girl gone.

I look out the window, and the trees are waiting like a collection of needles, piercing the evening blue. It won't be fully dark out for a while. Twilight has separation anxiety; it sticks to the trees.

I close my eyes, but I don't fall asleep.

Danny
THE LAST FIVE MONTHS

I would get out of bed in the middle of the night, and they'd find me three neighborhoods away. I dragged myself toward the fistful of lights at the center of town, down sidewalks and street margins so skinny my body barely fit. When I walked through the liquor store parking lot, I sliced my heel open on a broken bottle.

I called Dad that time.

He called Mom.

In the emergency room, she asked in a ragged voice, "Were you sleepwalking?"

I had done that. Torn up her hope that things were going to get better. And even worse: I couldn't name what I was doing, or where I was going, or answer the most important question, the one that started gushing out of people like blood from an unexpected wound.

Why?

The school counselor asked it when she handed me a calendar of the month of May, with the days that I'd missed school blacked out. It looked like a building with half the lights off.

"Where did you go?" she asked.

"Nowhere. Anywhere." I had mostly been in the fields outside of town, the abandoned barns with sunlight pushing through slits between the boards.

"Why did you feel that it was acceptable to leave?"

"I didn't," I said.

The counselor wrote a report that said I was *obstructing the process.* My teachers were asked to report it to the office immediately when I didn't show up for class or if I took more than two minutes to use the bathroom.

Which meant no more kissing Hallie Carpenter when I was supposed to be taking history quizzes. That turned out to be a stupid worry, because Hallie didn't want to kiss me anymore. She told me one day that we'd made out twenty times and she felt like if we did it again, it would actually mean something.

Apparently twenty-one was the magic number.

After that, I had to work at the edges of Mom's schedule, find time when I could disappear into the woods or the back seat of a car. The people I went with didn't care if we made out once or twenty-one times.

They barely cared if they knew my name.

I ran my hands over hips and under shirts and waited for excitement to take its rightful place. But all I felt was skin. I was trying to chase a feeling backward. I strained through each moment, hoping that if I worked hard enough, I could end up in that place where finding someone to kiss was enough.

A girl in the class above mine with a blunt black bob and a history of staring at me drove me out to the lake and threw me into the back of her Jeep with a pile of blankets. A half an hour in and a few items of clothing down, she flicked my hair with her breath as she laughed. "You're so lucky you're a girl slut. If you did this with guys, you'd be pregnant by now. Or worse."

I sat up so fast I almost threw up. I got out of her car and walked the rim of the entire lake before I called Mom to pick me up.

I didn't feel lucky.

"You're depressed because you're having random, meaningless . . . *hookups*," Mom said an hour later as she paced around my tiny room. She looked mad, but I knew the anger was just something she'd slapped on over her guilt so she felt fully dressed.

Guilt was a naked feeling.

"I'm not depressed," I said. I clicked open the metal tab on a can of Vernors. The ginger ale sizzled down my throat, coated my nervous stomach without shaving off the sharp edge. "And please, please don't say *hookups*."

I wanted to be better for her. But I kept getting out of the car at red lights. Walking through private property at dawn. Knocking on strangers' doors in neighborhoods where people owned multiple guns and would have been happy for an excuse to take one out.

And then: suspension, grounding, screaming, apologies.

And then: California.

A four-hour flight where, for once, I didn't want to run. Which was good, because there was no escape. Nowhere to go except into the howling sky. Pinned to my seat, I watched the landscape change beneath me. Rising, falling, endless curves and shadow-rich valleys. I put one finger on the window and traced everything beautiful.

The Grays
NOW

In the morning, long fingers of cold rake across Tempest, forcing the Grays into jackets and sweaters. They stamp their feet in the corner of the senior parking lot, four pairs of hands wrapped around steaming, sweet-smelling cups from Coffee Gods.

"Coffee is magic," Lelia mutters, sticking her face into the steam. "I will fight anyone who doesn't believe it."

June bumps Lelia's hip with hers. "That's what caffeine does. It triggers your fight-or-flight impulses."

"Good," Lelia says. "I'm a fighter, not a lover."

Rush tugs at the bottom hem of her long maroon sweater. It goes almost to her knees, worn over black velvet leggings with her silver-laced boots. She looks fancy, by Rush standards. She's clutching an extra cup, sipping from the one in her right hand and leaving the left outstretched. "I hope Danny shows up soon. Her latte will get cold."

"Let's focus on the rest of Danny's dowsing rod," Hawthorn says. "That's what she really needs."

"Yeah," Lelia says. "We got sort of interrupted yesterday."

They've been doing a decent job of not mentioning Neil, but the idea of him keeps gnawing at the edges of the conversation.

"Could Danny use a redwood branch?" June asks. "For the dowsing rod? I mean, it makes sense, if our magic is tied to Tempest."

"But the branch can't be just some random chunk of redwood," Hawthorn says. "It has to *mean* something."

The parking lot ripples as someone moves upstream through the crowd. Danny comes into view, and at first the Grays are proud — she must be using her dowsing sense to find them. Then they notice how deeply sunk the lines in her face are, how hard she's gripping the strap of her bag, how lopsided her breathing is. Big inhale, very little exhale. She's holding something in.

"We were just talking about you," June says too brightly, overcorrecting.

"What happened?" Rush asks softly.

Danny looks down at her feet, then snaps her neck back up with force, like she's decided not to hide from this particular truth. "I woke up in the woods."

The Grays hover around her with concern, not sure what she needs. They don't know Danny well enough to rush in and take care of her, and the slight distance between her and the rest of the Grays is almost as bad as knowing that Danny is terrified.

"Are you okay?" Lelia asks, her voice tight as fists.

"It was a bad night," Danny says, her voice split open at the seams. "The hermit took me for a spin."

Danny
THE NIGHT BEFORE

I didn't fall asleep, even after Mom's soft snore blanketed the cottage. The moon rose in the window, through the bottom square and then the top one. I flipped slowly from one side to the other like I'd trained myself to do when I felt restless. The feeling had vanished when I first got to Tempest, but it was coming back night by night. Waxing into fullness, like the moon.

My feet worked lightly against the thin standard-issue hotel sheet until I thought I might wear straight through it. I wondered how many miles I would have gone by now if I'd let myself stand up. I didn't stand up. I didn't let my thoughts wander through a forest of vanished girls and dead boys. I pulled darkness and nothingness over my mind like a blanket, like ten blankets.

That's when the hermit, or what was left of him, slipped into me. He didn't wait for an invitation, as if letting him share my mind once meant that he could do it again. I didn't know what he wanted or where he was taking me as my limbs swung toward the edge of the bed, heavy as wet sand.

I had worked so hard to stay put, and now I was passing Mom's bed without really meaning to. I was walking out through the screen door to the porch, down the steps, gathering splinters in my feet.

The woods greeted me with a forgiving bed of pine needles. I felt myself swell back into the proper place, shoving the hermit to the edges of my body, my mind, and I almost turned around and walked back to the cottage. But the fog breathed toward us, and the hermit pushed me forward. His fear slid through my mind like a shadow of my own. He knew where he was going, and he was afraid to lose this chance.

I was afraid to lose everything. My control, my mom's trust, my life. An ocean of panic rippled inside me, but the hermit didn't feel it, or the hermit didn't care. He believed he was doing something that needed to be done.

The fog closed in around us, and it would have smothered us, but the hermit wouldn't let it, and he wouldn't let go. He pushed me until I was running. He pushed me until I couldn't take a full breath.

And then, blackness.

At first I thought I had passed out.

Then I saw every shade of darkness, and light coming in through an enormous scar.

I was inside the hermit's tree, on the damp ground. It hadn't dried, was saturated in a way that brought me back to the ground beneath Sebastian's blood-soaked body. I held myself as I shivered, still in my tiny shorts and bralette, the T-shirt peeled off when I was sweating and not-sleeping. I was alone in the woods at night, wearing dangerously close to nothing.

The hermit wasn't in my mind anymore, but his presence stayed close, sticking to me like cold sweat. He had brought me here, which left a single question throbbing through me, like it was trying to pass through a too-small door.

Why?

I looked around at the dull black everywhere. Lelia's nature lessons came back to me — this tree was dead on the inside. A curl of coldness tugged at the back of my neck, and I tilted it back. Above my head I saw words that hadn't been there the night of the fog dance. They had been cut into the tree, more like a scar than a secret message. Thin, black on black, barely there. But the pale scrap of moon cast enough light to reveal a phrase carved unevenly in the same handwriting I'd seen on Imogen's notebook.

You're going to get hurt.

The Grays
NOW

The Grays look at one another, trying to decide who has to say the obvious thing. June sets her coffee cup down on the asphalt lip of the parking lot and steps toward Danny. "*Imogen* sent you a message?"

This should be good news.

If Imogen warned Danny that she was in danger, it means that she knows at least part of what's happening. She's still with them, even if it's in tiny chopped-up pieces instead of her whole self. But the message hovers around them like smoke.

You're going to get hurt.

The bell rings, and everyone else scatters. The parking lot is dead water in thirty seconds flat. Danny starts to move toward the buildings, but Hawthorn grabs her by the hand. "We can't wait until after school."

"Should we go right now?" Rush asks.

"It's worth skipping Econ," June says, Danny's schedule committed to memory. "I promise."

Lelia picks up her feet and starts them running. "And if you only want to skip one class, we're leaving *now*."

"I don't really want to be taken somewhere without my knowledge or permission again," Danny says, trying to sound sarcastic, but her voice crawling toward tears.

Hawthorn twists her hands together, wanting to touch Danny on the arm or shoulder — some comforting, non-threatening place — knowing that she has to wait for Danny's okay. "If Neil wasn't dead, I would ruin his life."

"Really?" Danny asks. "I thought he was your . . ."

"Nope," Hawthorn says, clapping her hands clean. "I didn't know him. The Neil I thought I knew would never do that."

"Witches before bitches," Lelia announces, her voice taking over the empty parking lot.

"I *hate* that word," June says.

Lelia ruffles the long side of June's hair. "Please let me reclaim it. I'm a bitch. I'm proud to be a bitch. Besides, you say *cunt* every day."

"And twice on Tuesdays," June informs Danny with a smile.

Danny looks grateful for the distraction of Lelia and June — which is exactly what they were going for.

Rush edges forward, holding out the hazelnut latte she bought for Danny when she thought this was going to be a standard morning. It seems like a meager offering all of a sudden. "We want to take you to Imogen's house."

Danny takes a few desperate sips as the Grays break away from the parking lot, away from the stores, toward the residential parts of town. They stagger down a little gully and over the spittle of a stream.

June gasps at how much her leg hurts — a nine on the

scale, maybe a nine and a half. It never healed after she went climbing with Imogen, or the original break healed but her nerves didn't really get the message. There's no painkiller that can dull what she's feeling. Any worse and she'll have to sit down right where she is. Her ankle turns in the mud, and she has to bite her arm to keep from crying out.

Danny lags, forcing them to a stop. They're safely off the school grounds now, and no one will come after them. Not that getting detention is their main concern right now. "Tell me what we're going to Imogen's house for. I . . . I don't want to get hurt."

"That's *why* we're going," June says.

"We're going to Imogen's house because she has spell makings there. You'll be able to find them. We'll show you how to use them."

"We'll *all* use them," June adds.

Danny looks around at the Grays, slow and suspicious. "What kind of spells?"

"Wards," Rush says.

Danny infuses her hazel-brown stare with a question. She is part of this now, the way they get their points across without speaking. She has been pulled into everything about them. Folded into their lives. The light and the dark. The gray swirl of storm winds that has been growing ever since Imogen disappeared.

"It's protection magic," Hawthorn says.

"Why didn't you lead with that?" Danny asks, grabbing Hawthorn's hand. Now the Grays are the ones running to keep up.

Danny
NOW

As it turns out, the reason I couldn't picture Imogen's house is that it's so intent on being nondescript. It comes into view at the end of a shaded cul-de-sac, small and green and sunk into the woods. The house is split-level, not big or small. No path of stones leads to the front door.

There doesn't seem to *be* a front door.

As soon as I've taken it in, I blink and forget the whole thing. I have to start looking at it all over again.

Green, split-level, no door.

I keep the facts firmly in my mind, but even as I stare right at the house, they start to drift. If someone asked me to describe the Lilly house, I would let out a mouthful of nothing.

At first I think maybe Imogen's parents are so boring that they chose the world's least exciting house without meaning to. And then I wonder if Imogen's magic did this, made my eye keep slipping away.

Is this what protection looks like?

Learning to be invisible?

Once we reach the yard, I let the Grays take the lead. Hawthorn knocks on the side door, and we all wait.

A small version of Imogen answers the door. "Hey," she says. "Imogen's not here." She's the kind of pale that looks sickly, the kind of pale that shines. She has the same curly red hair as her sister, limbs so skinny they look ready to break at the slightest suggestion. She must be thirteen or fourteen, though something about her skews younger.

"Hi, Haven," June says in a slightly cute version of her voice. It's probably how she talks to her own brothers and sisters. "Can we come in?" She eyes the inside of the house. We're one tiny girl away from getting what we need.

"Why?" Haven asks.

"We have to find something," Hawthorn says. "Homework. It's due next period. Rush left it, but she can't remember where."

"Why are there so many of you?" Haven asks, narrowing her eyes. "I mean, if it's just Rachel's homework?"

Rachel? I've never heard anyone use that name, not the other students at school, not even the teachers. Her nickname seems to have dug in, like a thorn, and stuck. I never even wondered if it was made up.

"There are this many of us because we travel in a pack," Lelia says. "We're called Bel's Hells."

"I thought you were the Grays," Haven says with a few hard blinks.

"Oh, we are. Unless we're cracking skulls," Lelia says. "Then we're definitely Bel's Hells."

Haven's eyes flit upward. She clearly wants to roll them but can't quite manage — as if she's too afraid of the Grays to give them a full eye roll.

"Why aren't you at school?" I ask her.

Haven looks at me for the first time, like I wasn't even there until I interrupted.

"I'm sick," she says, and I take in her intense pallor, the scrapes of darkness beneath her brown eyes. In a quick swerve, she turns to the Grays and adds, "Mom and Dad don't like it when you're here." She looks at me for a wavering second, like she's not sure if I'm included in this statement.

"Yeah," Lelia says. "But are *you* Mom and Dad?"

"Leave her alone," I say. She doesn't have her own set of Grays at her back. She doesn't even have her sister.

Haven looks at me differently now that I've stuck up for her. "*You* can come in," she says, pointing at me, one pale finger hovering. "And Rachel. Since it's her homework. The rest of you have to wait outside."

Lelia groans. Hawthorn looks between me and Rush like we're the last two people she would have sent in.

"Hey," I whisper. "Dowser? Remember?"

"Yeah, and Rush knows Imogen's bedroom better than anyone else," Lelia says.

Rush turns an ungodly shade of red. June smacks Lelia in the chest with the back of her hand. Everything is clawing its way back toward normal, and then I remember why we're here. Wards. Protection.

Rush must be able to see how close I am to falling into a panicky abyss, because when Haven turns to lead us in, Rush grabs my hand. "We'll find it," she says, her thumb circling my palm. Heat fills a hundred unexpected places in my body.

Is this another thing the Grays do for each other? A scrap

of magic? Or is this something Rush came up with just for me?

She pulls me into the house, and when Haven turns the corner toward the kitchen, she reveals a figure with the same red hair standing in the arch of the living room, watching Rush work circles into my hand.

Imogen.

Haven and Imogen
FOUR YEARS AGO

They went to the Eel River every summer when the water was high and the temperature broke ninety, because otherwise it was basically an icy wading pool with a current that stung their ankles like a billion hornets.

Imogen took Haven to the same swimming hole every year. That was what sisters did. They broke up the world and picked which pieces belonged to whom. They looked around and pointed and said *Yours. Mine. Ours.*

This trip was a secret one, because Haven's parents didn't want her to go out too often, especially in the summer. They said she was too pale. They hated dealing with it when she got overheated, as if it reflected poorly on their parenting skills. Haven's mom and dad treated her like she might break if she got breathed on the wrong way.

Pretty much every way was the wrong way.

Besides, Imogen was out all summer, plus every other season, and apparently having one daughter who did that was enough. Imogen had filled the wildness quota, leaving nothing but boring old *good* behind for Haven.

"Mom and Dad think your new friends are a problem," Haven said, letting her toes touch the water. Not really wanting to jump in.

"Did you know the Eel River flooded once?" Imogen asked, ignoring what Haven had actually said, as usual, and talking about whatever she wanted to. "At that elbow ten miles up, the one with the bridge. It swept away everything. People and houses and horses and cows. You can go to the Tempest visitors' center and ask the historians if you don't believe me."

Haven curled her toes away from the bitter cold water. "You tell me that story at least once a year."

"Yeah, and Mom and Dad decide something's *a problem* at least once a year. It's part of the life cycle."

"You should be careful what you say about them."

Imogen's scowl hardened into a threat. "How would they know unless you tell them?"

"They always know," Haven muttered. "They look at my face and figure out everything I did wrong."

"That's bullfuck," Imogen yelled, filling the whole landscape with her voice. She was experimenting with swears that summer, taking them apart, putting them together backward and inside out, trying to see which ones got the biggest reaction.

That one just made Haven snort.

"Maybe you shouldn't worry so much about Mom and Dad," Imogen said. "Maybe you should be careful what you say around *me*." She leaped off the rock and just missed the bite of another one in the water. She came up sleek and smiling. "I'm a witch."

Rush drops my hand. Of course.

Imogen gives us a look like a guttered-out candle, and for a moment I imagine it's because she caught the two of us holding hands, because she's jealous of me or she cares so much about Rush — or both.

But there's nothing inside that stare.

"Why isn't Imogen at school?" Rush asks.

"Ask her yourself," Haven says, pulling out her phone and thumbing through messages. "She's standing right there."

Imogen wears a creamy nightgown with lace at her knees and the thinnest black pinstripes. Her red hair collects in whorls on her shoulders and then spills over her back, her chest. I avoid her eyes because I don't want more evidence that she can't see us, when we're forced to see her, over and over, even when she's not there.

Purple darkness has gathered beneath her eyes, brutally obvious against her pale skin. I wonder if she was out last night, wandering through the woods to leave a message in the hermit's tree.

Or was it there already? Waiting?

Rush's breath sticks halfway through an inhale. I want to run my hand up and down her back, free whatever is caught inside her. But I don't touch her. Not in front of Imogen and her sister. "What are you doing?" Rush finally asks in a smoky rasp. "Why aren't you . . . where you're supposed to be?"

Imogen doesn't respond.

I think Rush is going to choke up, to visit the verge of tears, but her eyes turn to liquid fire.

"Ouch," Haven says. "Looks like someone isn't interested in giving you the time of day." Haven walks over to her sister and goes up on her tiptoes. "Imogen, you don't have to stay. Rachel's leaving soon."

Imogen turns and drifts out of the room. Rush and I share a questioning look. Imogen clearly just responded to what Haven told her, even if she didn't speak to us. Maybe she can follow directions, as long as they're simple enough.

Haven gives us another glare, and then she leaves, too.

Rush closes her eyes, and the pain on her face is so clear, I feel like I could gather it in my hands. A song simmers on her lips, the song that I heard pouring out of her that first morning in the woods.

"What are you singing?" I ask.

The question breaks her song midnote. She presses her black-cherry lips together. "Imogen."

I stand very still, waiting for her to explain.

"I took her name and turned it to music," Rush says. "I used a cipher. Letters to notes. I picked the Mixolydian mode, because it's hopeful, and added a few embellishments that . . . sound like her."

I prickle with the heat of the Lillys' sunny house, and a sudden rash of jealousy. I want someone to know me well enough to turn me into music. To melt me out of this body and pour me into pure notes and warm breath.

I work my way back to what matters. Rush's songs are spells. "You've been trying to sing her back."

"It was all I had until . . ."

Until I showed up. Until I failed to bring her back, too.

No point in pretending otherwise. Right now we're on damage control, trying to keep any of us from following in the footsteps of Sebastian and Neil. We head in the opposite direction from Imogen, stepping into the slightly higher half of the split-level ranch. Three white doors in a row. I point to the one in the center. "Imogen's?"

"You're good at this," Rush says, running a hand down my arm, giving me that hot staticky pressure between my legs. In another world, that would be flirting. But Rush and I live in a world where Imogen is missing, and no one can disappear too far into a good feeling.

"Thanks," I say, taking the compliment and trying to leave the rest of my response behind.

As soon as we're in Imogen's room, the generic feeling of the house slips away. I've only seen Imogen wearing black and white, but her room is a violent splash of color. Loose-leaf drawings overlap on every wall, a lot of them probably done by Imogen. Rivers in deep red and royal blue — or maybe they're veins. Cracked skies in livid colors, like birds' eggs opening. And there are grave rubbings, the kind that kids learn to do in elementary school, only Imogen has hot-wired the idea, stolen it from its boring, humble beginnings and turned it into electric art. She's as present in this room as she was absent from her body. Everything here looks like Imogen. Like she's stamped her name on every surface.

And when I look at Rush, she's part of the room, and Imogen's name is stamped on her, too.

Imogen and Rush
FOUR MONTHS AGO

Imogen kept pulling away, and Rush couldn't figure out why.

The rain gave way to a wickedly dry summer. Heat pushed the rest of the Grays into their skimpiest shorts and wafer-thin tank tops. June considered shaving her entire head. Hawthorn put contacts in every day because her glasses kept slipping off her nose. Imogen and Rush did their best to pretend that nothing had changed.

Heavy sweat and thick silence kept Rush and Imogen company on a drive to the movie theater, where they settled into a pair of seats with a huge soda wedged between them.

But halfway through the movie, Imogen couldn't seem to keep her eyes on the screen. They left before the hero and the girl even managed to kiss. Rush drove Imogen back toward Tempest in yet more silence.

"Pull over," Imogen said.

She walked through the weeds at the side of the road, all the way down to the Eel River, where she took off her clothes. She looked as if she were carved from a piece of moon. Rush thought she'd finally gotten it right, given Imogen the time she needed. She closed her eyes and waited for the waiting to be over.

When she opened her eyes again, she found that Imogen had left her behind to stare at her naked backside as she lowered herself into the water. Rush sat on the bank and pulled her knees up. The dry summer had come hand in hand with a drought, but the river seemed to inch up until it almost touched Rush's sandals.

When Imogen came back, Rush asked her, "Why are we here?"

Imogen scraped up a smile. "I thought you liked night swimming."

Day after day above a hundred degrees gave Imogen an excuse to slide away whenever Rush sat down next to her, to give them both a little breathing room when they stood side by side, working a spell.

This was why Hawthorn didn't want any of the Grays to date each other. Most of them had kissed each other. Sometimes as part of their spellwork. Sometimes just to do it. When Lelia discovered she was on the ace spectrum at fifteen, she let everyone know that kissing was fun, as long as it wasn't about sprinting to get to other bases. Hawthorn and June kissed every time Hawthorn brought June a good piece of rose quartz — her favorite. The Grays took each other to school dances, brought each other corsages, held each other tight on dance floors while people laughed. They ignored the whispers about orgies. They were in love with each other, and that was good.

Love wasn't the problem.

It was losing it that could hurt the Grays.

Rush still wanted to believe that this was going to fix itself, but as week after week went by, her hope dissolved. The worst part was that Imogen kept kissing her. Dull, dutiful kisses. Kisses that had so little of Imogen in them they might as well have been the wind against Rush's lips.

And then she mumbled another girl's name when she thought Rush wasn't listening.

And then she disappeared.

Danny
NOW

I pace in knotted lines around Imogen's room as Rush tells me about her and Imogen. How it started. How it soured.

"That other girl," I say. "Who is she?"

Rush goes into Imogen's drawers and looks around. She pulls out a notebook. It's not the leather kind that Hawthorn uses, adorned with stitching and stones. This is a plain book with a cardboard face. Inside, the pages are clouded with scribbles.

Emma Hart. Emma Hart. Emma Hart.

It's the handwriting I saw pressed into the bark of the hermit's tree. The handwriting stamped into the cover of Imogen's school notebook.

Overwhelmed, I sit down on the bed, which dips under my thighs.

"Who is she?" I ask again, not meeting Rush's eyes. She's still giving off unhappiness like steam. I stare at the notebook, page after page scrawled and looped with the name *Emma Hart*, until it feels like my eyes must be broken. "Did you ask?"

Rush sits down next to me and touches the imprints on the page. Imogen used a black ballpoint pen, pressing hard. "I was too afraid to ask," Rush says.

It's not hard to understand what she means. At the time, she was only thinking about the kind of hurt that comes with being replaced.

Now there are bigger things to worry about.

"Do you think she's . . . like us?" I ask.

"Queer?" Rush asks.

"A witch," I say, laying out the words as carefully as I've seen the Grays lay out candles and herbs and polished stones. "It could explain some of this. What if Imogen knew someone else who had power? Someone who might be willing to use it in ways the Grays won't?"

"You're ignoring the obvious," Rush says, picking at the neck of her sweater. "Imogen met someone else. Someone better." Her voice fades until it's nearly gone. "She was just . . . killing time with me."

"That doesn't sound like Imogen," I say, although I don't really know her. But I think they cared about each other. If they didn't, I would have closed the space between us on this bed. I would have fistfuls of Rush's dark hair running through my hands like water.

"You think this other girl . . . Emma . . . hurt her?" Rush asks. She twitches, shaking her head. "If Imogen knew another witch, she would tell the Grays."

"Really?" It's starting to feel like I could dig a grave and fill it with all of Imogen's secrets. "Let's find the wards," I say. I rattle through the belongings in Imogen's drawers, her clothes that only come in shades of black and white. Cream, snow, crow, coal. Rush checks the closet. The more she looks around, the more sharply I realize that she's avoiding a certain spot — the far side of Imogen's bed. I get the feeling it might be the spot where Rush's most personal memories of Imogen are hidden.

I climb over the mattress on my knees, slow and clumsy, and dangle my hand into the crack on the far side, where the bed doesn't quite meet the wall. My fingers skim air until I feel something. I start grabbing and I don't stop. Rush stares from across the room. I beckon her to come closer. I don't want to do this alone. She sits down on the bleeding-sunset comforter. She crosses her legs. We're stuck in the middle of Imogen's bed together.

Staring at her magic.

Haven
NOW

Haven's parents are home.

Mrs. Lilly parks at the end of the driveway. Haven expects Imogen's friends to scatter and flee, but they're the kind of stupid that passes for loyal. They stay right where they are on the front lawn. Lelia even waves at Haven's mom, baring a smile. Haven watches from the shadows of the long, cracked-open window in the living room.

Mrs. Lilly snaps her car door shut. "Are you here to bother my daughters? They're sick."

Haven touches her clammy cheek. She smells like old sweat, like salt, no matter how many times she showers. It didn't take much convincing to get her parents to keep her home. If she's not at school, Imogen can't go, either.

Haven's dad grabs grocery bags from the hatchback. "Do you mind . . . ?" he asks, breaking up the cluster of Grays, his arms full. He passes through the front doorway, and startles when he sees Haven watching.

He nods, his dark-dark eyes — Imogen's eyes — already moving on to something more interesting. They used to hug every time they saw each other. Now Haven's dad is polite, as if she's a stranger who wandered into his house.

Haven turns back to watch Mom through the window. At least she'll put on a show. Her face has tightened; her hands are two tight coils. "Shouldn't you be at school?" she asks the Grays, the threat in her voice as polished as her freshly done, peachy-pink manicure.

"Is Haven okay?" June asks.

Haven swallows painfully. The Grays don't care if *she's* okay. That's not part of the story.

Mom wedges her way past the Grays. "She just needs a few days at home."

"Because of Imogen?" Lelia asks.

Mom blanches, almost white enough to match her platinum hair, dyed twice a month. She's been covering the dark red roots for so long that they seem almost shameful now. Haven inches forward, not sure what her mom will say about Imogen. She's lost in the house somewhere. She doesn't care what anyone says about her — not that she ever did.

Dad passes through again, coming back with more groceries. He might as well be in a different dimension.

But before Mom can decide how to take on the subject of her older daughter, Rachel and that other girl, the one with the off-kilter haircut, slither out of Imogen's room, their faces down. The new girl is carrying a bag.

Haven leans over as they pass through the living room, looking down into the depths of the bag. Knots of string. Knives and wax. And the vials of water. Always, those vials, clinking in Imogen's pockets, glaring at Haven. Their mom used to pour them down the drain like she'd caught Imogen with alcohol. When Imogen got more, Mom would break them on the decorative stones in the backyard.

But more would always surface.

Imogen was unstoppable.

Rachel and the new girl emerge from the side door into a standoff between the Grays and Haven's mom. When Mom sees the obviously stolen magic crap, her throat turns into a tight cable. Haven inches forward so she can hear what's happening outside, waiting for the moment when someone loses it.

"I could bring the police into this," Mom says.

Haven smiles for the first time in days, and it feels warm on her face, like the sun finding her after being gone forever. Punishing the Grays is only fair. They shouldn't be able to walk into this house and take whatever they want — including her sister. Even Mom and Dad know there's something wrong with Imogen, and her nonresponsive ways, and her sea-glass eyes, and that the Grays must have something to do with it.

Mom looks at the bag again, shaking her head. "You're lucky I didn't want any of that in the house to begin with." She steps inside and slams the side door. Haven's disappointment closes in on her.

Mom was supposed to do something.

"Haven," Mom says, slipping out of her shoes and walking to the living room in her peach-colored socks. Haven is still bingeing on the sight of Imogen's ex-friends like a bad television show. "Come away from that window."

"But they're not leaving, Mom," Haven says, pitching her voice just so, to make sure Mom understands.

They're the victims of the weirdest girls in Tempest, California.

Imogen appears in the background, still wearing her dirty old nightgown, hair unbound. Haven pulls hers up into a neat bun as she watches her dad put away the groceries and her mom weigh the options.

Mom picks up the phone and calls the school.

The Grays
NOW

Danny is shaking by the time the Grays gather in detention. The teacher in charge, Ms. Lefevre, settles behind her desk, one eye on the possible panic attack in the third row, the other on a thick detective novel she clearly wants to read.

"It's just detention," Lelia says to Danny, but Danny's breathing stays jagged.

"The school has a red flag planted in my behavioral issues," Danny says. "They called my mom already. She left me a message. I'm in trouble, but she wants to talk about how much."

Rush has been in so many forms of trouble with her own parents that she remembers that feeling, even if it's a little dusty. She stopped caring a long time ago. She puts one finger on the spiky bone of Danny's wrist and rubs.

Danny closes her eyes, looking relieved. But then a desk screeches as Hawthorn drags the Grays into a circle. The other students seem determined to ignore them. Two skinny freshman boys are eyeing each other like they've recently indulged in a fight, and there are three sophomores who, judging by how vigorously they're texting under the desks, probably got in trouble for taking out their phones in class.

Lelia hovers her fingertips over a girl's hair, thick and gold and rippled. It's probably what hers would look like if she didn't chop it with kitchen scissors and dye streaks with Sharpies. "Don't worry," she says with a cartoon witch–worthy cackle. "We won't eat you."

"Stop," June whispers. "They don't need any more reasons to treat us like we're going to cause trouble."

"You worry too much about people treating you like shit," Lelia says.

Hawthorn gives Lelia a bored glare. "And you don't know what it's like to be treated that way without even trying."

"No talking," Ms. Lefevre says without looking up. "And sit down, Lelia."

Lelia sits cross-legged on top of one of the desks instead of sliding into the attached chair. June takes a water bottle out of her flowered backpack. She faces the back of the room, steals a sip, bars a cough with her dimpled elbow. She holds it out to Danny beneath their desks and shrugs when Danny gives her a confused look. "It's gin. As long as I'm in trouble, I might as well roll around in it," she whispers. "Otherwise it's like building a leaf pile and not bothering to jump in."

"Ms. Ocampo," the teacher snaps. "No. Talking."

June takes out a sheet of paper and writes, in sweetly looping cursive, *At least she didn't say no drinking.* She takes another tiny swig.

Hawthorn grabs the paper, spinning it with her long fingertips, and adds: *What now?*

She nudges the bag full of Imogen's spell makings into the center of the circle with her foot. It makes a soft clinking sound. Rush watches the teacher, who seems on the verge of looking up and confiscating everything in sight.

Ms. Lefevre licks a finger and turns the page.

The bag in the center of the circle gapes open slightly, revealing Imogen's collection of bottles and pitchers and vials.

Lelia grabs the pen out of Hawthorn's hands. *Can't do wards here. The school is like a sinkhole for magic.*

June takes a turn. *Woods? Tomorrow?* Her handwriting has a hopeful bent to it. It's also slightly wobbly, as if just a few sips of alcohol have gotten her drunk. Lelia swipes the water bottle, and when June opens her mouth to protest, Lelia drinks the rest in a single, throat-bobbing gulp.

Danny takes the sheet and scribbles with a vengeance. *Today. Before sunset. The hermit isn't stealing me from my bed again.*

Hawthorn's lips twist. She does not like the notion that Neil could still be out there — it means he's not at rest. Considering what he did to Danny, he doesn't exactly *deserve* rest, but even so, a restless spirit is not a good sign. She sits down and rubs her fingers at her temples, a slight trace of coconut oil coming away on her fingertips.

Rush grabs the paper, and her long brown hair swishes against the desk as she writes. Everyone's eyes stick to her. That's the power of being the quiet one. When Rush is finally ready to talk, the Grays listen.

She pushes the paper forward.

I've got a way to get us out. If it doesn't work, I might be in bigger trouble.

Danny scowls at the paper. Hawthorn is unwilling to

sacrifice one of the Grays, even if it's just to more detention. They need to stay together. It's one of the only things keeping them safe. Witches are always in greater danger when they work alone.

But they don't have anything else.

Rush opens her mouth and starts singing. The sound rises, smudged and warm as smoke from a chimney. And suddenly the room that was soaked in October sunlight becomes even warmer, the air wrapping around them like a blanket.

"Last warning," the teacher says. "No talking."

"With all due respect, Rush isn't talking," Lelia says.

Rush's voice fills the air as the teacher turns back to her. Ms. Lefevre's neck wilts. Phones drop to the linoleum as the muscles of the students go slack. Eyes closed, breath slow.

Rush picks up the bag of Imogen's spell makings from the center of the circle, careful not to break anything as bottles slide and settle. Rush knows they don't have much time. She crouches in front of Danny's desk to wake her.

Danny doesn't look peaceful even when she's sleeping. It hurts Rush to see her like this, eyes tracking behind her closed lids as if someone is chasing her through a dream.

"Danny," Rush whispers, and her mouth fills with a tousle of ripe flavors. Strawberry, lemon, mint.

It's dangerous, how good that tastes.

She can't bear to say Danny's name again, to think she might get to keep it. Rush didn't want to tell Danny about Imogen and Emma — not because she was scared to be honest with Danny about the feelings she'd had for Imogen. It was more a wretched attempt to avoid remembering how Imogen didn't feel about her. How easy Rush was to move on from.

She flutters a hand on Danny's shoulder. If she lets herself touch Danny with pressure and purpose, she might not be able to stop.

Danny's breath slices in half, quarter notes to eighth notes.

She wakes up with the heavy work of dark-brown lashes and touches her mouth, confused. Does she think Rush had to kiss her to wake her up? Her lips are glossy, smooth, unkissed.

Rush says, "Let's go."

Danny
NOW

When the mother tree comes into sight in all of its rotting, life-giving glory, Hawthorn dumps out the bag.

"Hey!" June shouts. "Be careful with those." She kneels, and I can see that pain follows her down as she touches Imogen's possessions, pushing her lips together and keeping her face smooth by force.

"Do you want help?" Lelia asks.

"No," June grits out.

Lelia steps back. From what I can tell, Lelia's hardness is mostly bluster. June's is not.

But I can't stay away from Imogen's ward makings. I'm drawn in by a clock with a broken face. A bundle of white sage. Red string and melted-down wax. Lots of tiny bottles, each one filled with water. "So how is this stuff different from what you already have?" I ask. "Or what Ora keeps in her magical barn?"

"Have you ever looked at something and had an affinity for it?" Hawthorn asks.

"Like, a pull that felt completely out of proportion?" Lelia translates.

My eyes dart to Rush before I can stop them.

"Yeah," I say. "Sure."

"Those things can be prepared for spellwork," Hawthorn says. "But it takes time. Moon phases. And then whatever you put all of that energy into is primed."

"So these have Imogen's magic in them," I say, touching the piles like I might be able to pick up on it. "And she used these to make wards?"

"Imogen has a big, bleeding heart," Lelia says. "She mostly made wards for the same girls who stare at us in school like we have tentacles where our heads should be. They would hear that Imogen could get rid of a guy who was bothering them, and all of a sudden they'd always been friends."

"Why water, though?" I ask. "I mean, I know Imogen has a connection to it, but what turns water into a ward?"

"Moving water can stop an enemy," Hawthorn says. That word, *enemy*, simmers in the heat as Hawthorn stirs her fingers through the bottles. "Imogen collected these everywhere she went."

"Which one do you think we should use, dowser girl?" Lelia asks.

I arrange the tiny mismatched bottles into a lineup and run my fingers over them, like playing scales. My interest spikes when I hit a diamond-shaped bottle. I look up at Hawthorn, eyebrows raised. "This one is powerful."

Hawthorn works her lips into a frown. "Eel River water. It's tied to Tempest, but it's unpredictable. It might bring on calm, or it might be ferocious and unforgiving. Depends on the spell and the water sample. We need something deep. Dependable."

I don't like that I picked wrong the first time, but I go back to the bottles, quickly pulling down a few from the original lineup and creating a new one. I run my fingers over the four bottles in that group. Each is strong in its own way.

I pick up a round green glass bottle with a tiny cork stopper.

"Pacific Ocean," Rush says. She doesn't need to check the labels. She probably helped Imogen bottle most of these herself. I picture it quickly, two girls at the shore, red hair dipping toward waves, Rush kneeling in the surf. I feel like I'm there with them for a second — and then remember that I wasn't, and I could drown in the shallow water of my jealousy.

Hawthorn nods, approving my choice. "Now we have to make a likeness of each of us."

"You mean like a doll?" I ask, deeply creeped out.

Hawthorn lets out a long breath. "Just . . . something that stands for each of us. It helps if you add a piece of yourself."

I look down at myself and scowl. "What kind of piece?"

"A *symbolic* one," Lelia says. "When are you going to get the fact that we don't do blood and body parts? This is magic, not a horror movie."

"Blood is powerful," Hawthorn admits. "It's just not very creative."

"Watch," June says. She cuts off a swatch from the end of her hair and lays it in the dirt, combining it with silver string from Imogen's bag, setting down the shape of her body. Rush takes a small round cake of amber from her pocket. It takes me a second to figure out what it is — rosin from this cello she plays, even though I've never seen her with one. She borrows the small wood-handled knife from Imogen's collection and carves the rosin, one sharp nick at a time, until there's a crude version of her curves worked in it.

Hawthorn takes the flowers out of the spread of her hair, picking them carefully so the delicate pieces stay intact. She lays them down, constructing a person, all petals and sepals and circles of grass around her eyes to stand for the glasses. Then she adds mica-flecked rocks as her hair.

Lelia spits in her hands and combines it with the crumbly dark dirt under her feet and some wax from a black votive in Imogen's pile, working it until it is a kind of dark clay. She makes a mound at the far end of the mother tree, shaping it into a tiny Lelia.

I could stay here for days watching them work magic like this — like a dance they know by heart — but when it's my turn, I freeze. "What am I supposed to do?" I ask, feeling more lost than the morning they first saw me.

The Grays look at me. They look at the pile of spell bits Imogen left behind. Rush picks out a set of rubbed-down oil pastels in forest colors. They immediately leave their mark on her hands. She sits down at my feet, staring up at me. The world narrows, until all I see are her Pacific-blue eyes.

"How much do you care about these shoes?" she asks. "Would you call them a piece of you?"

"Sure."

"Can I . . . ?" She sets a finger to the canvas, and I freeze up.

These are the shoes that carried me all over Michigan, the ones I was wearing when I almost left in a stranger's car. These are the thin rubber soles that brought me to California, the heels I sank back on when I kissed Hallie Carpenter. Rush wants to know if they're part of my story, when they could probably tell the whole thing.

"Go for it," I say.

Rush starts to draw on the canvas, and I try to crane around the view of her dark hair, but it doesn't work. I have to wait. June gets the idea and picks out one of the pastels. "Hey, let me," Lelia says, grabbing the dark green. Hawthorn crowds in last, picking up my soles one at a time so she can draw on those, too.

I wobble.

I wait.

When they kneel back, I pick up my feet and inspect what they've done. Here is a girl, more or less flying. Her clothes are a dark blur. Her short, unevenly chopped hair is yet another blur. There are redwoods, and sky, boiling blue day shading into night, stars everywhere. The Grays, below her, are waiting. When I pick up the soles of my shoes there's Imogen. She's with me, every step of the way. One dark eye with a strong brow staring out from each shoe.

"That's me," I say, my voice thawed by wonder.

The Grays
FOUR YEARS AGO

Hawthorn knew every single place in Tempest that could offer a thirteen-year-old some privacy. *Alone* didn't really exist in her mom's world. Ora wanted to put her hands in her daughter's life up to the elbows.

So Hawthorn disappeared a lot. Not in a big, showy, gone-forever sort of way. Little trips to various nowheres. The High Point was good enough when she couldn't leave the farm. But her favorite spot in the world was the mother tree, so that's where she took the new friends she was making.

Hawthorn didn't know how this was supposed to work. She had been homeschooled most of her life, until Ora cast her into the deep end of eighth grade. Hawthorn got the sense it was her grandparents' idea. They were the furthest thing in the world from witches — lawyers. Ora's rebellion had started with a spellbook purchased at fifteen and lasted the rest of her life. It became Hawthorn's life, too. Her first and only real rebellion was finding friends and not immediately telling Ora everything about them.

"Why did you bring us all the way out here?" Lelia asked, panting from the hike, her face and neck and the backs of her arms stung an angry crimson.

All five of them sat on the fallen tree's trunk, their feet off the ground. "The coven never comes here," Hawthorn said. "They call the mother tree a place of death. They think the energy's *too dark.*" Her voice swirled with excess drama.

"What about you?" Imogen asked.

"White magic, black magic," Hawthorn said, her hands flying. "That's the kind of stuff people make up to sort us into piles." What witches could do wasn't good or bad. It just *was.*

"Well, I love it here," Imogen announced, reaching her fingers out as if she were trying to grab the whole woods.

It hadn't escaped Hawthorn that Imogen had raw potential for magic. She smiled at someone, and they were happy for days. When she frowned, the world inverted. And there was the water. No way of saying if Imogen was drawn to the water or it was drawn to her, but Hawthorn took note of how the Eel River pulsed on the days when Imogen was upset. How the school's sprinklers went off unexpectedly the day that Imogen wore black lipstick and declared that the world was *completely fucked.*

"Hey," Hawthorn said. "Let's do a spell. To bottle up this feeling."

She wasn't trying to start a coven. Spells were just what she did, the way that some kids played sports and others took dance lessons or learned French or played every video game in existence. And she wanted to remember this moment. It was the first day she'd felt not-alone since she was little. Which made no sense, because she was always surrounded by Ora. Ora's magic, Ora's friends, their feral kids.

"A spell?" June asked. "My parents would not like that."

"We're not asking your parents," Lelia said. "We're asking you."

"So that's a yes?" Hawthorn asked Lelia, just to be sure.

"I'm up for anything," Lelia said with a shrug of her razor-blade shoulders.

Hawthorn dumped out her bag and stirred through the selenite wands and scraps of leather for her boleen, the small knife her mother had given her when she turned twelve, the one she used to trim wicks and slice through knots and whittle shapes out of soft-skinned pieces of redwood.

She used the knifepoint to draw the outline of a human-size bottle into the dirt, and then lay down on top of it, fitting her body to the drawing. "I invite you in, I invite you in, I invite you in," she said to everything around her. She looked up at the whole sky and waited for it to shrink down inside of her.

Imogen went next, and then they each took turns lying on top of Hawthorn's outline and drawing the day into them. The other four hovered over the one inside the bottle and let her drink in the sight of them. Their nervous, excited faces.

"That was weird," Imogen said in a way that made it clear she approved. She stretched her arms way up, like she might accidentally stay bottled if she wasn't careful. "Can we do more stuff like that?"

The second Hawthorn heard the question, she knew it was the one she'd been hoping for.

Imogen gave them a secret kind of smile. "I do things like this when I'm alone sometimes. Go to graveyards and touch every grave to see if any of them feel different. Or, when it rains, I catch the drops on my skin and if they make a shape, that shape will be a message about what's happening in my life, some kind of secret. My parents don't know what to do with me," she added with very specific intonation, as if quoting something they said a lot. "They think I'm a bad influence."

"On who?" Lelia asked with a snort.

"Haven." That was Imogen's little sister. The group had met her when they picked Imogen up from her house. Haven had red curls and cream-top skin. She had wanted to talk, so they all sat around the kitchen island for an hour, letting Haven be precocious for as long as they could stand. It had been almost impossible to peel Imogen away from her little shadow.

"So what?" Lelia asked. "We're witches now?" She ran her fingers over the ferns on the mother tree where she was sitting.

"I want a name that's ours," Hawthorn said.

Imogen nodded with a grave sort of understanding. Everyone else watched closely, in case she leaked something brilliant.

Then Rachel leaped in, her voice soft and unsure. "*Magic* tastes like a spoon dipped in honey. Solid and liquid, silver and gold. *Witch*, though . . . It's like when you go to the beach and the sea is gray and the sky is gray and you can't tell which gray is which. That's how *witch* tastes."

"What are you babbling about?" Lelia asked.

"Rush has synesthesia," Imogen announced proudly.

"Is that contagious?" Lelia asked.

"Who's *Rush*?" June added, looking hungry for the secrets that Imogen and Rachel shared.

"That decides it," Imogen said. "We're the Grays."

"What do we do?" June asked.

"Anything," Hawthorn said.

"Everything," Imogen said at the same time.

"We live," Lelia shouted, standing up on the tree, stretching her body up toward the sky.

"We die," Hawthorn bookended.

Lelia tipped her thumb down. "Booooo."

"You can't live unless you're willing to die," Hawthorn parroted, not even knowing they were Ora's words until she'd already dressed them up in her own voice and passed them off as her opinion.

"What if there are other options?" Imogen asked, kicking her shoes off, anchoring her feet in the bark.

What if alive and dead weren't the simple choices everyone acted so sure about? The Grays were really thinking about it now, their eyes slick with possibilities. They all knew people who were technically alive but weren't bothering to live. They knew people who were dead on paper but whose memory lingered like sharp perfume after someone leaves a room.

Imogen closed her eyes. "If I turn into a ghost, I'm going to haunt you all so much."

"Fuck that!" Lelia shouted.

June laughed, hiding from the swear behind crosshatched fingers.

"Really?" Imogen's eyes snapped open, and the rest of the Grays focused on her pupils, slivered thin against the sun. "I thought it was a compliment. We're friends now. I would never give you up just because I was dead."

She smiled, and the line of her lips was a thread, binding them.

The Grays
NOW

Danny slips out of her shoes and stands in her bare feet, adding her likeness to the other four. They gather in a circle around the pile, but not in the usual way. Now the Grays spin outward, their backs to the center, arm pressed to arm, protecting everything inside that circle.

Rush sings a song that is made of thorns. Of *Don't come closer*.

Hawthorn weaves words through the notes, stitching together a warning as she sprinkles water from the Pacific vial on top of the shoes and the rosin, the flowers and the wax and the hair. Her fingers shake, but her voice is steady. "You will not touch what is not yours." She passes the vial, and they all dip their fingers in the water and sprinkle it, repeating the words. "You will not touch what is not yours. You will not touch what is not yours."

Even though sunset is hours away, darkness drops. The Grays have time to share one panicked look before the water they're dribbling catches fire, and the fire eats everything it falls on. The Grays are pitched out of the circle, away from one another. Danny cries out, her fingers singed. Hawthorn catches herself on her palm, bloody where it hits a rock. June falls, her leg twisted beneath her. She gasps, but the wrench is too sudden to feel how bad it is at first.

And then, it's a thousand hornets stinging. It's having your leg fall asleep hard and wake up harder, the pins and needles staying hours or days past the time when they should have faded.

This hurt is going to stay with her.

The unnatural darkness lets up, leaving the Grays in the standard blue of late afternoon. When the Grays put themselves back together, they turn to find that, where the likenesses were a minute ago, there are only five marks of scorched earth, like dark sunbursts.

"Did it work?" Danny asks.

June takes Danny by the arm, even though she's the one limping, and says, "Magic tells you when it's working."

"So what was that?"

The Grays look at one another, trying to nominate someone to give Danny the bad news. But there's no obvious choice this time.

"Blowback," they say, tripping over one another.

"Sometimes it's because you're trying a spell you don't have the power for," Hawthorn adds carefully.

"But you don't think that's what happened," Danny says.

Hawthorn touches the burn marks on the ground and winces. The Grays know that sometimes it's a gift to be read and understood, but just as often, it feels curse-like. There is no hiding when someone truly knows you. The lies you can tell narrow down, and soon nowhere is safe.

The only way to keep a secret safe is to say nothing.

"We couldn't do the spell because it had already been cast," Lelia says.

"Imogen?" Danny asks. "She put a ward on you?"

The Grays nod. They should have known. They'd felt Imogen every minute since she left, but they thought that was just a natural by-product of her being gone. A missing so strong that it filled every minute.

"That means Imogen knew something dangerous was happening *before* she disappeared," Rush says. She presses her lips together and casts a glance at Danny, a silent apology for not believing her in Imogen's bedroom.

June touches the shaved side of her head, which is already growing out to a stubborn, prickly length. "It means Imogen was doing magic without us."

"Is that really such a big deal?" Danny asks.

"Yes," Hawthorn says. "It's one of the most important rules. If you want to do little bits of everyday magic by yourself, fine. A ward for one of the girls at school to keep away an ex-boyfriend is one thing. But a spell to protect five witches from the entire world?" She shakes her head. "Way too dangerous."

It's more than being left out of Imogen's spellwork, though. If Imogen was doing magic without the Grays — if she could spin something they were supposed to do together into a secret — maybe they didn't know her as well as they thought they did.

The Grays push through anger, confusion, disbelief, as Danny stares into the dark sunbursts. Then she looks at her bare feet, already battered from last night's walk in the woods. "I have to go. Sorry. You'll be fine, I guess. Imogen is keeping *you* safe."

Hawthorn shakes her head, the blink of her eyelashes bitter. "When we used her magic to set another ward, we negated the first spell." There is a dark silence as everyone works out what this means. And then Danny says it, because, as the Grays have noted, she can't keep anything important inside of her for long.

"So no one is protected."

PART THREE

NIGHTFALL

The Students of Tempest High School
NOW

At the start of senior year, when Imogen Lilly showed up without her personality and with eyes like sea glass, everyone noticed.

And then weeks went by and friendships demanded their attention and tests annexed their brains and the fear of college tugged at their collective heart. So when Imogen actually went missing, they didn't see it.

Not at first.

A day off meant nothing. The second day went equally unnoticed. But as Imogen's absences pile up, they become officially worried.

"How long will it take before her parents admit she's missing?" asks a girl with an online girlfriend somewhere in Montana.

"A month," her straight friend says. "Maybe two."

"Has anyone talked to her sister?"

They track Haven down, corner her by her locker in freshman hall, and ask her the same pointed questions that half a dozen students have already asked. She sighs, twisting red hair around her finger like string. "She ran away, I guess. I don't know. She usually stays close to me, and then I woke up and she was just . . . gone."

Some of the girls with bottles of water sloshing around their necks want to believe it's true. They text each other endless possibilities.

Maybe she went to San Francisco

Or LA

The Rockies?

Tempest was never big enough to hold Imogen. They imagine her into epic new settings, a spiral of red hair and a challenge of a smile against the background of pastel Victorian row houses, neon-laced strip malls in pink and mint, mountains that rise high enough to put even the redwoods to shame.

No matter how many lives they brew up, they can't quite shake another vision: a headstone with her name on it, a grave with no body. That's what happens to the people in Tempest who walk into the woods and never come back.

On their way home from school, as the autumn days trim down shorter and shorter, Imogen's classmates look at the redwoods out of the corners of their eyes. They'd gotten used to coexisting with these beautiful monsters. But now the students side-eye the trees as if they might grab someone.

In the daylight they tell themselves they're being ridiculous. Imogen was too savvy to do something as dumb as get lost in the woods — not when GPS exists. There has to be another explanation, a finger to point. And the students of Tempest High know where to point it.

They pull the new girl aside. They drop notes in her locker, visit her when she's frothing milk for lattes at Coffee Gods. "Be careful," they say, looking around to make sure they're not being overheard. "The weird girls are at it again."

"At what?" Danny asks, acting stupid on purpose. The Grays already have their sparkly black nails in her.

The girls who are going out of their way to help her really don't need this kind of denial. "They did something to that new kid, Sebastian. They did something to Imogen. They'll get you, too."

"Someone is messing with Tempest," Danny says, handing the girls their extra-hot lattes. "But it's not the Grays."

She waves her nails as she dismisses them. Sparkly. Black.

She really believes she's one of them.

Her funeral.

Danny
NOW

The Grays and I only have five minutes together before classes start. We gather at the end of the hallway, where it opens up into the lawn. Lelia is a walking haze of pot smoke. Rush looks too nervous to speak. June is standing on one leg and leaning the rest of her weight on Hawthorn as they frantically try to concoct a new plan to get Imogen back, to keep us safe. Nobody looks at me directly. Nobody blames me for not finding her.

But it's there between us, thick as fog, even if I can't touch it.

"Danny, when can we meet to . . . ?" June asks, letting the question dangle.

I shake my head. When I got home after the wards failed, Mom grounded me for the detention and the skipped class. There's not going to be enough time for spells. Not for weeks.

"It's fine," Hawthorn says, lying through her supremely white teeth. "We're all going to be fine." June hangs her head and groans. Lelia kicks a locker, sending a horde of sopho-mores scattering down the hall. Rush's silence, which is usually so deep and peaceful, turns malignant. She stares a hole into the ground, and I wait for it to open up.

If this is a preview of how the Grays will break up when Imogen's gone forever, I have to stop it.

So I start searching.

In that sliver between day and night, between school and grounded, I go out with my dowsing rod, Lelia's raven feather set against a long redwood stick I picked up in the woods.

I hold out the dowsing rod, the road and trees blurring into the background. I take step after step, but the rod doesn't feel quite right. Maybe I'm just not used to it yet. Maybe it feels wrong to wield it without the Grays around me.

They said it's dangerous to do magic alone, but I don't have time to care about the rules. Of course, that might be exactly how Imogen felt right before she disappeared. I push those thoughts away, focus my entire mind to a point as small as the end of the dowsing rod, and look for the truth about what happened to Imogen.

I look for three days in a row.

Every day, I find Rush.

The first time, I'm passing the Tempest Diner. I feel a prickle at the back of my neck and turn. Rush is perfectly framed in the front window, waiting for an order. Like so many people do in California, she keeps her sunglasses on — aviators tinted saltwater green. I'm busy staring when she catches sight of me. Even without her eyes to give her away, I can see her face light up. But I'm afraid to be near her without the insulation of the Grays, the safe distance they create when they're standing between us.

I act like I didn't see her and hurry down the row of shops.

The second time, she's sitting in her car in the trailhead that leads to one of the least popular redwood hikes. The car looks abandoned at first, and my heart skids. What if she went into the woods looking for Imogen and didn't come back? But no — she's slouched in the driver's seat, smoking a cigarette, which I've never seen her do. It's like watching someone speak a language you didn't know they knew. She tips the ash out the window. Pulls so hard that the end lights up an angry red. Then she stubs it out, somewhere out of view. She lifts a jar of honey from the passenger seat, tips her throat. Her lips reach for amber droplets that are sliding down, down, down the glass. It's not a black-cherry lipstick day. Her mouth is stripped, soft pink. The droplets are stuck.

I run away fast, as if I've been caught staring in her window at night.

And then I find her in the graveyard, singing for an audience of trees. Rush's voice is a ribbon, shiny and unspooling, leading me forward. I don't stop until I'm up against the fence, standing behind her, the dowsing rod pointed at her back. The tips of Rush's long dark hair reach for the ground. Her music rises.

This is a melody I've never heard before. Imogen's song was powerful but trapped. This makes me think of wind and freedom. It skips through the air like a kite, brighter than anything around it.

This time I don't have to run. Rush is so bound up in the music that she doesn't even notice me.

Imogen and Rush
FIVE YEARS AGO

They met in fall, not long after school started, on a day that smelled of sweetly rotting leaves. Imogen Lilly wasn't new in Tempest, and neither was Rachel Downing, but they were new to each other.

Imogen had outgrown childhood friends, the ones that had been chosen for her. Rachel didn't have time for friends. She had music. Rehearsals, recitals, dreams that were shoved full of difficult runs that woke her up with aching fingers and sweat on the back of her neck.

She was in the cemetery that day, sitting on a headstone, playing Tchaikovsky. She had always liked him, as a composer, for the obvious reasons (his work was lively and his name tasted like almonds, both bitter and sweet) and the other reason (he was gay, which made Rachel feel a kinship she didn't fully understand when she was twelve and more focused on whether she won first chair than figuring out who to kiss). The problem was that Tchaikovsky never completed his own cello concerto, so she was actually playing the Leonovich, based on a fractured set of bars from Tchaikovsky's papers.

It was murder on her hands, and she wasn't very good at it. Or she was technically good, but Rachel knew about the huge leap between mastery and the magic that comes with playing with a piece like it *matters.*

Like playing it is the difference between life and death.

She was fretting about it when a girl in a white overall dress and a black T-shirt and the big spilling tongues of boys' work boots came wandering out of the woods and sat astride the fence, stripping the petals off flowers and watching her play. It was nice for a few minutes, and then it was irritating.

Rachel ripped her bow away from the strings. "How long are you going to stay?"

"Until I'm sure you're real." The girl stared at Rachel, and a name came to her in a sudden burst. *Imogen.*

Rachel laid her bow down in the long grass and set the cello on its side, carefully, as if she were putting it to sleep. "Why wouldn't I be real?"

"Sometimes I hear things in the woods," the girl said, waving vaguely at the redwoods behind them. "It sounds like the trees are talking to each other."

"You don't think it's real?" These questions were there when Rachel opened her mouth. She didn't have to reach for them nearly as hard as she did for fifth and seventh positions. They slid out, like notes that played themselves.

"Ummm," Imogen said. "Trees are just wood."

"So is this," Rachel said, rapping the side of her cello with her knuckles.

"Yeah, but you're the one *making* it make that sound," Imogen argued.

"Maybe there are people in the woods and you can't see them." Rush tried to sound like an expert, because for some reason she cared if Imogen believed her. "People don't see other people all the time. I can stand right in front of my parents and they don't see me."

Imogen seemed to take this problem seriously. She devoured Rachel with her dark eyes. "You look really uncomfortable in that," she said, pointing at literally everything Rachel was wearing.

It sounded like a challenge, so without a word, Rachel tore the taffeta bow out of her hair, working out the stiff, tight architecture of the French braid. It left her hair rippled and loose. She took off her blouse, revealing the sigh of a loose white camisole. She left the short blue satin skirt on but kicked her jeweled black flats up so high that they looked like gleaming dark birds against the October sky.

"Better," Imogen said.

Rachel had to agree. "Yeah."

"Your music is pretty," Imogen said.

Rachel sighed. She didn't want *pretty*. That word was bland, and she craved something better. "I want to play like my sister," Rachel said. "She's in an orchestra. Actually, she plays in a lot of orchestras."

"Does she play the cello, like you?" Imogen asked, looking less interested in Rachel's sister than in Rachel herself. Which was rare.

"The clarinet," Rachel said. "She's going to leave someday and do a tour of the whole world, and I'm going to be stuck here. Forever. Alone."

"What's your name?" Imogen asked, leaning down to kiss a flower and then taking it apart two petals at a time.

"Rachel Downing."

Imogen shook her head, red curls clutching sunlight. "Nope."

Everything about Rachel's proper upbringing came back to her at once. "You can't tell someone that their name is not their name."

Imogen wasn't having it. She jumped off the fence and landed inside the cemetery with a decisive crash. "It's like those clothes you were wearing," she said. "There's nothing *wrong* with them. They just don't match you."

Rachel pursed her lips. She picked up the cello again, spinning out a few bars of the Tchaikovsky, her fingers rushing over the dark wood, the indents in her fingertips lighting up with a fresh sting, the notes burning so hard that Rachel almost expected them to leave scorch marks on the air. "How about that?"

"I like it. Why *can't* music be your name?" Imogen asked, twirling the idea around like it was another flower between her fingers, something to admire and then take apart. She turned back to Rachel. "But I still need something to call you."

Rachel thought of the heady feeling she got when she was playing a favorite bit of one of her favorite songs. When the music wasn't flowing through her like a calm river but pushing toward a destination.

"Rush," she said. "You can call me Rush."

Danny
NOW

Imogen has been missing for ten days, and whatever I feel for Rush is clouding my ability to find her.

I can't imagine seeing Rush again and not talking to her. Not touching her. When we sat on Imogen's bed together, Rush's leg rested against my arm, two parts pressed that I'd never thought to put together. That felt like a revelation. That felt like enough.

But *enough* takes up more and more space, fast.

After the last bell rings on Monday, I avoid the Grays and take out my dowsing rod yet again. I've been frantically trying to graduate from babywitch into serious dowser. At first, the decision to search on my own was just practical. But now I want to find Imogen myself. I want to give her to the Grays, like a present. Then I want *them* to unpack her. To ask their perfect, pretty witch what the hell is going on.

I walk over the lawn and plant myself at the very edge of the soccer field, which is maybe a weird place to start, but it feels neutral to me. No Rush-related longings. I draw the dowsing rod out from my red canvas backpack, which can barely hold any books now that it's home to an enormous stick lined with a long, delicate raven feather.

I hold out the dowsing rod and think about Imogen. I've only seen her a few times, but I remember her as if she's carved into my brain. Taller than I am by at least four inches, tall enough that it makes her seem older than seventeen. Her body scrolling with endless curves. Her white skin offset by the exclusively black-and-white wardrobe, and a rainbow of chakra stones on her fingers, her wrists, at her neck.

Red curls, everywhere.

My feet start to traipse over fakely green grass and white painted lines. The dowsing rod is tugging me back toward school. There are almost no students left, but the few who are are definitely staring.

I stare back.

I let them see exactly how little I care.

The flame on my life has been turned up, and what I care about boils down to three things: Keep Mom happy. Keep the Grays safe. Find Imogen.

The dowsing rod stops, twitches, turns me around a corner into freshman hall. I see a girl with red hair standing with her forehead resting against a locker, eyes closed, and for a second I think I did it.

"Imogen?" I ask.

She spins fast, her hair slicing the air, eyes panicked. They're also perfectly clear, without the mist that clouds Imogen's. This is Haven, Imogen's sister. I realize I'm standing in the middle of the hall with a dowsing rod in front of me. There's no hiding the weird right now. Haven swallows so hard that I can hear the dry, painful sound.

"What are you doing?" she asks.

I could lie to her. But it seems like she lives in a house where people tell her less than the truth all the time. Or maybe they only tell her the truth according to the Lillys, and that's nothing like mine.

"I'm a dowser," I say. This is the first time I've said it to anyone but the Grays, and I thought it would come out sounding weak or ridiculous, but it feels solid in my mouth. "It means I find things that other people can't."

Haven looks less sickly than she did the last time I saw her, some of the purple swept away from beneath her eyes. They skitter up and down the length of the dowsing rod. It's still pointing at her. I lower it slightly. "You're looking for my sister, aren't you?"

I check all around us, like admitting it in front of the wrong person might be dangerous. But we're alone. "I need to find her."

Haven sinks against her locker as if she's melting. "Why do you want her?"

It's a good question. One I've asked myself a dozen times, always finding a different answer. *Because our friends are in trouble. Because it's in my nature to find things. Because I want to kiss her maybe-ex-girlfriend.* "If I was missing, that's what I'd want someone to do for me."

Haven looks up at me, her dark eyes unnaturally calm. When I stare too long, I unbury the feelings she's hiding from everyone. The turmoil of losing someone she's known all her life, the loneliness of going through it with those parents. The guilt of not being able to fix things. I want to tell her I'm feeling the same guilt, but I'm afraid she'll run, like a deer scared off by the touch of headlights.

"You were nice to me," Haven says. "So I'll tell you the truth."

"About what happened to Imogen?" I ask, my chest filling with hopeful static. Maybe that's why the dowsing rod led me here. Maybe Haven knows where her sister is. Maybe she really *did* run away.

"No." Haven narrows her eyes. Even her freckles pinch. "You don't know her."

"I'm learning fast," I say.

Haven hunches her shoulders so hard, it looks like she might fold in half. "You believe what the Grays tell you," she says. "But I'm her sister."

Haven and Imogen
FOUR YEARS AGO

Sitting on the bank of the Eel River, Haven felt as uncomfortable as if a hornet were buzzing around her, refusing to go away, refusing to sting.

"I'm a witch, I'm a witch," Imogen sang.

"Stop it," Haven said, curling her knees tight to her chest.

"Why should I?" Imogen asked, kicking through the water in a slow circle. "It's who I am. You can't just stop being who you are."

Haven very, very much wanted to disagree. She also didn't want to start a fight. So she stared down at the pale-mint water. She stared up at a canyon of sky between the treetops on both sides of the Eel River.

She looked everywhere but at her sister.

They swam for a while, or Imogen swam and Haven watched. Imogen's legs were strong, and she didn't seem to feel the cold.

Haven sunned on the river's margin, made of all kinds of pebbles. Dark and pale pebbles. Scratchy and smooth.

Broken from glass or chipped from cement or made when the earth pushed down on itself for thousands and thousands of years.

Imogen looked over with her dark eyes, fighting to keep them wide when the sun was blaring. "You can be a witch, too."

"Maybe I don't want to be one," Haven said. Even though she really, really did. But she also wanted to be normal like her parents. Imogen had everything easy. She couldn't stop herself from doing what she wanted.

"You should try it," Imogen said. "It's fun." She smirked at the water, and it flicked onto Haven's feet, getting her icy and wet.

Haven snatched her toes back. "Hey! You did that!"

"You can't prove anything," Imogen said, but a second later, water that had been totally calm slapped at the shore and then broke over Haven in a cold, glassy sheet. She shrieked. Imogen laughed as she bobbed in the water.

"Stop," Haven said.

"Okay," Imogen said. She swam in a little, found her footing, and stood up. The water was building, slapping Haven over and over.

"Stop!" Haven screamed. Her voice rose, but it was their special swimming hole and there was no one around to hear except Imogen.

Haven started to cry.

"I'm trying," Imogen said, looking upset but not actually stopping the water. "Everything was fine until I tried to control it."

"Shut up," Haven said. "You're lying. You're doing it on *purpose.*"

"Why don't you believe me?" Imogen asked as the water rose and rose, as she swirled her hands in strange shapes, and the water swirled, too, until it was a hand grabbing for Haven's throat.

Haven screamed, and the sky went white.

Danny
NOW

I wonder how long she's been keeping that story in. Haven has a shocked look on her face, eyes hard with shine and chin jutted so her mouth is still open an inch.

"Do your parents know about that?" I ask.

"Seriously?" Haven asks. "If I told them, they would have had Imogen taken away." She looks down at her fingers, twisting them into a pale knot. Then she looks back up at me and does damage control. "I woke up and everything was fine. We told Mom and Dad that I got heatstroke. I didn't get to go outside for the rest of the summer."

"That sounds bad," I say. "And not really fair."

Haven looks at me like I single-handedly turned night to day. "That's what *I* thought."

I take a step closer to Haven. Just one. I don't want to scare her. But I need to know more about the Imogen that only *she* knows. "Did she ever use her magic on you again?"

Haven stares down the length of the open hallway, toward the woods beyond the school. "No."

I think about Neil. Did he steal me away from my bed, steer me through the woods, to tell me who had killed him?

Imogen's words there in the bark. His actual death, the voice in that memory, the one that said *I'm sorry, Neil.*

But I've never heard Imogen's voice. Only memories translated through a dozen different minds, pouring out of a dozen mouths. I've seen the versions of her that other people remember, and none of them match up.

"Can I go?" Haven asks, as if I'm keeping her there by force.

"Of course you can," I say.

She runs off, a scared animal. When I get back to Tempest Gardens, I trap myself in cottage nine for the afternoon, doing homework for a class about California's history and geography. It's stuffed with facts about redwoods. They *drink* fog. That's why they love the valleys of the Lost Coast, which always seem to be filled with it. They're fickle about climate. They like to be near salt water but not too near. They send each other messages, keep each other safe. And they only thrive with other redwoods around.

The Grays are like that. Hawthorn, June, Lelia, and Rush need each other to thrive. I've seen the way they help each other stand tall. Because they have each other, they can be who they are in the largest, most complete sense. But I don't know what happens if I don't find Imogen. Does the whole forest come down?

I rush to the end and open my math notebook. I flip into the depths of the pages and scribble questions.

Where is Imogen now?

Is she alone?

Do her parents even care?

If she ran away, where did she go?

There's a knock on the door. I climb over the little table where I've set my dowsing rod next to my homework and open it.

It's Rush, wearing the Tempest Gardens apron over shorts and a fluttery tank top. Her hair, dark as wet earth, spills down past her pockets. The dowsing rod on the table is pointing straight at her. Apparently I'm going to keep finding Rush no matter what.

I step aside so she can come in. She gets right to work, making herself industrious.

"I thought you were working at Coffee Gods today," she says.

"Veronica needed to switch. She said I could take her Saturday morning; it's the shift with the best tips. And we definitely need the money, so . . ." My sentence trickles out to nothing.

"Veronica," she says slowly. "Her name even *tastes* like coffee."

I can't help but fall into the beautiful trap of it. "What do I taste like?"

It must be nice, because Rush's lips loosen into a smile. It's new to me, but somehow this looks like her natural state. I wonder if this is the girl Rush was before Imogen went missing.

"*Danny.*" I watch her rolling my name around in her mouth. Tasting it. Then she opens her eyes fast, wiping dust from the windowsill as she recites, "Strawberry and lemon and fresh mint leaves."

"What about Imogen?" I ask.

"Licorice and cream," she says automatically.

I get what I asked for — a hard pebble of jealousy lodged in my throat. But I notice that she doesn't say Imogen's name.

Rush cleans the knobs on the gas stove, opens the oven, and wipes down the inside until her cloth is oily black. She works through every area in the cottage until there's only one left — the love seat where I'm sitting. I keep my feet bolted to the ground. I'm not leaving this time.

She considers me carefully. Then she goes back to her cart, picks up her spray, and thickens the air with it.

"That stuff is unbreathable," I say.

"Then come outside," she says. "There's real air and *October*."

"You know I can't leave."

She comes right over and sits down with me, hip pushing at mine until there's room for both of us. Barely. I can't imagine Mom would let me bring a girl into the cottage when she's gone, while I'm being punished. But this is a different kind of punishment: sitting this close, my thoughts turned to glue, my skin informing me how close her skin is.

"The wards are broken," I say. "Aren't you afraid that we'll get hurt if we go out there? If we attract the attention of . . . whatever Imogen was trying to protect you from?"

Rush draws spirals in the margin of my homework. "Sometimes hurt is better than nothing."

I don't think we're talking about magic. Or maybe we are. A different kind. Just as dangerous. Just as likely to have rules that make you feel like you're safe until you're fumbling around in the dark, chanting breathy words, more potent then you've ever felt, with no idea how you got there, no way of knowing if you're going to be the one who hurts or gets hurt. The one who leaves or gets left behind.

"Come with me," Rush says, her fingers sliding lightly along the backs of mine.

And I stand up, spilling homework everywhere. I look until I find the not-very-creative spot where Mom hid my phone in a drawer. I grab my bag and slip the dowsing rod inside. Rush doesn't seem to care what happens to her cleaning cart. I leave a note for Mom.

I'm alive.

It's never felt this true.

I follow Rush, one stone at a time, down the path. She looks up at the trees, down at her feet, working them out of her sneakers, hanging those sneakers from one hand so she can feel the slate on her arches, the mulch between her toes, the hard kiss of the parking lot as she leads me toward her car. The Deathmobile. Her hair swings darkly, back and forth like a metronome, keeping its own time and not anyone else's. The way she walks, at home in her skin, with all the doors open wide, is what I want. She turns back to me and smiles.

Rush wants me with her, and she doesn't have to cast a spell to convince me.

She *is* the spell.

Emma and Imogen
FIVE MONTHS AGO

Emma Hart loved the Grays, though she sometimes felt as if she were on one side of a thick-paned glass staring in at them. Outside in the cold as they talked and danced and chanted and kissed.

Their kissing started out as innocent as anything else. It made Emma happy to see the Grays so free with one another, love flowing around them in eddies and swirls, never trapped in their hearts with nowhere to go.

Then Rush and Imogen started looking at each other in a way that Emma knew painfully, perfectly — from the inside. She was the first to understand what was coming next. She saw it from a mile away, a storm on the horizon.

The first time Rush and Imogen kissed in the woods, Emma vowed never to speak to Imogen again. It was best for both of them.

"But that's not what I want," Imogen said, her stubbornness putting small cracks in Emma's resolve.

"What *do* you want?" Emma asked.

"For you to be with me," Imogen said. "Always."

Emma remembered someone else telling her they would always be together, a very long time ago.

It hurt just as much the second time.

Imogen visited Emma as much as ever — more, even — but sometimes she came fresh from kissing Rush, her lips swollen and cinnamon pink.

It was the worst when Imogen tried to talk to her about kissing Rush. Imogen thought that Emma was only sad about the past. As if seeing her with Rush could fill the emptiness of what never happened with Ada.

"It's amazing, the way I can tell when she wants to kiss without her even saying it first," Imogen gushed. "It's like I can hear her entire body asking me." Emma's heart raged, an overfull river, but Imogen couldn't see that. "Rush is always so quiet, but her body's not quiet at all. It's making music and talking to me and shouting. When I kiss her, all of that pours into me."

"Please don't tell me more," Emma said, a strained whisper.

Imogen was free, and she was choosing someone else. Someone who could be with her in a way that Emma never could.

Danny
NOW

I hold my breath as Rush steers the Deathmobile one-handed through town, past the shops and the school and then a little farther, sliding us into the dirt tracks alongside the cemetery.

When she stops the car, I get out. Fast.

"What are we doing here?" I ask, pretending I haven't already followed her to this exact place. It's an old patch of graves, barely cared for. The wildness at the edges is gnawing inward, toward the center. A little fence pretends to be the boundary, but mostly it's an excuse for wildflowers to grow along the posts. The headstones aren't planted in rows, but wherever people thought to put them. Some are the old-fashioned kind with grimacing angels. In one corner is a little blocked-off section where the stones are tall and white and wafer-thin, all done in the same stark style.

"I met Imogen here," Rush says, her soft voice blanketing the cemetery.

"Of course you did," I mutter. It would never be something boring with Imogen.

"And *this*," Rush says, popping the trunk and letting it whine open, "is why I don't let the Grays ride in my car. They would find what I keep in here."

"You mean the bodies?" I ask.

It's the worst possible thing to say, but somehow it earns me a quiet laugh.

Rush pulls out a black cloth case by a handle. It's as wide as a body, with curves even more dramatic than hers. When she sets it to the ground, it clunks in a distinctly wooden way.

"Is that . . . ?"

"A cello," she confirms. "I don't really play much anymore, unless I'm upset. It's like comfort food. I used to come here because I thought I wasn't good enough for living audiences yet. I made dead people listen to me instead. They had to deal with a lot of Dvořák."

She finds a headstone to sit on, not setting her full weight against it but leaning so gently that I can't imagine the person buried there minds at all. She unzips the cello from its case, peels away the cover, and centers it between her bare legs.

I blush so hard that I'm competing with the sunset. Rush doesn't seem to notice. She stares down at her hands, one of them pressing the strings, the other one working the bow. A chord slides out, bursting with unexpected harmonies. She grates the bow across the strings on purpose, then smooths the sound over. It brightens the air, wakes up the birds. They take to the sky. The wind picks up, shaking the flowers at the edges of the cemetery. Rush's playing is a call to everything around us—living and dead. "Imogen wandered out of the woods one day."

The birds flock above us. Ravens and crows and smaller ones, starlings maybe. A dark swirl of birds.

I close my eyes and listen as Rush plays herself into the past.

Emma and Imogen

TWO MONTHS AGO

Rush and Imogen were together. Pasted to each other's sides, always kissing. Those weeks of wandering were the worst Emma had ever known, a doubled pain pressing down on her.

She felt like crying, but she couldn't cry. Instead, the world filled with a stinging-cold rain. When she was stupid enough to follow Imogen through the woods one day, she found Imogen and Rush pressed against a tree, untouchable. Every drop of rain that flowed around their skin was a reminder.

They had what Emma never would.

She left that clearing in a hurry, not wanting to see the rest. The inevitable, perfect moments of love. Emma waited for time to sweep this whole thing away like a rough broom. In a few years, Imogen would leave her behind. Someday she would die. There was no real comfort for this, only an inching away from pain.

The next time Emma visited the mother tree, Imogen was waiting. She sat on the mossy center of the fallen trunk, wearing a loose creamy-white dress with an eyelet pattern.

"I missed you," Imogen said the moment Emma came into the grove.

"That doesn't change anything," Emma said, instead of what she meant. She meant, *I missed you, too.*

"I can't keep doing this," Imogen said, and Emma waited for the moment when Imogen announced that she would leave forever, that she would never visit the woods again. Imogen looked down at the ground, then up at the blank space where Emma should be. "I need to see you. *Really* see you. I think I found a way."

Danny

NOW

The last note from Rush's cello haunts the air, and then we're sitting in the kind of tense, breakable silence that makes me realize how natural and calm the silence of cemeteries usually feels.

"When did you stop playing?" I ask, pointing at the cello with my sneaker. "I mean, officially?"

"When I met Hawthorn, she told me about chanting. I loved the idea. I'm not even a good singer, really."

"You are," I say, the dark burn of my feelings leaving a mark on my voice. "Really."

"Thanks," Rush says, looking embarrassed and pleased, her eyebrows scrunching in a way that I enjoy far too much.

"Did your parents get mad?" I asked. "When you stopped playing?"

"They don't really *do* mad. They do disapproval. They thought that I was going through a phase." Anger is coming off of Rush in sheets, and after a second of heat, I realize that I'm feeling it, too, for her parents — and mine. They didn't ever use the word *phase*, but there were times when it seemed like they were waiting for parts of me to disappear. "When I quit orchestra and skipped all my private lessons and started spending my time with a bunch of queer witches, my parents weren't exactly happy. My mother said that as long as I was living in their house, I would keep playing. So I stayed with the Grays, couch-surfed for a while. That's when I learned how to ride motorcycles with Lelia."

There's a delicate silence as I realize what Rush just told me: her parents kicked her out, and she would have been on her own if the Grays hadn't taken her in. I'd thought leaving Michigan for California was a big deal, but I'd never had to leave Mom. She'd stood by me, even when she didn't understand, well past the time when she had solid reasons to trust me. The anger from a minute ago vanishes, leaving an empty space that I want to fill by running back to cottage nine and finding Mom right there, waiting. But I also have Rush standing in front of me with her pain on full display as she toes the dark dirt under the rough cemetery grass.

I want to find out everything about her, not just gawk at her while she eats muffins. "When you were staying with Lelia, that's when she decided you're a rebel?" I ask.

Rush laughs. "I also babysat June's brothers and sisters and learned how to make desserts from the Philippines with her mom."

"What about Hawthorn?"

"I was on the farm for a few weeks, but it didn't feel right to stay long. Ora is . . . a force," Rush says. "She wanted to train me as a chanter. I loved waking up early and sitting with Ora and drinking this tea she makes, with dandelions and a thousand different herbs in it. But it wasn't easy for Hawthorn, I think."

"She probably just didn't want to lose you," I said.

"It's a good thing Ora hasn't met you," Rush says, giving me an all-over look. "I think she'd claim you for her coven."

"Why?"

Rush blinks at me as though she can't believe I'm making her say it out loud. "You're powerful."

"Not like Imogen," I say without thinking.

"Why does it have to be a competition?" Rush asks. "Maybe we need everyone's power, not a fight over who has the most."

"Sorry," I say. "It's just . . . I've never been around other people like me before."

Rush isn't letting up with the intense blue staring, so I look at the ground, but that's no real relief because there are dead people down there. Can they feel the echoes of what's happening above them? Does it trickle through soil and caskets? Do they remember what it's like to be alive? To want too much?

You're going to get hurt.

"So you still come here and play?" I ask, sitting down in the grass, sliding closer to Rush. I follow in Imogen's foot-steps. I follow my hard-beating heart.

"Yeah," Rush says. "Secret playing."

"The Grays have *never* heard you?"

"Only one of them. Once," she says, and I don't have to ask which Gray it was. The last of the birds above us slide away, leaving the sky empty of everything but sunset. "My music used to belong to my parents. Sometimes I want to have things that don't belong to anyone else. Not even the Grays."

I have two thoughts.

The first is that I've been working so hard to do the exact opposite of Rush, to have things that aren't *just* mine.

The other is that Rush played for me. She broke her own rule. Or maybe when she lets me listen, the rule stays magically intact. Maybe the music stays *hers* in a way that it wouldn't with other people.

That idea is way too tempting, so I run away from it at top speed. "But you're sharing with all of these lovely people." I open my arms, flourishing them at the graves. I grab Rush's bow, spring up, and start pointing it at headstones, reciting names. *Valerie Moore. Elizabeth Livingston.*

At first I'm doing it to put on a show, but with every etched name, the show becomes more serious. The bow feels right in my hands, like a piece of fruit that's reached the perfect ripeness. It tugs me over toward the little patch of graves with the stark matching headstones.

"Don't," Rush calls out. "Nobody goes over there."

I spin around, drawing a circle in the air with the bow. "Why not?"

"Those are hollow graves."

"What do you mean *hollow*?"

Rush gives the patch a sideways glare. "No one's buried in those. They're markers for people who've gotten lost in the woods and didn't come back."

I keep walking. I tell myself that it's the bow leading me forward, pointing the way. I step over a line of stones on the ground, and the air changes. It feels dense here, colder. My skin ripples. It must be the sun going down.

I move the bow from grave to grave, focused on the empty space between the horsehair and the wood. Before, I was shouting names, flinging them toward the sky. Now I'm whispering, cold as fog.

Evelyn Stuttgart

Rosa Ramona Díaz

Matthew Blackall

Emma Hart

Danny and Rush
NOW

Rush can't believe the name was there the whole time, only a few yards away, waiting for her to find. She's been afraid of it for so long — wanting to know who it belonged to, and not wanting to know, both forces dragging her down. She crouches to touch the writing on the headstone, carved so the actual letters are just hollow space.

Emma Hart

Danny touches Rush's back but doesn't say anything. She gives Rush a second to process, even as her own mind sprints from one strange truth to the next. Maybe when she found Rush over and over, she *was* dowsing. Maybe it had nothing to do with Danny's oversize crush. Her impatient heart. Rush led Danny to hidden pieces of the story, pieces no one else had.

Together, they ended up here.

Stuck on that name. Breathing it in. Letting it out.

Emma Hart

The whole world narrows down to the size of that name on a headstone, and then it starts to ease open. Rush can hear the wind again, lacing through the trees. Danny watches darkness flirt with the edges of the sky.

"Do you think that's why Imogen left?" Rush asks. "Because of . . . her?"

Danny can't answer that. She doesn't know Imogen's heart. She only knows her own, and it's starting to hurt. She helps Rush to her feet but tries not to look too deep into the shifting blue of her eyes. Danny holds out the bow, pressing it forward, trying to hand it back to Rush.

"Keep it," Rush says, putting her hand over Danny's and pushing the bow back toward her. "I think it's supposed to be yours."

Danny knows Rush wants her to have a dowsing rod, to find Imogen — but maybe Rush also wants Danny to have her own power. Danny touches the silk of the horsehair bow, sticky with rosin. She doesn't fight back against the sudden tide of Rush's generosity. She'll take anything Rush will give her.

She'll give anything Rush will take from her.

Rush's hand is still on hers. Their bodies turn before their thoughts catch up. In a second, they are softly aligned, touching their mouths together, testing to see if either of them will stop this.

One touch. Two.

Neither girl backs off.

Danny has been trying to reason it away, and Rush has been afraid to let herself feel this again but it rolls over both of them as their lips open and a secret warmth passes between them. The dull, obvious reasons they shouldn't do this still exist, but there is no room for them as Rush's hands claim Danny's hips, and Danny's fingers slide over the pink silk ribbons of Rush's cheeks. She sinks fingers deep into the earthy brown of Rush's hair.

Danny thinks, wildly, that she is finding one more thing that she needs, even if she has to keep it a secret, even if it never happens again, even if no one else cares.

This matters. *They* matter.

Rush and Danny kiss and kiss so they don't have to talk about Imogen or Emma. They kiss and pretend, for a minute, that they are the only ones who matter. They kiss as night coats them in a first, thin layer of darkness that feels like it could be peeled off with careful fingers.

But it's only going to get darker.

Danny
NOW

When I spin away from Rush, I'm aware of so many things. The first is that she kisses like a wave breaking.

The second is that if I don't stop, *now*, I might never be able to.

The third is that every cell in my body is awake, and when I feel like that, magic can't be far behind.

"I need to dowse," I mutter, running toward the Deathmobile.

"Now?" Rush asks, close at my heels.

"That kiss . . ." That kiss was a million things. It was everything I needed and wanted and shouldn't have done. But I don't tell Rush any of that. "I'm pretty sure it gave my magic a boost."

When I get to the car, I grab my bag and pull out the dowsing rod. I untie the black string holding the raven feather, careful not to ruffle it. Then I settle the feather into the crook of the bow, messing up the knots because my fingertips have gone numb and stupid at the touch of Rush's skin.

Rush comes up behind me, slipping her cello back into the trunk. After she bangs the lid of the trunk down three times to close it, she offers me a soft black case that matches the bow.

"Thanks," I say, pinching the final knot into place.

I want to grab her again and kiss her until our minds drain of every thought, every memory of dead boys and lost girls. Instead, I hold up the new dowsing rod, and power sings through me.

"It's a few miles," I say, as confidently as if I'm looking at a map. I point past the cemetery, away from Tempest.

"Can you feel her?" Rush asks, leaving Imogen's name unspoken. "Did she send another message?"

"I don't know yet," I say, still supercharged from the combination of dowsing and Rush's soft kiss. "But this is important."

We get back into Rush's car and she drives north, following the curves of the highway as slowly as she can so we don't miss whatever is calling my name.

"There," I say, and she spins a sharp turn into a gravel parking lot. There's a low building on one side with a massive cross section of a redwood in front of it. I've never been inside it before, but I'm pretty sure this is the Tempest visitors' center.

The same one Haven mentioned when she told me that story.

I'm out of the car before Rush can bring it to a full stop, running to the door. The hours stenciled in white on the glass are 9–5. I don't need to check my phone to know that we've missed the cutoff.

Rush leaves the Deathmobile in the middle of the lot, right next to the ancient chunk of redwood, not even bothering with a real parking spot. She runs up and starts knocking on the door.

"What . . . ?"

"You know how to dowse," Rush says. "But I know Tempest."

A woman in a woodsy-green polo looks out with a frown. "Closed," she says, muffled by the glass.

"Please," Rush says. "We have to do this research project and we both had work. . . ."

There's a long pause, and then a longer sigh as the woman comes around the desk and unlocks the door. "I'm not turning the lights back on. Close the door behind you when you're done, Rachel Downing."

Rush's lips tighten with a fake smile as the woman disappears behind the desk and then through a door into some back room. Rush gives me a real smile, gathering dusk along her lips. "Small towns do have their benefits."

I almost kiss her, but she turns away.

I wonder if that's something I get to do again, or if it was a one-time deal. All the certainty I felt in the graveyard is gone. Except, of course, for knowing that I want to be closer to her, touching if at all possible.

I follow Rush through the metallic trees bearing T-shirts and sweatshirts in green and purple and red. The colors look different in the low light, as if their cheerful daytime saturation was a lie.

I bring out the dowsing rod and spin a circle in the center of the space. It pulls me into a nature room for kids — a table covered with redwood pinecones, another bearing sculpted leaves from various native plants. A table filled with very real bones that belong to the animals that live here, and a little game to match them up to species names.

What does this have to do with Imogen? I want to ask.

But the dowsing rod is tugging. At the very back of the visitors' center, under a few streams of pitiful light, I find a room that looks more like a historical society than anything else, with little exhibits and large stacks of binders and record books. There's a display about the worst flood on the Eel River, the one that washed away a whole town. Prospero, California, according to copies of articles about the flood sitting under shiny glass. There are tiles from the roofs of houses that people ran up and stood on when the floodwaters rose. There are pictures of the rooftops, small unnatural islands in the swirl of water.

"Did you know about this?" I ask.

Rush nods in a vague way. "Everybody knows about the flood."

I turn from the exhibit to the record books. I slide the dowsing rod over the stacks, and everything feels smooth and normal and there's nothing strange here, nothing worth a second look.

Then I feel a snag, like a stitch that doesn't line up with the others.

I slip the dowsing rod back into its case and pick up the brown leather book that caught the rod's attention. The book feels good in my hands, perfectly weighted and solemnly right, so I turn back the cover. It opens clean in my hands, like someone cracked the spine to a certain page a long time ago.

It's from the year of the Eel River flood: 1926. Most of the page is taken up by pictures of the relief efforts. The bodies of houses washed up far down the river, wrecked on the shores.

My eyes keep moving until they reach a tiny paragraph at the bottom.

A young woman was declared missing: Emma Hart, daughter of James and Laura Hart, engaged to Robert Mason. She disappeared shortly after the flood, after the waters stopped rising. It was believed she ran off into the woods. There's no reason given, no source for the strange certainty, when she just as easily could have fallen into the still-high waters of the river. That's the whole story. Next to it is a picture, clearly taken before they started telling everyone *Smile for the camera.*

Robert Mason has a face that I've forgotten before my eyes have traveled all the way across it. But Emma — Emma has a hurricane of dark hair and a stiff white shirt. Her body fights the tightness of her blouse. The color of her eyes is impossible to tell, but they stare through the thin yellow paper, through the years between us that suddenly feel thin, too.

She looks at me the way the Grays do. Like I might save the world or I might be a complete disappointment.

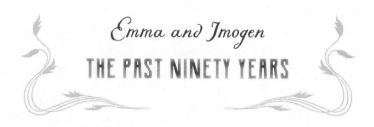

Emma and Imogen
THE PAST NINETY YEARS

The Eel River rose and rose. It was swollen and angry and it wanted everything. But Emma's house remained strangely untouched. Her beau was in the parlor, watching the engorged river with a fascination that made Emma's stomach turn.

She sneaked to the kitchen door, choosing to leave behind every concern about her parents, what they would think of her, how much they might worry. She ran all the way to Ada's house. It was right on the riverbank. It was dry as a bone.

Emma waited in the bushes outside Ada's house. When Ada didn't appear, she smacked Ada's window with pebbles, too hard, cracking the glass. Then Ada came out and shouted at Emma. "Go home. You need to stay safe."

"We don't have to fear anymore," Emma said, the water rushing by her feet without so much as touching her stockings. "If we lived through today without being touched, we must be a miracle."

Ada brought Emma inside and tried to warm her up by the fire.

"I'm not staying here another day," Emma said. The words wavered slightly, so she said them again, to turn them solid.

"I'm leaving, and you should come with me." She pounded up the narrow stairs to Ada's room and grabbed Ada's favorite drawing brush and ink. Then she drew a map on Ada's arm, as she had when they were little girls playing at being prospectors. She formed a big black X at the spot where they were supposed to meet.

Ada held her breath. She watched Emma as if she wanted to believe all of this was real, and not just some game concocted by a nervous, dramatic girl.

She watched Emma as if she didn't believe it at all.

That night, Emma spun through the dark woods. She waited at the place she'd marked on Ada's skin. Emma was alone for hours, and then days, but Ada did not come, and the world grew cold.

She stayed in the woods, only she didn't have her black shiny shoes anymore, or her heartbeat, or the hunger that had killed her.

At first, she clung to the spot where she'd died, an uneven basin where a mighty tree must have lived at some point. She thought staying there would help her move to the next thing, to pass to heaven or, more likely, hell, considering everything she'd been taught in her church pew on Sundays.

But she didn't pass on to any kind of *after*. And the longer she stayed, the more she came to understand that she wouldn't be leaving. Sometimes, Emma could feel other spirits thickening the air. They became part of the fog, drawn into the trees, a resting place for those without graves.

Emma stayed separate, different.

The years passed with the sticky crawl of molasses. Emma

did not grow older, and she never tried to find her way home. There hadn't been anything there for her, except Ada. Without Ada, she was lonely. When living girls wandered past Emma, she took to saying hello. Most of the girls looked up for a moment and then went on their way.

One day, Emma saw a red-haired girl walking with her shoes off. After decades of mostly silence, Emma's own voice sounded odd in her ears, like the rustle of dry leaves. "Hello? Hello!"

This girl's head snapped up. This girl didn't stop searching even after she'd looked over every inch of the grove. She called, "Who is that?"

Emma started talking, and her words flooded the woods. This girl, this *Imogen,* heard her, followed her, nipped at her heels. Asked her a hundred questions and then heaped on a hundred more.

Imogen's life and Emma's death wove together. Emma was older than Imogen at first, and she thought of her as a sweet playmate, a lively spark in a cold world. But as Imogen grew, her beauty and wildness wove together, too. Emma noticed. Imogen started asking Emma new questions. "What did you look like, when you were alive?"

"I had dark hair, I think. I never could get it to stay put."

Imogen laughed. "I can picture that. What else?"

"I . . . don't remember."

"You're *afraid* to remember." Imogen smiled, privately. "I'll bet you were soft and had the smoothest skin. I'll bet you were lovely."

Imogen visited Emma in the woods often, sitting by her

side with little more than a whispered greeting when someone else was near — most often Imogen's friends, the Grays. Imogen asked, more than once, if she could tell them about her. Emma didn't want that. She was afraid the Grays wouldn't believe in her, and it would break her heart all over again.

What do you want?" Rush says, not to me, but to the girl in the picture, running her hand over the article, using one fingertip to blot out Emma's face for a moment before she pulls it away.

I flatten my palm on the page with the news clipping about Emma's disappearance and pull it away from the binding of the book, wincing as the tear goes jagged. I make sure that the book is tucked back where it came from — not that I can imagine anyone noticing a single page being gone.

Rush and I leave the visitors' center without bothering the employee in the back room. Outside, the sky has committed to darkness.

I pull out my phone. Two dozen texts, half as many missed calls. It's a good thing I kept it on silent. Mom wants to know where I am. She wants to know who I'm with. She wants me to come home. *Now.* And then she unleashes the threats. She's getting better at them.

I never promised this would be permanent.

If this isn't working, we have to leave Tempest.

Back to Michigan?

I can't go back. Not now that I have the Grays. Not with my dowsing rod pulling me closer and closer to the truth of what's happening in Tempest. But there's also no way I can explain any of that to Mom. I fumble the phone into my pocket, lodging it there and trying to forget.

But Rush has noticed the state of my face. "Should I take you home?" she whispers, her soft disappointment cutting deeper than any nasty comment would have.

I stare at Rush, not even bothering to hide the force of how I feel. I might not have many more chances to look at her like this.

"No," I say. "If we're going to find Imogen, we have to do it now."

"Where to?" Rush asks.

I let the dowsing rod make that decision. I can tell from the feeling that I get inside, a long, stretched-out feeling, that we've got to cover some distance, so we get back into the car. As Rush drives, I text the Grays, telling them to meet us at the entrance to the nearest trailhead.

I let myself imagine that Rush and I might get a minute alone before everyone else shows up, but Lelia and June are already waiting for us at the turnstile with the NO WALKING AFTER DARK sign. Rush's headlights spill over them — Lelia's leather shorts and fringed tank top, June's star-spattered dress and navy knee-highs.

Hawthorn pulls Ora's truck in behind us and starts unloading bags of magical supplies from the back. Bottled cuttings of flowers snipped at just the right time of moon, pungent homemade oils, ten different kinds of salt.

I want to grab Rush's hand, gather some of her soft confidence, but I don't know what we are in the context of the
Grays. Alone, there are certain rules, and ways to warp them.
When we're with everyone else, it's probably best to keep
this quiet. Which makes me want to shout that I'm about to
kiss her.

I wait until everyone is slightly settled, and then I lean
back against the metal bars that separate us from the woods.

For the first time in my life, I don't feel like wandering
away from the topic. I explain what I know about the *why*
of Imogen leaving. I tell them the strange cut-short story of
Emma Hart. "I'm going to dowse for Emma," I say. "I think
that's what I did after I found her grave."

"What about Imogen?" June asks. "Wouldn't finding her
be easier than connecting to a spirit? I mean, she's still alive."
The hope in her voice could destroy a small town.

I finger the dowsing rod, the new combination of bow and
raven feather. "I tried to dowse for Imogen, but the trail went
in loops and circles." I skip over the part where my dowsing
kept throwing me headfirst at Rush. "It led me here, to Emma.
I think if we find Emma, we find Imogen."

"How does this work?" Hawthorn asks. It's the first time
she's looked to me to explain and not the other way around.
It reminds me exactly how much I'm making this up as I go.
I'm not the expert they need, the witch they wanted. I might
not even be here tomorrow. There's a good chance Mom is
furiously emptying her bank account to buy us plane tickets.

I open my mouth to tell them all of this, but then I look
around at Hawthorn's pressed lips, Lelia's cutting stare, June

fiddling with the zippers on her backpack. Rush lights one of the votives from Hawthorn's stash as she waits for me to reveal the plan. When I first got here, I thought the Grays were perfect, that they always knew the right thing to say or do. Now we're all huddled around a tiny black candle, trying to invent the next minute.

"Emma Hart died a long time ago," I say. "Searching for someone who's been gone for a hundred years is going to be hard. Her grave helped, but that can only do so much." I had the hermit's bones, but Emma's grave is empty. It's not really a physical piece of her that I need, though — more like a piece of her past.

I turn to Rush on a fresh wave of realization. "That book we found in Imogen's room," I say, grabbing her hands and hoping the other Grays think it's just overexcited Danny. Rush's fingers are warm, stirring, ready. "That wasn't just Imogen spilling her lovesick guts. It was a spell."

Rush shakes her head, not understanding. Or maybe she's still too afraid to let in the truth.

"Think about the likenesses we made," I say. "They required a piece of us. But . . . if you wanted to do that for someone who's been dead for a long time, and you didn't have anything left of them physically, you would need a symbol."

"Emma's name," Hawthorn says. "Imogen charged it like atoms in a storm, gave it power."

"We don't have time to build up to that." I slip my hand back into my pocket to make sure the flimsy page from the visitors' center is still there. I rub it between two fingers, in circles, the way you'd rub a charm. "But I have Emma's picture now. And . . . I might be better at this kind of spell. Imogen isn't a dowser."

It feels like blasphemy, admitting that there might be something I'm capable of that Imogen isn't. But whatever doubts the Grays are feeling, they bury them under six feet of longing.

I jump the metal bars onto the hiking trail and walk into the dark welcome of the woods. The massive trees seem more like living creatures at night, not just scenery. They stay awake and vigilant while the rest of the world sleeps.

I hold out my dowsing rod and chant, "Emma Hart, Emma Hart, Emma Hart."

The dowsing rod pulls me with a certain, almost vicious wrenching. A mile later, I've been keeping up an impossible pace, and I don't know how much farther this hunt will take me. I look back at the Grays, catching slips of them in the fog.

I'm leading them to Emma, but she could be the one who killed Sebastian and Neil. Who stole Imogen. She could be stealing us now. I do desperation math, hoping that five witches against one will keep us safe. That the Grays will forgive me if I'm making every wrong call.

The dowsing rod pulls until I'm breathless and my calves want to snap with the effort, but eventually dullness arrives in my chest, and I stop. I'm standing on the verge of a bowl of earth, shallow and wide, a place where a great tree used to stand.

"Death," Lelia says coldly. "This is where things come to die."

My heart suspends all beating.

"How do you know that?" I ask.

"Believe me," Lelia says, and I remember her mother. She knows the rough texture of the quiet here.

Lelia drifts away from the Grays and curls up in the basin. Her stillness scares me.

"Lel," June says. "Lelia, come back."

I've been sticking close to a tree with a thick, alive smell, loam and lemons. I step into the basin. I take out the thin sheet from my pocket and press it to the earth. "June, can I use your knife?" I ask.

She's behind me in a wordless second. "Pin it there," I say. "Please." She spears the page through the center, leaving Emma's picture untouched beneath the blade.

"Are you there, Emma Hart?" I ask. "Can you hear me?"

Fog moves in fast, rolling over the lip of the basin. The Grays disappear into it, one by one.

"Emma." My voice strains. Tips toward breaking. "Help me find you."

The space around me floods with fog, white as mushrooms and rich with damp. I blink, but I can't find any kind of balance as light swallows the darkness. I feel a strange prickle on my right arm. I look down, but I can't see my own body past the hollow spot where my neck meets my chest.

And then the fog snatches back, leaving the world a clean, starry black.

There is a map on my forearm. A map made of simple black lines. And up near my wrist, at the end of the path, is a juicy black *X*.

PART FOUR

BEFORE
MIDNIGHT

Emma and Ada
ONE HUNDRED YEARS AGO

Emma was born on the rainiest Tuesday in the bounds of memory or belief. Pellets of water left dents in the earth, turned the redwoods a sullen black. It ate the banks of the Eel River, but by some grace the river didn't flood. The town of Prospero, California, clung to life on the verge of the water.

Tiny Emma clung to life, too.

She grew into a red-faced child, prone to harsh moods as well as cyclones of glee. Her parents would come to wish, in quiet moments after she was abed and darkness had beset the world, that one of her brothers and sisters buried in the yard, marked by nameless stones, had lived in Emma's stead.

Her mother looked for ways to put things right. She found hope at the end of the lane, in the form of Ada Moore, a girl her daughter's age with straight pale hair and a disposition to match. She treated Ada like medicine for her sickly daughter. A dose for bad days. Two doses for impossible ones.

Emma and Ada took long walks, tracing the river from Prospero to the nearby town of Tempest. Emma wore her best shiny black shoes and her most intent frown. She handed Ada pebbles, but only the ones that glowed yellow or pink when they were wet. Like magic. She tugged the collar of her dress away from her sticky neck. She was not allowed to take her shoes off and splash in the water.

She was never, never allowed to go in the woods.

At school, Emma and Ada shared a desk, their hips fitted together snugly. When the teacher struck an iron bell and the students of Prospero carried lunch pails outside, Emma and Ada sat on the same stump in the schoolyard, their arms touching from shoulder to wrist. They spoke only to each other, always in whispers.

Emma's mother began to worry that she'd given her daughter too much medicine. "Is this typical?" she asked the schoolteacher. "Should we be troubled?"

"Girls are soft, sensitive creatures, prone to close friendships," the schoolteacher said, clasping her hands around Mrs. Hart's as if gifting her some natural truth. "Soon enough, you'll remember these days fondly. A girl like Emma is destined to become a handsome woman."

The teacher's prophecy came true with a frightening quickness. A year later, Emma walked arm in arm with Ada down the main street of Tempest, holding her sharp chin high but casting her eyes down whenever a young man looked at her. They checked to see if her cheeks had gone that telling rhubarb pink.

They hadn't.

"It's one thing to be humble and chaste, but you can't look away from every one of them," Ada said one night as she stabbed a pin through Emma's hair. It did nothing to restrain the great pool of it.

"*You* don't smile at any young men," Emma challenged.

Ada's frown thickened to a paste. "I'm needed at home." Ada's mother had died two springs ago of a fever that also took her brothers. "I don't have to worry about marriage. I won't have time for it."

The next day at school, Emma traced the word *spinster* on her paper over and over, though it wasn't one of the spelling terms.

That night, the schoolteacher paid the Harts a visit. Over dinner, when Emma had gone to the kitchen to fetch a plate of rolls, she leaned toward Mrs. Hart and said, "You might have cause to worry."

Less than a month later, Robert Mason, a young man from town who Emma barely knew, arrived at the Hart house for dinner. After stew and potatoes and pie, Emma found herself in the parlor with this stranger and his sickly pale face as he lowered himself to one knee. Her parents hovered in the background, donning masks of happiness so Emma would know how to look.

Before they took the engagement photograph, Ada spent an hour on Emma's hair and fussed over the mother-of-pearl buttons on her collar. She stood beside the photographer and blinked a little too often, blaming it on the great flash of the camera, rising in a puff of smoke.

Robert kissed Emma on the cheek. She shuddered. Girls in the schoolyard said that shuddering when a boy touched you meant that you were destined to be his wife. It meant Emma would love him soon.

Later, in Emma's childhood bed, she cried with her head

in Ada's lap, her body curled tighter than a young fern. Ada stroked her hair and told her in a low voice that everything would be fine, and Ada would help Emma raise her babies.

"We'll never be apart," Ada vowed, her hands cupping Imogen's face as she thumbed tears away. She kissed the most perfect one, and it tasted as salty as she imagined the sea. Neither Emma nor Ada had seen the Pacific. It was thirty miles away, through untamed redwood forest.

"Will I be happy?" Emma asked.

She waited for Ada to say *Of course*. When the pause drew on too long, her hopes narrowed. A simple yes would do. Emma looked up at Ada from where she lay on the bed, so that Ada's face took up the entire world.

Ada's fingers trickled through Emma's stubborn hair. When a few minutes had wafted past, Ada pressed a kiss to Emma's lips, and with it, she sealed every one of Emma's hopes. "I choose to believe you will," she whispered. "Someday."

The Grays
NOW

I t's a good thing we came prepared," June says, tugging her backpack straps. Her bag is deceptively large, fitting worlds of helpful items. She brought her athame, a tumbled piece of pinolith to keep her third eye open, black candle stubs to banish bad energy, a matchbook from the diner, one steel flask filled with water, another with gut-twisting cheap whiskey, and enough snacks to keep them going on a long, uncertain hike.

Lelia grabs Danny's arm and takes stock of the situation. She knows this map, or at least other maps like it. It's the shape of the Lost Coast. "Look," she says. "The X is more than half-way to the water. That"— she runs a finger along a dark, craggy line —"is the Pacific coast. Between Tempest and the Pacific is one of the oldest and most important stands of coastal redwoods in the world. Only trees. No towns, no roads."

"What does the X stand for?" Danny asks.

The Grays look at one another and take stock. They're all pretty sure they've made an important connection, but they want to check with one another before they share it. It's getting harder to give away pieces of Imogen. It feels like the pile is dwindling, and soon they might run out.

"Imogen drew a map like that once," Lelia says. "It led the hermit to the tree where he . . ."

The words *lived* and *died* blossom in the air.

"I'd call it a coincidence, but witch logic says otherwise," Lelia adds.

"Are we sure it's Imogen who drew the map?" Danny asks. "I mean, she's not the one I'm dowsing for."

"You think Emma did this?" Hawthorn asks, pushing her doubts around her face, twisting her features.

Danny stands there, clearly waiting for one of the Grays to tell her that she's ridiculous. Even if they're witches — Emma Hart has been dead for almost a hundred years, and there's no such thing as a dead girl drawing a map on your arm, leading you into the deep, deep woods.

June pulls out a granola bar and chases down a bite with whiskey. She definitely shouldn't have skipped dinner. Her confidence is not holding up to the notion of chasing a spirit into the depths of the Lost Coast. "Why would she draw a map exactly like Imogen does?"

"Maybe Imogen taught her," Rush says, trying to keep her words light. But it's all weighing on her — the secrets, the kisses, the places where the two overlap.

"Let's move," Hawthorn says. "If we're going to find anyone tonight, we have to get started."

The Grays head away from Tempest, their sandals and sneakers and boots marking the earth in a way that will be instantly brushed over, forgotten. They take turns using their cell phones as flashlights until the batteries start to die. They decide, one by one, to save their last sliver of a charge, just in case they need the phones in an emergency. Not that there's any service where they're headed.

Danny leads them down a slope into a great valley, each step plunging them deeper into a place that shouldn't exist in the modern world. This is one of the last places that people don't trespass, don't harm, don't scratch with their steps and clutter with their lives.

If the Grays get lost here, they are well and truly lost.

They've been walking for over an hour when Danny stops.

"We're looking for a special tree?" June asks, inspecting the tree trunks. Some are breathtakingly high, others are as wide as buildings. A few have bark that grows in straight strips, while the patterns on others twist in a tortured spin. Needles cluster high overhead, thickening into clouds. "They all look special to me."

"I don't think we're even close yet," Danny says, and the Grays' frustration gathers around her. "It's hard to be exact with an arm map." She pulls out the dowsing rod and holds it out, straight and certain. The Grays can tell she's been practicing without them—the way Danny carries the rod is starting to look natural, balanced.

But June thinks there might be something missing.

She digs in her bag and grabs her athame, feeling the lines of the labyrinthine pattern carved into the handle. "Here. Try this." When she sets it to the bow and the raven feather, it becomes a sort of handle and a point all at once. It gives the dowsing rod a focus, but also a dangerous edge. June can feel potential along the edges of the knife. It looks as if it could work its way through anything.

The other Grays are giving her a collection of doubtful looks. "Unless we're completely off base here, we're dealing with spirits," June says. "And spirits are somewhere else. Well, a somewhere else that overlaps with here. An athame can find where the worlds are thin and cut through to other places."

"Theoretically," Hawthorn says, the snag in her voice betraying that she doesn't really believe this — that her understanding of magic has clean lines. Boundaries.

Danny steps closer, closer, tugged into the circle of June's nervous breath. "Tell me everything."

June tells her about climbing and falling, slicing and seeing. About towers of fog where there used to be trees. She touches her leg as she talks, feeling it all over again. She hears Imogen say *It's okay. I saw it, too,* her fascination as sharp as June's athame. "I know there are ways in. I cut a window, but there have to be doors."

Danny
NOW

As Tempest loses its grip on us, it's like a hand that's been around my throat eases up for just a second. Which isn't fair, because I love Mom, and that same hand is probably closing around her throat instead.

Tighter and tighter, for every hour that I'm gone.

I look to Rush for some kind of comfort — or even just to share this new sense of fear — but her face is darkly shuttered. She closed up shop, and I don't know when she'll open up to me again. *If* she will.

I know she hates the idea of following Emma Hart, of messing with this spirit who messed with Imogen, but it's the best chance we have. Sometimes what you want and what you don't are knotted like that. Sometimes there's no real undoing them. I could explain that to Rush. I could tell her how I'm falling for her, and how Imogen is bound up with that whether I want it or not.

The closer we get to Imogen, the farther away Rush feels. For one foul pit of a moment, I think about turning back.

Preserving what I have with Rush, even if it's almost gone. They'll never find Imogen without me. If I leave now, they'll wander in circles all night and trail back into Tempest by morning.

I would never do that, though.

I would never leave them.

I set the path and the pace. The farther we go, the more fallen trees we find, slashing across the woods in great, sudden lines. They look like broken statues, fractured pieces of a lost world.

"Stop here," Lelia says when the moon is hanging straight above us, bright as a warning. "This is where the map ends. More or less."

"More or less," Hawthorn mutters, holding her hand out for June's water. The Grays are starting to look exhausted, and more than a little afraid.

How far would we have to walk before we died of dehydration? Exhaustion? How far do we push before we try a new direction? How do we avoid the death sentence of going in circles? Does Emma want five more dead bodies, to match the first two?

No one in Tempest would seriously question what happened to us. The weirdos wandered into the woods, thinking they could do magic, and never came out.

I hold the dowsing rod straight in front of me, locking my elbows. It droops and weaves. I stutter in one direction, then another, and the Grays try to follow me, but there's nowhere obvious to go. I stop in front of tree after tree after tree, watching each one like it might swing open a secret door. But the trees are silent, their faces blank. This feels like the night of the fog dance, when Imogen was nowhere and everywhere at the same time.

I grab Hawthorn's wrist. "You can scry trees, right?"

"Anything with a pattern in it," she says, looking excited to be doing something other than hiking.

I point at the newest tree the dowsing rod has picked, and the three before that. "Do they have anything in common?"

Hawthorn draws a line with her fingers. Her breath comes harder as she studies the trees.

One of them has bark that shoots straight upward. Another's bark is more cracked and crumbled, like the face of someone who has been alive too long and seen too much. The bark of the third spirals around the trunk. The fourth is softer, with deeper grooves, enough room for shadows to collect like rainwater. I've never noticed how different all of the redwoods are until this moment. I've seen them as part of a group. Like the way I saw the Grays when I first met them.

But they're each as different as they are the same.

"Birds," Hawthorn says, touching the bark of the final tree. "I see a flock of huge, dark birds with their beaks open."

Lelia's posture, which has been slouching lower and lower inside her thin jacket, shoots up tall. She runs behind June and without saying a word, unzips her backpack with a low metal growl.

She grabs a compact and flashes the mirror at the sky.

The Ravens
NOW

They lift. Wind and effort and the tilt of wings. The delight of dark against dark. The slide of body against sky. Silver flashes below them. Brighter than moon. Sharper than moon. It cuts into their eyes, pricks their hearts.

They want it.

They dive fast.

Holding silver, like a splinter of moon, is their friend Lelia. Known, good, help.

"What do you have there?"

They show what they found. *Who* they found.

Red hair. Bright, bright.

"Imogen," the others say. The Grays are known, good. They are Imogen's flock. "That's Imogen's hair," they say.

"Where is she?" they cry.

The raven with the curl snatches it away. *Not yours,* it screams. But it will take them to where they can find the rest. They lift — wind, effort, wings — and fly a straight line toward copper-girl.

Danny
NOW

We run.

We are mindless streaks. Muscles and blood. We run and we run and we run. The birds are a straight dark line above the woods, and I can't even begin to keep up with their confident glide. I weave around trees and climb their fallen sisters, leap and hit the ground.

"Slow down!" Lelia screams at the sky, flashing the mirror again. June is working hard to keep up, but her leg is obviously giving her hell. The ravens don't care. They've probably dragged us a mile, and now, with one last flash of black feathers against the night, they leave us behind.

"I need to see where they went," I say, looking up. "I need to get higher."

June grabs my hand and looks at me with all of her best, raw eagerness. "What you really need," she says, "is to fly."

"Is that something you can help with?" I ask, trying not to sound doubtful. I'm so tired of doubt. It's always dragging me in the wrong direction.

June does a quick scour of the trees around us and points out one that's thinner than most, dense with branches. "That's climbable." She shakes out her leg a few times. "I can't go with you, though."

"I don't do *up*." Lelia puts both arms around June, encircling her.

"I'm going," Rush says. "Obviously." That word darts around all of the defenses I've been putting up. My heart tells me two stories at the same time. In one of them, Rush is falling in love and she'll do anything for me. In the other one, Rush needs to get to Imogen and she will do anything for her.

"Quick," I say. "Before the ravens are out of sight."

I leave the dowsing rod with June. Lelia gives me a push that helps me reach the first branch. It takes a few more for me to find a rhythm. Reach, grab, step, breathe. Reach, grab, swing up, breathe. Rush is not the fastest climber, and I can't wait. I strike out quickly, seizing branches in a sloppy but powerful grip. At first I don't let myself think anything but *up*. Fear is one branch behind me, catching up fast.

"Danny!" Rush calls, but she doesn't say anything about going back down.

I can't wait. There is no more time to make this happen. The ravens will be gone soon, if they aren't already.

I grab for the biggest, heartiest branch above me. The one that's so thick I can scrape my whole body onto it, belly-first. Rush catches up to me, straddling a branch, both hands on a smaller branch above.

"Look out there." She points away from the body of the

tree. We've broken through into a layer of the world that most people never see. Needles and branches form a spidery sort of ground below us. Clouds above us, the color of smoky quartz, look touchable.

"Have you ever heard of astral projection?" Rush asks.

"Seriously?" I ask, my voice dropping several stories to the ground.

"Listen to me," Rush says. "Listen and don't lose the thread of my voice. I'm going to keep you safe. I'm going to keep your body here so the rest of you can wander. Can you do that?"

As Rush speaks, I imagine walking out on this branch, brushing lightly to the next tree. I think about branches dipping and skimming below my feet, and it's almost like it's happening. I test the air, and it's not solid, but neither am I. This is the dream that little kids have about flying — not a hard rush of wings, but a simple floating.

"Find the ravens," Rush says. "Find them and come back to me."

I take a few steps like walking across an old, worn-out mattress. I don't look down, because there's no reason to. The world I need is laid out in front of me. There's a dark smudge in the distance. The birds.

I arch my feet and strain forward. The air around me doesn't rush and tug as I expect it to. It's buoyant, with little swirls of motion. But somewhere behind all of this ease, I have a single fear, lurking.

Imogen.

She's out there, and the closer we get, the more fear hits me, cold droplets running together.

"Find them quickly, Danny," Rush says, and the rough confidence of her voice is rippled with worry. There is no real boundary between us right now, because our bodies aren't standing in the way, and her fear floats into me.

Something is wrong.

I try to turn around, but I can't. The needles on all sides are dark as inkblots. The sky is suffocating, the moon crouched low.

"Find the ravens and come back," Rush says. But backward is a different sort of magic than forward.

I know how to find people, how to leave people, not how to come back safely.

So I do the one thing that feels right. I cling to the little piece of Rush that I have — I hold on to her voice like a rope.

"Danny, come back," she says. "Danny!" And then I'm crashing through the air, blurring breathless past the trees. I come back into myself hard, and there is a moment when I'm so sickeningly solid, I think that gravity is about to claim me, that falling is inevitable.

Rush grabs my arms. She holds on to the branch with her legs. We're holding each other up. Our weight balanced. Our bodies keeping each other from falling. Our foreheads pressed together, gently.

The cold droplets I felt weren't just fear. Rain is hitting my skin, icing me through, attacking me in tiny cold bursts, and then the sky opens.

The Grays
NOW

The storm comes on so fast, it gives the Grays whiplash.

Hawthorn looks up at the sky, her glasses freckled with water, then streaming. June's eyes catch the sickly light of a storm. Lightning fills the clouds, brilliant through the gray. It rips out and strikes at the world.

Rush and Danny are tiny in the face of it. They are so far away, and the Grays can't do anything. It's the same helplessness they've been battling since the minute Imogen left. They can't lose anyone else. They can't walk back to Tempest with a smaller number of weirdos than when they left.

"They have to climb down," Lelia says. "Before . . ."

Thunder cracks the quiet night to pieces, shaking the ground so hard that the whole tree sways.

The Grays grab for one another, Lelia and June and Hawthorn holding on tight even though they're not the ones who need the safety net. June pours out the contents of her flowered backpack, but nothing in its depths can help them now. The wind is so spiteful that they can't even light candles to help draw Danny and Rush down safely. Hawthorn hands out luck crystals: the jagged citrine points shading from clear to yellow to purple, the smooth tree rings of tiger's eye. The Grays palm them with sweating hands.

That's small-time magic, though. It's more for their own comfort than it is for Rush and Danny's safe return. Lelia has never seen a storm like this one, and she keeps a record of every storm in Tempest. This moved in faster, roared down harder, and won't let up, no matter how hard they rub the stones. The rain grows into white fury. This storm is messing with them in a way that feels personal.

Lightning showcases Danny and Rush, stuck on a branch that they can't climb off without free-dropping to the one beneath it.

"This is what nobody ever mentions," June mumbles, as her leg sparks, hitting the top of her pain scale — part exhaustion from the hike, part anticipation of Rush and Danny crashing. "Down is much harder than up."

A voice slices through the clamor of the rain. "That's Rush," Hawthorn says. "Is she hurt?" But she's not screaming. She's singing as the girls drop, branch to branch. The notes are high and slippery and strange. And the feeling in what she's singing isn't *calm* or *safe* or even *down*.

It's *You can't catch me.*

Rush is turning the storm. The Grays lose the melody as lightning strikes the tree next to Rush and Danny, blasting the treetop bare, and thunder fills their bodies.

Danny slips, hanging one-handed. June's entire body fires

up with memory. With a perfect understanding of how this moment feels.

"Don't be afraid, Danny," she yells. "Fear is what fucks you over." If she clenches up now, she'll smack into branches on her way down, hit the ground tensed and hard. She'll shatter.

"Go loose all over, and then let go," June instructs in a hoarse scream.

Danny eases out of her grip.

Slowly.

She drops and hits the branch beneath her. The air is a tangle of screams. But Danny has gotten one arm and part of her chest curled around the branch, and slowly, painstakingly, she pulls herself back into control.

The fear leaves Rush's voice, and now she's not screaming but she is crying out, wild and fluttering and free. The Grays pick up that sound and throw it back at the sky. Louder. Harder.

Danny helps Rush down, giving her a place to step, a body to hold on to. She helps Rush all the way to the final branch, and then Rush is letting go. Hitting the ground. Rush is back with the Grays, where she belongs.

She looks dazed with fear and triumph.

Danny slides to the ground, cringing against impact. The Grays catch her. It's the least they can do. June pulls small, sticking bits of Danny's wet hair from her face and hugs her, jumping to keep warm, and kisses her, cold wet lips against cold wet lips. Hawthorn and Lelia do it, too. Then they tip their heads back and scream at the thunder.

"I didn't find the ravens," Danny shouts over the full-throated storm, the raging Grays. But no one is disappointed. That's a small-time feeling compared to what's coursing through them right now. Rush grabs Danny by the wet straps of her tank top and kisses her. Everyone has been kissing her.

But Rush doesn't stop.

Danny
NOW

I'm waiting for the end, but this kiss sprawls into a messy, beautiful beginning. Rush crowds my hips with hers, fists in my shirt like she's in the middle of an invisible fight and she can't tell if she's winning or losing. Her breath falls warm on my neck, and then she's kissing me at the soft branching place between neck and shoulder, working her whole body against mine, like she might be able to pass through me if she tries hard enough, like I am a doorway to somewhere she wants to be.

The Grays are watching.

They are silent, unblinking, blurry because nothing else can be perfectly in focus when Rush is kissing me.

"Whoa," June whispers.

"Wait a second," Lelia says, raising her hand. "I have questions."

"What about Imogen?" June asks, and I snatch back from those words like they're trying to burn me. I wonder how long I'll have to be here, how special they'll have to believe I am before anyone asks *What about Danny?*

It was bad enough in Michigan without having to worry about losing this feeling. The one I just got when I touched the electric arc of Rush's lower back and opened my eyes to find her face so close, eyes open and staring back at me, so blue I can't imagine any other color. It takes me back to the first time I saw the redwood trees. The scale was shattered. My heart couldn't adjust.

A feeling this big shouldn't exist.

It shouldn't even be *possible*.

I'm about to walk away from it, but Rush takes my hand and slowly, carefully, leads me away from the rest of the Grays.

"I'm sorry, Danny!" June cries after us.

Rush laces us between trees. Soon we are in our own grove, rounded on all sides by tall, thin trees — ones that look young, somehow, even though they're already a hundred times taller than we'll ever be.

Rush takes my hands in both of hers.

"Remember when you kissed me in the cemetery?" she asks.

"Of course." I remember every movement, every breath.

Rush inhales, like she's going to need the full strength of her lungs for what she has to do next. "You said it made your magic stronger."

"Yeah . . ." And then I see the rest. Rush wants me to kiss her so we can find Imogen. And part of me — the part that's made of magic — wants that, too. But the stupid boring Danny part is heartbroken.

"I love her," Rush whispers, and those words hit my heart like a widowmaker. I'm pinned to the truth. "I love her, and

I'll always care about her, and I'll never stop looking for her." She starts shaking, probably because she's wet and cold, and I put my hands on her upper arms, rub up and down slowly. Maybe it's strange that I'm taking care of her while she's saying these things, but she's got this look on her face that keeps me right where I am. "Imogen was never really with me. She was halfway gone before she disappeared, and I didn't want to admit it."

"And now?" I ask. I'm shaking, too, like it's contagious.

"Now I want something new," Rush says, her voice unfinished, unpolished, raw.

I push forward and kiss her. I can feel every layer between us. Flimsy wet fabric. Clammy skin. Fear. And none of it matters, because I'm grabbing Rush and kissing Rush and I'm not stopping.

Not for Imogen.

Not for anything.

She dances me backward. Even in deep silence, she has music in her bones. And then I'm pressed between Rush's softness and the soft bark of a tree. My head knocks back, and my teeth clamp down on my tongue, drawing out blood. My mouth goes salty-hot.

"Sorry," Rush whispers.

I don't want *sorry*.

"I want this," I say.

"Yeah," she says, kissing all along my collarbone. "I got that feeling." Before embarrassment at how unsubtle I am sets in, her smile curves and she's grabbing at her clothes, grabbing at mine. I feel like she would undress the tree and the ground and the night sky if she knew how. I tug at her hair, her hips, her thighs. I try not to think about her doing this with Imogen. I throw rocks at my thoughts, scatter them hard.

Rush stands back from the tree, taking on a silver glow that comes back now that the clouds are parting. The thunder and lightning have finally given up and the rain is starting to die off.

Rush's naked body is like the world at night, moon-brushed hills and soft, dark shadows.

"I'm ready," Rush says.

And I believe her.

When I push my hand between her legs, they fall open like a book that's been waiting to be read. She covers my hand with hers, gives me a guided tour of what she wants. I make circles to keep her safe. I make figure eights, tiny eternity symbols. I'm afraid, the whole time, that I'm on the exact edge of losing her.

But she said this is what she wanted.

And I believe her.

I lift away from the tree because I can't ignore how uncomfortable the bark is, all the places it doesn't fit my body. I'm a mess of bark, and Rush quietly brushes it off me until I'm naked again.

Then she lies down. And she waits for me, with a look that is patience and impatience in perfect tension, about to explode. I kneel, and the ground roughs up my knees. I remember that Rush hasn't done this with anybody before (not even *her*), so when I take hold of her hips, bend low, and brush a kiss on the inside of each thigh, touch my tongue to the exact place I've been aching for, I keep it slow. Gentle and lulling and sweet. She is earthy and salty, she is the dark forest near the sea, and I want to stay here, live here, never come back. Soon she's pushing against me.

And then I find it.

And she is flying. I slide my hands beneath her as her stomach rises, hips completely off the ground. She kept me safe when I was out beyond the trees, and now it's my turn. I hold on to her as she strains. Rush makes noises that are pure sound, not even an attempt at words or melody.

Then she blinks like she's just woken up from a very long sleep. I ask if she's okay, and she responds with the widest smile I've ever seen, shine moving over her face slowly as she reaches for me. She gives me a little nudge, moves me so I'm positioned over her, her body stretched long beneath me. Her hands move up and all over me, exploring unknown territory. She's not the first person to touch me, but no one has ever mapped my skin like this.

She pauses long enough to look up at me. "Hi, Danny." Somehow I know that she's tasting my name.

Her fingers spread over my hips, and I tip forward slightly, anticipating the warmth but still not ready for how good it feels, sounds rushing out of my mouth before I can stop them. I don't need to see Rush smile now. I can feel it. I can feel *everything*. It takes Rush a minute to find a beat that she likes, her hands pulsing on my hips. When Rush gives me a feeling so good that it's like crying from relief, I stare up past the forever-trees, to the pinpricks of stars, shaking as I take in the light of long-gone places.

I whisper her name — the one she chose — and try not to think of Imogen right there, helping her find it.

The last of the rain comes in ragged drips as we pull on our clothes. I stop to kiss freckles of rain off Rush's back, her shoulders, before she shrugs on her sweater, and all I can think is how strange the timing of that storm was. My thoughts are waterlogged. My skin is still soaked. No matter how hard I try, I can't seem to get dry again.

"Imogen was a water witch." The words came out of my mouth unbidden.

Rush doesn't say anything back. She's too busy pulling her boots, looping the silver laces and knotting them tight. When I look at her, I want to keep her safe. And all I can think is: What if Imogen caused the storm? What if she was the source of the salt water in the hermit's tree?

What if *You're going to get hurt* wasn't a warning, but a promise?

Imogen saw the same thing June did when she fell, and she was on the hunt for Emma Hart. What if Imogen believed that the way to cut through, to get to Emma, was less about a knife than the fear that came from falling out of a tree?

Near-death fear?

She cast a ward to keep her friends safe. She didn't really want to hurt them.

She just wanted Emma Hart.

With the Grays protected, she could have brought the wind, hoping that their fear and magic would open the way for her. But Sebastian was unprotected, and the widowmaker found his heart. She could have tried the same thing with the hermit — but Imogen's magic was difficult to control. It got away from her sometimes, like the day she almost killed Haven on the Eel River.

"What's wrong?" Rush asks, putting a hand to my wrist, over the blue spot where veins sit too close to skin.

"Nothing new," I whisper. The pieces have all been there, even if I'm connecting them for the first time. Maybe I've brought Rush — all of the Grays — into the depths of the Lost Coast so they can see who Imogen really is. So they can finally let her go.

I grab the dowsing rod. The bow with the athame strapped to it spins me in a vicious, dizzying circle, its magic stronger than I've ever felt. I don't think I could deny the direction it wants me to take next.

Rush grabs my arm. She's fully dressed, but her stare hasn't caught up. It's still bare of everything but wanting.

"I know where she is," I say.

The Grays
NOW

Rush and Danny come back looking exactly as mussed and breathless as the Grays expect. They've been huddled together as the rain drips to a stop, trying to figure out how long they should wait before interrupting. But now the missing pieces of the group are back, and moving fast.

"Come on, come on," Danny says, pushing them all away from the tree she and Rush climbed. "Imogen is this way."

"How did you . . . ?" June asks, letting the question dangle.

"I'll tell you later," Rush says, with the blush they've all been waiting for.

"Ohh, sex magic!" June says, clapping. "I've always wanted to try that."

"Is it really so obvious?" Danny asks.

"You might as well put a neon sign over your vagina," Lelia says.

Now it's Danny's turn to blush, a quick stripe across each cheek.

Her steps are so confident that the Grays can't keep up.

They form a fraying string behind Danny, Hawthorn and Lelia first, Rush falling back to help June.

June's leg has announced that it's done. "Please," she says, holding her thigh as it stings and sparks with pain. A nerve block might help, but she can't get one of those in the middle of the woods.

"Slow down, please," Rush yells ahead to Danny.

"Sorry, sorry," Danny says, lowering her pace from impossible to frustrating. June scrapes forward, one step at a time. She isn't going to be left behind, not when Imogen is this close.

"Listen, when we get to her, she's probably still going to be . . . partial," Danny says without turning back. The words float to them in dark wisps. "I think the rest of her is with Emma Hart."

"What do you mean?" Hawthorn asks.

Danny spins to face the Grays. She keeps moving, walking backward at almost the same rate she was going forward, picking her way around obstacles without seeing them. The pull she's feeling toward Imogen must be strong enough, clear enough, that she doesn't even have to look. "When people get lost in these woods, when they die here, I don't think they leave. Well, not completely."

June crashes forward a few steps, each one costing her a hundred quick-stabbing needles. "That place I saw with Imogen."

"Imogen told Rush she heard voices in the woods years ago. I think she's always been able to feel that place. And now . . . I think she's there. The part of her that's missing. I've been able to feel her all over these woods since I got here, but it's like feeling fog. It's everywhere and nowhere."

"We need to bring Imogen back," Hawthorn says. "The *whole* Imogen. That's the point."

"I'm not sure that's a fantastic idea," Danny says, her feet catching on a branch. It clacks like teeth biting down. "There's still someone causing problems. Someone who killed Sebastian and Neil."

"Right," Lelia says. "Imogen knows who. When we find her, she'll be able to fix things." She can feel, even as she says it, that her reasoning is thin, but she doesn't want to admit that. She tugs at her jacket as if it's armor against more than the damp night.

Danny stops walking. She looks at Rush and makes some kind of decision. A *no turning back* look. "Remember how upset you got about Imogen keeping secrets?"

"Yes," Rush says.

"I'm not going to do that." Danny talks directly to Rush, even though the rest of them are there. "This is going to be different."

Rush nods, but it's choppy.

"I don't want you to get hurt." Danny looks around at all of the Grays now, giving them a stare that they recognize, because they know Danny. She's asking them to banish their doubts and believe her. "I don't want *any* of you to get hurt."

"Of course not," Hawthorn says, urging Danny toward the point. She can't let Imogen's trail to go cold while they stand here.

But Rush needs more time.

Rush isn't ready.

She tries to tell Danny that without saying anything. She tries to spin a connection as strong as the one she has with Imogen, but that takes long-stretched years and the tiny stitches of moments.

"Danny —" Rush says, desperate.

"I think Imogen wanted to get to Emma Hart," Danny says, cutting her off. "The only way she knew to break through was for someone to be in danger. Falling-out-of-a-giant-redwood danger. Almost-dying danger. So she used her magic to . . . scare people. I don't think she meant to hurt anyone. It must have gotten out of control. It's happened before. She almost killed Haven once. And . . . I heard Imogen in the hermit's vision. She said *I'm sorry, Neil.*"

The silence of the woods feels so deep that the Grays could dip their hands into it, like dark water.

"How do you know it was her?" Hawthorn asks at last.

"She's the one with the water magic." Danny waits, clearly wanting someone else to lend their own belief to her theory. The Grays give her silence. "I mean . . . can you really not see this? Not even think it might be *possible*?"

The Grays would never think that. They would definitely never say it. Especially not Rush. *Imogen killed Sebastian and Neil.* Rush clenches, confused and angry. She can't believe that Danny would kiss her, touch her, take things so beautifully far — and then follow it up with those accusations.

Danny takes a step forward, and Rush takes one back, a reflex as deep as breathing.

"Why are you trying so hard to find her if you think she's a murderer?" Lelia asks, crossing her arms.

The Grays close ranks. June staggers over to Rush, who puts an arm around her waist. Lelia drapes one of her long skinny arms across Hawthorn's shoulders. They don't leave a space. Not for Danny. Not for Imogen. Not for anyone.

It keeps getting them hurt.

Danny finally slows down, stumbling toward an apology. "I wish there were another explanation. I thought you should know in case . . ."

Lelia and Hawthorn and June turn and walk away from Danny. They don't even have to discuss it.

"Where are you going?" Danny asks, her voice groping after them.

They don't turn back. They can't go soft.

"We're going to find Imogen ourselves," Hawthorn says.

"How?" Danny asks. "That's why you brought me here. That's why you need me."

"Maybe we only needed you to get this far," June says, picking up a walking stick and stabbing it into the ground.

Rush runs after Hawthorn, Lelia, and June. "We can't leave Danny in the woods alone." That word, *alone*, tastes hard and sour, an apple that will never ripen.

"She's a dowser," Hawthorn says with certainty. "She'll find a way out."

Danny
NOW

The trees close in quick, sew up the space where the Grays used to be, make themselves into one dark quilt.

I walk faster. The dowsing rod pulls me across the woods until I'm running, mindless and breathless to match. I don't know how many miles I am from the sea, but it's close enough that the air prickles with salt. Through the fog, I get a flash of what's going to happen next.

I'll find Imogen.

I'll drag her back to Tempest with me.

I'll show the Grays that I was right.

I've been running with my eyes closed, which I realize only when I trip. I have a red palm, a turned ankle. I get up, keep going. Pain distracts me and I lose my way. I focus on Rush, let the memories burn through my body, giving my magic something to run on.

I wonder how long it will last before it fades.

How long *I'll* last.

The dowsing rod tugs me hard and fast. And then, after all of those days I burned up looking for her, those nights I fell asleep with her red curls spilling into my thoughts, I break into a clearing and find a girl moving in a slow, vague circle around the most massive redwood tree I've ever seen. It could swallow all of the Grays. It would flatten stars if it fell.

Around the base, sticks have collected in a feral tangle. The thicket is a dark crown of branches, cracked and broken. I remember Lelia's words — a faerie ring. People thought it was possible to walk around one and find a way into a very different sort of place. A world of mist and trouble.

Another world. An overlapping truth.

Imogen's feet drag on the ground, caking dirt on her toes, as she walks around the faerie ring. She isn't traveling the secret inner circle between the tree and the ring. She must have gone in once, though, and wandered out like this. I don't know why she came back to the tree, leaving Tempest behind. But I do know one thing. This is Imogen's doorway. She found a way in that had nothing to do with hurting people.

The truth gets both hands around my lungs and squeezes.

The Grays were right.

Imogen didn't attack them or kill Sebastian or drown Neil in the hermit's tree so she could reach Emma. But I know her magic troubled the sky, summoned the water.

"Imogen," I say. "Imogen."

Her muscles stay slack, the red whorls and eddies of her hair streaked with mud.

"Imogen." I run to her, the dowsing rod between us, pointed straight at her long white throat. "Imogen, come here. Come back. The Grays need you. *I* need you."

Imogen blinks her way to the surface, dark eyes gathering force and personality. She points past me, at a spot behind me. I can't turn away from her, not while she's staring at me for the first time, truly seeing me. Pain slides over her face. "Danny. You brought her with you."

Then she's gone again.

And I know, completely and truly, that her voice is the one I heard in the vision. The tone was the same, blurry and afraid.

"Danny," says a second voice, and it's like someone held up a strange mirror to Imogen's.

You brought her with you.

I turn and find Haven standing in the negative space between two trees. She is wearing a dark-green hooded sweatshirt that makes her skin look viciously pale. I've seen it before. I've seen *her* before. She was walking under the tree I climbed with Sebastian that first night in the woods.

"Thank you for finding her," Haven says. She approaches Imogen and parts the red mess of her sister's hair down the middle. "Nobody would have done that for me." Haven's pain is clear and shimmering, almost something I can see.

"Haven," I say, taking a step closer when I should probably run. "You know what happened, don't you? With the boy who died?" It's not just my stubborn heart pulling me toward these questions. It's my dowsing sense. My magic tells me that the way to the truth is giving Haven a chance to tell it.

While Haven was making a bowl of cereal and spattering it with blueberries, she asked Imogen questions about what she'd done with the Grays, what big spell she'd been planning, and got no answer.

That was normal. Imogen had a policy of blackout silence when it came to magic. She pretended it was about Mom and Dad, but Haven knew Imogen was still punishing her for that day on the Eel River. Haven only knew about what the weird girls of Tempest did through the whisper-chain of other kids at school.

Haven put her bowl into the sink a little too hard, on purpose. She thought it might get Imogen's attention. She kind of wanted the bowl to break. It stayed frustratingly whole.

"Can you at least put the rest of the groceries away?" she asked as Imogen stared at the patterns in the marble on the breakfast bar.

Imogen stood up and did it, without hesitation or a single complaint, as if Haven had stuck a hand up her back.

As weeks went by, and Imogen remained blank, it became clear that Haven was the only one who had this effect on her. When anyone else talked to her or asked her to do things, they got the Nothing Show. At first, their parents thought this was a new brand of defiance. But soon they noticed that Haven could get Imogen to do chores around the house, to take out her homework at night, even if she left most of the spaces for her answers snowy white, untouched. Mr. and Mrs. Lilly liked the newer, blander version of Imogen. They also liked that they could put Haven in charge of her, like reverse babysitting. It was completely unfair. Imogen had taken up every breath of air in the house, every bit of attention at school, every inch of Tempest. Now she was mild and boring, and Haven still wasn't free to do what she wanted.

Every once in a while, when Haven was sitting at the end of Imogen's bed or walking her home after school, Imogen flickered through whatever was holding her back, like a moth struggling toward a candle.

Every once in a while, Haven missed her sister.

But most of the time she hated having to take care of Imogen after all of the years of living in her shadow. She *was* Imogen's shadow, flimsy and quiet, always where people expected her to be.

And then Haven got an idea. If she was going to be in charge of Imogen, she might as well have a little fun. She asked her sister to take her to the Grays.

Haven put on shadow clothes — quiet sneakers, a dark-green sweatshirt. She told Imogen to do the same. Haven moved like she would never be seen. Imogen had always moved like everyone was looking at her, and they usually were. But that night her sister was a murmur in the woods, leading Haven to the clearing filled with witches.

All Haven wanted to do was scare them. She wanted to punish the weird girls of Tempest, just a little bit. They did what they wanted, kissed who they wanted, called on magic like that was something you could just *do*. Like there would be no consequences.

Haven had seen what happened if you said you were a witch.

If you lost control.

Danny
NOW

You know what happened," Haven says, her voice so thin it has an edge that I could easily get cut on.

Imogen vanishes behind the monstrous redwood. It feels like she'll never come around the far side.

It's just me and Haven.

I keep one hand on the dowsing rod, afraid to move closer to Haven. Afraid to turn my back on her and run. "I need you to tell me what comes next, Haven. Because my guesses right now don't look very good."

"I'm not bad," Haven says, the words shivering out between locked teeth.

"I never said you were."

"A person can't spend every minute trying to be good and then turn out to be bad," Haven says, but the words are muttered, and they sound like they're mostly for her own benefit.

"You can fix this," I say, feeding her a lie and a truth at the same time. There's no changing what happened to Sebastian and Neil. She can let me walk away, though. She can bring her sister back. "Don't you want to help Imogen?"

Haven turns even paler than before, her freckles standing out darkly, her breath coming harder and harder until I think she's going to have a massive panic attack. "Imogen. Imogen. Imogen," Haven says, each repetition more biting. Haven points at me, one skinny finger straight at my face. "The storm was supposed to stop you. You didn't pay attention. That makes it your fault."

"That was you?" I ask. "The storm?"

"No," Haven says, twitching under the weight of my accusations. She locks her arms across her body. "No no no."

But I know now. She's been using her sister's magic.

Imogen comes into sight from behind the monstrous redwood, ringing toward us on her endless loop. Haven grabs her sister around her waist, hugs her tight.

"Tell her to come back," I say. "She'll listen to you."

"You're fucking wrong," Haven says, swearing in a way that reveals how little practice she has, the word exploding from her as if it's been waiting forever. She hardens her hold on Imogen, pale fingernails digging at her. "She ran away from me." Then she whispers in her sister's ear.

The ground that is supposed to stay under my feet rises up, inch by inch, a dark tide crawling up my legs. It froths like the edge of a wave, delicate-looking, but when I try to walk, to break away, the earth wraps tight. It holds me in place.

Haven takes a step back from Imogen. She walks around me in the same direction that the earth is wrapping me like dark, smothering cloth. "You were nice to me. No one is ever nice to me. I don't want this to happen."

"Then stop," I say as the earth grabs for my waist.

"It's too late," Haven says. "I can't stop it." As if she isn't the one who made this happen. As if she has no power at all.

I'm up to my chest already, being buried standing up. When I fight back, the dirt just crumbles toward me and fills in faster. It edges up to my chin. I have thirty seconds, maybe, before I can't speak. The dowsing rod is buried at my side, but I can still feel its power humming.

I look at Haven and I dowse, searching for the hidden words that will keep her from hurting me, but I can't find them. All I see is her paleness, her pain.

The dirt reaches my bottom lip. The smell of rich, potent soil fills my nose, drowning out the salt of the far-off sea. I've only seen the Pacific once, the day I got to California, when Mom and I walked all the way down to Ocean Beach.

Mom. She'll never know what happened to me.

The Grays will split apart, one of them gone and three people dead in their wake.

These aren't hard truths to find.

I can't talk now, can barely breathe through my nose, pulling in the last of the air as everything fills in, dark. This is the last thing I'll ever see, a tiny girl with red hair staring death at me. Dirt bricks over my eyes. Everything in me wants to scream, but I fight to keep myself silent. To control it. Keeping it in is almost as hard as dying.

The Grays
NOW

"**T**his is over," Hawthorn says, stepping into the clearing, using her most commanding voice, borrowed from Ora. She doesn't mind being her mother's daughter in a moment like this one.

The Grays emerge from between the trees, each one winding a piece of string around their forefinger, the tips as white as roots until they turn blood-choked purple.

"You can't kill all of us," Rush says.

"Someone will find out," Lelia adds.

"You won't be able to stand it," June finishes.

Haven cries out. She crumples to her knees. "I didn't kill anyone. I'm not a witch. Imogen is the one . . ."

The dirt covering Danny's body loses its hold, falling away. Danny breaks from it, collapsing. She slumps to the earth, breathing too hard, but at least that proves she's breathing.

This moment has the peace of an ending—but as it turns out, the silence and stillness are only the eye of the storm.

Haven crashes forward, her hands tossed out in front of her, palms to the ground. Dirt covers her. It swarms over her back, binds her to the earth. "No," she says, the word muffled, almost lost, as the earth presses her down. "No, you can't do this to me."

The Grays look at one another, trading strength.

"All we're doing is telling you the truth," Rush says, soft as lullabies, mild and sweet as warm milk.

"We're binding it to you," Lelia says.

"So you can't forget," June finishes. "Or look away from it."

Hawthorn crouches so she's right there in front of Haven, staring into the darkness this girl has gathered. Hawthorn takes Haven's chin in her hands. "So sure you're the victim that you won't look at the harm you've done, can't even name it. You let it loose on the world, though. You used magic — your sister's magic. You're not a witch, but the rules hold true. Whatever you do comes back to you threefold."

"Stop hiding, Haven," Lelia says.

"Stop hurting people," Rush whispers, cold.

"Make a new choice," June begs.

The look on Haven's face wavers, and for a moment there is a chance that she'll come back to the Grays, that she'll stop pretending she has no power here, that she'll change her ways and do no harm. The magic might still change its course, if she can face the truth of what she's done.

Haven's eyes pierce theirs with perfect sincerity. "I can't control it. I can't I can't I can't I can't—" Her voice stops like a snuffed candle, starved of air. The earth pulls so hard that it slips out from under the Grays' feet, swarming over Haven until she is a lump in the earth.

A burial mound.

The Grays unwind the strings from their fingers, letting their blood return to its normal flow. Silence brushes over the scene, and the only sound left is the soft drum of Imogen's feet, dragging her around the faerie ring.

The Grays gather near Danny, curled on her side. They help her up to sitting, and she looks confused that they are bothering with her when Imogen is right there. But she's not there, really. Imogen's eyes are still as misted over as sea glass.

Whatever happened to her is bigger than Haven's betrayal.

Haven and Imogen
TWO WEEKS AGO

That night in the woods, with the Grays so close, only the body of a redwood kept Haven and Imogen concealed. Haven went up on tiptoes, chanted into Imogen's ear. "Make them scared. Make them wish they hadn't come out here. Make them want to take it all back, run screaming out of the woods." Haven's mouth went dry. She stole glances around the side of the tree, watching the Grays.

Imogen flickered into her body for a second, looking down at Haven through a fog of confusion, which quickly burned off. "What are you doing, Hav?" She'd always been afraid her sister would snap. That's why she'd tried to brew a little reck-lessness in Haven, but the more Imogen tried to help her, the harder Haven recoiled.

And Imogen couldn't stop her from snapping now, because a second later, Imogen was gone again.

But her magic wasn't.

A storm stamped all over the grove where the Grays were meeting. It didn't hurt them. But the wind grew way past what Haven had imagined, and Haven didn't whisper for Imogen to stop it. She didn't *want* to stop it. Once Haven got started, once she broke those tight tight bonds inside her, she couldn't force everything back into place.

The next day at school, she heard about Sebastian. About the widowmaker. She learned she was a murderer from some junior who flung gossip around like it was free candy.

Haven told herself that she was safe. They couldn't trace the storm back to her. It was an accident, anyway. A mistake. She would never use Imogen's magic again. Haven didn't want to play this game anymore.

Danny
NOW

You came back," I say. I can believe the Grays are here, but maybe I don't quite believe that *I'm* here. Like if I blink hard enough, this might turn out to be a really nice hallucination right before I die, smothered by dirt.

"Lelia found Haven's footprints in the woods," Hawthorn says, standing in front of the little rise in the earth that covers Haven thoroughly. It looks like a lump caught in someone's throat.

Lelia smudges at the dirt with the toe of her boot. "Simple tracking stuff. Haven had a tight gait, size-six feet. Her shoes were smooth on the bottom. All of Imogen's shoes have decent tread — she wants to be able to hike around at a moment's notice. Her strides are huge. So are her feet."

I spit out clear strings flecked with dark earth as June rubs my back. I look up at them, eyes and throat stinging. "I shouldn't have said that about Imogen —"

Hawthorn waves a hand, her tourmaline rings catching the harsh moonlight. "You were right."

"And wrong," Lelia adds with an edge, not quite willing to let it go.

"It *was* Imogen's magic," Hawthorn says, setting the argument to rest. "Haven was using her."

Imogen comes around the tree again, wandering even though the Grays are right in front of her. She looks tattered to the point that I'm surprised she's lived so long in the woods on her own. But that's the least of it.

Her sister stole her magic, and two people died. When the wards broke, Imogen must have felt it. So she ran away, afraid that Haven would use her power to mess with the Grays again. I can't imagine knowing that someone you love could do that. Take your power. Use it to hurt your friends. Use it to kill.

The Grays wanted me to use magic to help them, but they never forced me. I made every choice myself, including the bad ones.

Especially the bad ones.

Some of those are the choices I'm most proud of.

I look over at Rush, standing directly in front of the girl she loved, the girl who's gone. Imogen doesn't blink. Rush takes a step to the side and lets Imogen pass in her endless rounds. I get up, brushing dirt from every part of my body.

I walk to the place where the faerie ring opens. It's a tight, tiny corridor of sticks and shadows. I can barely see a few feet in before it curves. The secret inner ring is a place that would be slightly terrifying even if it *didn't* open onto another world.

Rush joins me, our hands sliding toward each other, knotting loosely. Rush whispers, "I can do this part."

I shake my head. "It's why I'm here. Besides, you saved me. I'll save her. Then we'll be even, right?"

Hawthorn picks up the dowsing rod and hands it back to me. "You need us on this side," she says. "To keep you anchored."

Rush hums a single note, and then she does something new: she instructs Hawthorn and Lelia to hum two others. Together they form a single, dissonant tone. A haunted sound that hangs in the air.

"What is that?" I ask.

"Locrian mode," Rush says, breaking out of the chord for just a second. "It's for opening up doorways."

June pulls black candle stubs from her backpack. She sets them around the outside of the faerie ring, three steps between each, kneeling to light them. A tear slides down her face, drops into a sunken cup filled with shiny wax. At first I think it's only the pain from her leg, but then she whispers, "Imogen didn't let us do this for her. She might have made it out safely."

"She was trying to keep *us* safe," Lelia argues.

"That's not how things work," Hawthorn says, threading her arms across her chest. "She should have known better. If you want to do big magic, you don't mess around, even if you think you have good reasons. You trust your friends, your coven."

"Imogen should have told us about wanting to find Emma," Rush says, tightening her grip on my hand. I watch her chest rise as she takes a deep, filling breath and adds, "She should have told me."

I twist my fingers in hers, finding a stronger way to lock them together. I don't want to leave Rush behind.

She nods me into the faerie ring. I take the first step, and then I can't help glancing back. The look that Rush gives me isn't a smile, but it has the seed of a smile in it.

"Don't forget to come back," she says as I disappear.

PART FIVE

MIDNIGHT

Danny
NOW

I leave the Grays and Imogen in the grove. As I step deeper into the faerie ring, branches leave tiny all-over scratches on my arms, whispers of touch, each one telling me to turn back. I push forward, giving myself over to the faerie ring's stifling dark. I hold the dowsing rod out like a weapon.

I think about Sebastian, and how scared he would have been if I had asked him to go into a faerie ring for our second date. I touch my lips. I should have kissed him while he was still here.

The air feels trapped, old, a musty sort of wrong. I try to convince myself that I'm not afraid of the next step, and the next. But the lies I tell myself are as thin as the space between worlds.

I walk in a wide curve, wondering how long it can take to wrap around fully, even if this is the widest tree in existence. I try to look up, but between the thicket and the tree all I get is a snatch of stars, like stealing one last good breath before dying.

I know what that feels like now.

I push forward with the dowsing rod, and June's athame catches on something. Then it slides through clean, sharp, fast, stabbing this midnight and spilling its gray blood. The world doesn't just fill with fog; it *becomes* fog, overwhelming my senses without giving me a single solid thing to hold on to.

I step out of the faerie ring. I should come out in the same place I entered — there was only one opening. But it's different here.

For one, the redwoods are gone.

Instead, there are towers of fog, each one the sum of the fog that a tree would need to breathe over hundreds of years to stay alive. They form a forest of wispy columns that stretch from ground to sky.

I've been holding my breath, and when I let it out and take in a new one, I learn that this place has secrets instead of air. I pull in regrets and partial truths, betrayals and hopes that never came to pass, wishes that never left anyone's lips, so thick that they go down like syrup, making me cough. None of these feelings have names or lives attached to them. They're in pure form — floating — everywhere.

I think I would choke if it wasn't for the joy.

The falling-star plummet of first love, a slow wade into a long warm friendship, babies cracking the secret of how to smile, art being coaxed out of hiding places, hope brewed from nearly nothing, and stories brought to life, told on dark nights around a candle or a fire or any kind of beautiful glow.

The spirits in the fog of the Lost Coast are here with me. But even as these spirits wander, lost, I feel them tugged toward the towers of fog that, in my world, are trees. The red-woods have found ways to carry the dead, to invite them into their skin, to offer them rest.

But Emma Hart isn't resting.

I leave the tower of fog that used to be the tree with the faerie ring, walking farther into a land that I have no way of mapping. And all of a sudden *now* feels like a lonely place to be, without the past reaching out to hold my hand and keep me company, no future glinting with promises that keep a person walking forward.

Imogen.

She is the promise.

I keep walking forward.

I try to keep track of which way I'm walking and for how long, but apparently being a spirit means that I have to leave those kinds of certainty behind. My body is probably still caught in the faerie ring, as blank as Imogen's. I look down at my hands. They're made of something less solid than skin but more than mist. The dowsing rod slipped out of my hands at some point, and now I don't have the athame or Rush's bow or the raven feather to point my way. I only have the moon — the same as our moon, a bright pin keeping the two places together. The dark sky is clear, glassy and black despite the towers of fog, but there are no stars here.

There is a strange claustrophobia to this place, one that plunges me inward. I still have my heartbeat, faint but louder than anything in this wordless, muted place. Or maybe it isn't my heart at all. Maybe it's a different pulse, a whispered truth.

She's here.

She's here.

She's here.

When I find Imogen this time, there is no question. There is only a wisp of fog, different from all the other wisps.

Imogen's spirit is wandering, and I know that feeling. We've all been acting like she must be in danger, or dangerous — not *lost*. The Grays worship Imogen so much that they can't see that she's like me, stumbling and searching, always looking for more, not always sure where to turn next.

"Imogen?" I ask.

When the wisp hears its name, it springs into a girl-shape, a vague and beautiful notion. She holds up her hand, and I match it to mine. Our fingertips kiss.

"Tell me a story," Imogen says. It's the voice from the hermit's death. It's the voice from the moment before Haven tried to kill me. I try not to be afraid.

"A story about what?" I ask.

"About Imogen," she says.

At first I don't understand. But she's looking down at her shape like it's hollow and meaningless. She needs to fill it. She needs to remember who she is.

So I tell her stories borrowed from Hawthorn and Lelia and June and Rush, even Haven. Ones about the girls at school who wear her wards in tiny bottles around their necks. Ones about the witch who beckons water and the girl who summons loyalty from people's stubborn hearts. Imogen, who wore black and white even though her personality blazed in every color, like the rainbow stones on her fingers. I give her the places she came from: the split-level house with no door, the town that's in danger of shrinking back to normal size without her. I give her the people she came from: the family that never built her a safe home, the friends that became an entire world. I give her the stories I found when I was looking for her. I give her back to herself, beautiful and confusing and more than anyone could possibly take in at once, the way the far side of a redwood can only be guessed about from where I'm standing.

Imogen listens. She starts to interrupt, telling me details that I don't remember or never knew. The more she speaks, the more solid she gets. Loose curls and wide, intent eyes emerge from the mist, followed by the angles of her jaw, her high cheekbones, her pointed chin. I can't wait any longer. "When you disappeared," I say, "you were looking for a girl named—"

"Emma!" The way she says that name turns it to wildflower honey. "Emma, Emma, Emma."

Another wisp draws across the woods, dotted and incomplete. It finds Imogen and clings to her palm, dances around her fingertips like a tiny moon. Imogen murmurs her name again and again.

Emma has been lost for so long that I bet it takes a lot to remember.

Emma takes shape, broad shouldered and fog bodied, and she smiles. First at Imogen. Then at me.

"This is Danny," Imogen says.

"I thought you might come," Emma says.

I hold up my arm. The map is there, faded but with the X still visible. Emma nods, her eyes two mistlights, the pupils so large from the darkness of this place that they're orbs of black ringed with silver. She puts up her hand, and I match it to mine. Our fingertips kiss. I think this is how people say hello here.

"Why aren't you in the trees with the rest of the spirits?" I ask Emma.

"Magic." She sighs.

"You did a spell to keep yourself like this?" I ask.

"No," Emma said. "Magic keeps me apart from the rest. The bits of me that were alive are gone, but magic . . ."

"You stayed this way because you're a witch," I say. It makes a strange sort of sense. Magic makes life different — why wouldn't it make death different? "And Imogen found you because she's a witch, too."

"We've been friends for the longest time," Imogen says, glowing at Emma. "She's like us."

I try to smile at Emma, but guilt smothers it. I don't know how much she knows about me — but she knew enough to lead me here. "I'm sorry I thought you were trying to hurt Imogen. Or the Grays."

Emma nods and closes her eyes with a calm smile, as though she's absorbing my apology.

But Imogen looks troubled. A memory is working its way into her, one painful breath at a time. "Emma wasn't hurting people. Haven was hurting people. The last time I saw you . . ." She gasps like I pricked all of her fingers at once. "What happened to my sister?"

I wince. "She's gone."

Imogen hangs her head, and her edges blur. I'm afraid

she'll disappear back into the fog. "Imogen!" I cry. "Imogen, I tried to stop her. The Grays tried. They wanted to help her, but she was . . ."

There is a sound around us, like great bones breaking. Imogen takes my hand, and her memories of Haven slide into me. She was so small, so contained, so angry and sad. "I ran away so she wouldn't be able to hurt the Grays," Imogen said. "It was all I could do. It wasn't enough. People are dead, aren't they?"

I nod.

"Tell me," Imogen says.

I realize that I left out all those bits of the story, the truly bad ones. I push my hand through Imogen's, and I push the story at her. I feel it pass into her like a river flowing into an ocean.

"Your wards protected the Grays until we found your message in the hermit's tree. And then . . . and then we tried to protect each other."

"Your friends," Emma says, smiling at the thought. "I never had those. I had . . . someone I cared for . . . but I didn't have *friends*."

I didn't have friends either, before the Grays. That word was an empty outline until they filled it in. "I'm sorry," I say, and it feels like I'm crying, even though there are no tears in this place. If there were, it might be an ocean.

Emma purses her lips and steps into me, overlapping me, so I can see her truth without anything standing between us. Two girls, holding hands along the banks of the Eel River, wearing high-buttoned dresses and crow-black shoes, everything about them proper except the look they are passing back and forth.

One girl, about to be married off. When she looks at the man she's meant to love, nothing happens in her heart. *Our* heart. We're overlapped, every emotion doubled. It's overwhelming, but I don't step away.

A flood.

The memories come faster, harder, sweeping me under. I am drowned in her past, years and years of pain.

And then Imogen. She was the first good thing that Emma Hart ever found. Imogen is the happiness she waited for, years and decades.

Almost a century.

I step back from Emma, finally understanding why Imogen risked so much to find her. Imogen lays her head on Emma's shoulder, and Emma runs a hand over Imogen's hair. I've found the heart of another secret: the Grays are always touching and kissing each other because so many before us couldn't. Each kiss carries the weight of so many kisses that never were.

Every touch is an invisible battle won.

"I first thought I might be able to bring Emma back when I saw the cut that June's athame made," Imogen says. "And then . . . and then after what happened with Rush, I didn't know if I should try it. But it always felt like Emma should be right there with me. Even when I wanted to kiss Rush, even when I dreamed of leaving Tempest someday. There was a space for Emma that wasn't for anyone else."

Emma looks at Imogen like she's the moon, shining hard enough to light the whole dark world.

Imogen gets lost in that look for a second, and then she comes back to me. "It took time to build the spell. I had to find Emma's name. She'd lost it a long time ago. It would have been easier to tell the Grays, to have them help me, but . . . I didn't think they would understand. Or they would, and then they'd be mad at me for keeping so much of my life a secret."

Imogen kept parts of herself hidden. Imogen did magic by herself.

Imogen was not the perfect girl the Grays needed her to be, and she knew it.

But Hawthorn was right: Imogen should have trusted them. She could have shown them every so-called imperfection, every strange longing and rough patch in her heart. They would have loved her anyway. Maybe they would have loved her better if they knew all of her.

"Why are you still here?" I ask. "If the whole point was to bring Emma back?"

"Blowback." Imogen hesitates, and I nod at her to keep going. I know what blowback is, thanks to Hawthorn and the failed wards. "The spell brought me here, to Emma, and I thought I would be able to carry her out with me. But I couldn't. My magic wasn't enough, or it wasn't the right kind, and I just . . . couldn't."

Emma gives Imogen a pained smile. She turns to me with a prim set to her features that I realize is worry. "We needed a witch with just the right ability." I look down at my arm.

Haven's storm washed away most of the map, but the last smudges are there, a faint but visible X lodged in the softness near my wrist.

Emma brought me here for a reason. Me, not one of the others. "You think I can help you leave."

Imogen looks at the map on my arm. "I didn't know you did that," she says to Emma.

Emma looks down at the ground, and when I follow her gaze I see that it isn't earth but a shiny black mirror. "I was afraid you would tell me not to."

"You're right," Imogen says to Emma, and then she spins to me. "It was dangerous for you to come. You have to go home before you get stuck here, too." She's staring at me as if it makes all the difference whether I make it back — and that look brings her fully to life, just for a moment. I want to see Imogen walking down the main street of Tempest or standing on the mother tree, blazing red-haired, leaving magic in her wake like a trail of coins dropped from her pockets. I don't want to leave Emma behind either. She waited even longer than I did to find the Grays.

"Come on," I say, holding out a hand for each of them. "We're leaving this party together."

PART SIX

AFTER
MIDNIGHT

Danny

NOW

How did you plan to do it?" My words sound tissue thin. The breaths I'm taking barely dent my lungs. Or maybe I'm just remembering breathing; maybe I don't breathe at all in this place. "How were you going to bring Emma back with you?"

"I was going to offer her a place in my body," Imogen says.

I nod, gulping air that feels like frosted glass.

"It didn't work," Imogen adds. "I wanted to do it, but that's not the same as being able to. I guess it's not the kind of thing that any witch can do. I thought . . . I thought that loving Emma would be enough."

I try to find something inside me, something that I can shine up and call bravery. If I want to get all three of us out of here, I need to offer them both a place. Find space for them. And if I carry them out, Emma still won't have a body, and Imogen won't be able to carry her spirit.

"You would have to stay with me," I say to Emma.

Emma bows her head quickly, keeping her eyes — her truth — hidden. "I want you to save Imogen. That's all."

But she's been stuck here for lifetimes.

I think of all the loneliness, all of the nights when I went looking for a feeling that was less empty. Maybe this is the reason the Grays' spell pulled me here, of all the possible witches, all the dowsers in the world.

"Would you give me some time to, um, be alone? If I needed it?" I'm already thinking about Rush, about making sure that I'll be able to kiss her and know that she's comfortable and safe and happy.

Emma looks up at me and nods, her eyes eager. They flicker as a stream of fog rolls over us. "Ada," she whimpers. "Ada, where are you?"

"Emma," Imogen soothes. "Emma, Emma, Emma."

We need to leave. I remember that. The rest of it, though, is starting to slip away. I remember thinking this place was strange when I first stepped out of the faerie ring, but what if the place I came from is the strange one? What if sunshine and two-thousand-year-old trees and skin holding you separate from other people are the things that don't make sense?

The faerie ring is missing, and my dowsing rod is gone, and I have found so much, but I still don't know how to get back to the Grays safely.

This is the thing I'm worst at.

I don't tell Imogen and Emma. I find something inside me shaped like confidence, and I spin it into a bridge that's not really solid but might be solid enough for three girls who aren't fully there. Our feet pound over it, as the fog pours in all around.

It rolls over me, stealing memories.

Mom. All her hope, all her sadness. The ways I've let her down filling the air between us, making it harder to breathe every day. I see her in that little cottage in Tempest Gardens, making phone calls and talking to herself about how I'll come home soon and shaking until she can't stand up.

I run faster, but it's nowhere fast, the kind of speed that eats itself up and then dies. I'm forgetting everything. My life is slipping through my fingers like water, and then my fingers are water, slipping away from me.

"Stay with us, Danny," Imogen says. She runs beside me. She grips my arm. She keeps me whole.

I've known this whole time that the Grays love Imogen, but now I finally feel *why* — and I get the first inkling that maybe I could love her like that, too. Maybe this was about more than just bringing her back to the Grays. Maybe I get to keep Imogen, too. If we both make it out of here.

I turn in a full circle once, twice, no way to dowse now that I need it more than anything. I have no direction, no tugging inner compass or hidden magnetic lines. I can't find my way back to the faerie ring, back to my body.

I've lost the one thing I always had.

Myself.

The Grays will forget about me soon, and then I might as well be gone.

I remember the Grays even as I'm losing the rest of myself. Rush, Lelia, Hawthorn, June. I let myself believe, at least for a second, that I'll get to keep them. That there will be other nights in the woods, howling and dancing and drinking and kissing. That there will be gold days soaking into us as we string together new spells.

I hear a voice lifting through the fog. Just a tiny sliver of it, half muffled like it's pushing through the crack in a door. It's sweet and wild and high, and it tastes like October sunlight cooked down until it's as sweet as caramel.

It tastes like *Rush*.

I know this song. She was singing it in the graveyard when I pretended I wasn't there and she pretended not to see me. This isn't Imogen's song. I couldn't hear the truth before because there was too much in the way, but in this spirit-made world, the song comes clear. It scrawls a picture for me, a picture of a girl with her skirt caught in a strong wind, her hand to her forehead. She's searching for something. Always searching.

Danny.

Rush has taken me into her lungs and turned me into music. She's taken me into her mouth and melted me into song.

I hold on to Rush's voice and pull myself along that rope. I drag Imogen with me, and she drags Emma. The dark mirror of the ground slips beneath us, grows treacherous. But I can see the faerie ring, and Rush is just outside of it, Rush is here, Rush is singing me home.

Emma and Imogen
NOW

Danny takes a deep breath and inhales the wisp that is Imogen and the wisp that is Emma. They slide, loose and slippery, down her throat. They settle into her heart. Their weight changes the way Danny steps. Imogen feels how hard it becomes for Danny to keep moving, but she doesn't falter. Danny learns how to carry them with her. She takes them through the door, into a strange, terrifying, beautiful world.

They emerge from the grip of the faerie ring, past the cracked branches. The moonlight hits Danny's skin and goes deeper. Emma looks up at the trees with a dreadful sort of wonder. The woods killed Emma once, but it wasn't their fault. She was alone then, and no one should come this deep into the woods alone.

Danny, a girl who hardly knows her, agreed to bring her back. To share an entire life with her.

Candles flicker near Danny's feet, throwing unsteady shadows.

Imogen can feel Emma curled beside her, not quiet, a sort of ecstatic presence — the feeling that comes with a first kiss. There will be endless firsts for Emma now that she's part of Imogen's world. Imogen always loved this place, but loving Emma grew and grew until she couldn't imagine getting through life without Emma in lockstep, like two girls walking alongside a river. Now the fight that she's been raging against time, against two worlds, goes quiet, a river settling back into its banks.

The Grays are waiting for Danny.

A ring of them, eyes wide and pained with hope. Hawthorn has her arms crossed tight, as if she doesn't want to let this moment in. June staggers forward a single step, pain clawing its way over her hopeful expression, and Lelia holds her up with a linked arm. Rush is running toward Danny.

Looking at Danny the way she used to look at Imogen.

Guilt and jealousy and relief flicker through Imogen, all at once.

Rush is the first one to speak. Rush is *never* the first one to speak. "Did you . . . ? Was she . . . ?"

Imogen can feel it in that moment, stretched long with anticipation. They haven't stopped missing her. They haven't let her go, even though she kept so much of herself as close and quiet as a secret.

She thought that finding Emma meant losing the Grays forever.

She was beautifully wrong.

Danny
NOW

When I leave the faerie ring, the Grays greet me with a trembling kind of need. I don't know what to say. Where to start. Everything has changed inside of me, but the world looks exactly the same.

Including Imogen, walking in a circle, blank-eyed.

I run to her, a burning deep in my stomach. I grab Imogen by the shoulders and try to remind her what *whole* feels like. Remind her that she did the same thing for me, in a place that is very far away and probably right where we're standing.

I push forward, toward her pale lips. I tip my breath into her mouth, and I tell myself that I will stop in less than a second if this doesn't work. But her lips come awake against mine. Automatically at first, then slowly, knowingly, she dives into the kiss until she's taken everything she needs from me.

Then she leans back, holding me by the arms.

Imogen is red-haired and dark-eyed, with cream-top skin and a way of twisting her lips that makes the feelings flood deep inside my chest. She is everything that everyone has told me.

But it doesn't make me feel like less to stand so close to her. Maybe this is part of her magic, or maybe this is just part of Imogen, or maybe there's no need to draw a firm line between the two. When she smiles, everything good in me rises to the surface and stays there, shimmering in the light. In the first second of seeing her, I want to know her forever.

Imogen touches my lips with two fingers, thanking me for what I did. Then her smile pricks deeper.

"It's nice to finally meet you," she says.

Haven and Imogen
TWO WEEKS AGO

Haven took her sister into the woods the day after Sebastian died. She walked to the hermit's tree, the one that looked like it was always screaming. Imogen had told her that the hermit could figure out things about people that no one else could. That's what made him the hermit instead of a dirty college dropout living in a tree.

"Can you tell me how to get her back?" Haven asked, pushing Imogen in front of her. But the hermit was staring at Haven, swerving to fix her with his long-lashed southern-boy eyes, which was weird because nobody looked at Haven. It made her angry that it was finally happening now, at the exact moment she didn't want it to.

The hermit always wore shorts with a rat's nest of white strings at the bottom, let his hair grow out until it was one stupid inch past his shoulders, and even then he was pretty. Haven hated how pretty he was. She hated how he paid so much attention to Imogen.

"You did something wrong," the hermit said. "How could you do that, Haven?" He kept talking even though Haven desperately wanted to shut him up. To control the vomit of words coming out of his mouth. "You know it was wrong," he said. "But you went right on and you took from your sister and you called up that wind."

Haven wondered if this was Mom-and-Dad *wrong* or Imogen *wrong*. Had she finally found something that was both? The one thing they would agree on? That made her laugh. A wild sound, one that scared her, but when she tried to put it back in her mouth, shove it down her throat, she couldn't. She'd been keeping it down too long.

Now it was all going to come out.

Haven grabbed her sister by the wrist, too hard, making Imogen sway. She tugged her down and said, through another laugh that was also a sob, "Make him stop." But that wasn't enough. "Make it so he can't tell *anyone* what he knows."

The salt water of the tears that Haven didn't want to cry ripped away from her eyes. It swirled and grew. The hermit backed up until he was standing in the nook of his tree, safe and dry, but Haven didn't want that. The water rushed in after him, and Haven finally stopped laughing and crying as it covered his face, pushed its way into his mouth.

Imogen snapped out of her nowhere state for a single second. Neil, the boy she had convinced to stay in Tempest, was dying. She fought against her own magic.

She told the hermit she was sorry.

But if Imogen was really sorry, Haven thought, she wouldn't do this. She would stop it somehow. This was *her* magic.

Besides, Haven was sorry, too.

But she couldn't take it back.

The Grays
NOW

The second after Imogen comes back, the Grays flock to her, crowd her on all sides. They fling their arms around her waist, hold her close as if they're trying to absorb her.

"Hi, witches," Imogen says, pulling Lelia into her side even though her elbows are too sharp, running one hand through June's grown-out hair. "How long have I been gone?"

"Fifty-six days," Hawthorn says.

"Forever," June hurries out.

Imogen scowls, but both answers must be true, because the Grays can feel them at the same time.

"Where were you?" Rush asks, finally demanding the truth that she should have asked for a long time ago. She gives Imogen a hug but then flits over to Danny, quick and certain.

"I promise I'll tell you, but only after I eat seventeen plates of pasta at the diner," Imogen says. She starts across the grove, only making it as far as the dark lump of earth. Haven's burial mound rises from the grove like a tumor.

Imogen kneels and touches the earth. It feels muted, silent. "I want to do a spell to bring Haven rest. When we're away from the faerie ring, though."

"Why?" Hawthorn asks, touching the frames of her glasses the way she does whenever she's off balance. It brings her back to herself. She can learn how to understand this magic, even if it's not part of what Ora taught her.

Maybe this is her rebellion.

"Magic brings the worlds closer for a second," Imogen says, biting her lip.

Danny closes her eyes, lids crushed. "That's why you came back when Haven . . . used you."

"And when we cast the spell that broke your ward?" June asks.

Imogen nods. "I felt it. I knew Haven might come after you again, and there was nothing to keep you safe this time. And she was getting worse. I could think again, just for a little while. I didn't know what would happen, but I had to leave Tempest. So she couldn't use me against you."

That was how Imogen ended up here, circling and circling Emma's redwood, drawn to the place where her spirit was trapped. That was why she almost died in the woods — to keep the Grays safe.

Danny

NOW

Instead of walking back to Tempest, we hike the last ten miles to the coast. It's closer, and the smell of salt is as tempting as anything at the Tempest Diner. June pushes the rest of her granola bars at Imogen so she'll be able to make it out of the woods. Hawthorn and Lelia take turns helping June keep her weight off her right leg. We walk and walk, and then we're standing on the edge of a cliff, at the edge of the world.

Lelia looks down at the churn of white against rocks below us and a deep pool just beyond. The water looks clean and cold, and it holds a dark mirror to the stars. "I don't do *up*," Lelia says, bouncing on her feet. "But down works." Lelia leaps off the cliff, and my heart flies with her.

She bobs in the water far below, screeching, slicking back her short pale hair. "Come on! The water is amazing! I mean, it's really fucking cold! But that feels *amazing*!"

The rest of us work our way down a sandy cliff path with ice plant on both sides. Lelia joins us when we make it to the beach, jumping to warm herself up. I hold the ocean in sight, a tiny patch of it, and I try to imagine the rest. The water stretches out, away from me, and I know that this is only where it starts.

Emma has never seen the Pacific before. Every time I stare, she asks me to stare a second longer. It's a sort of gentle nudge inside of me, strangely polite. I haven't told the others about her yet. Imogen knows, of course. But I don't want to keep secrets from the rest of the Grays. And Emma doesn't want to live a half-life.

"I brought her back with me," I say.

"You really did it," June says giddily.

Hawthorn and Rush and even Lelia grin at me — they think I'm talking about Imogen.

"Emma," I say. "I brought Emma Hart back from the place where Imogen was trapped."

"What?" Rush asks, suddenly nervous. She stares down Imogen, like it must be her fault. But this was my idea.

I take Rush's hand, carefully, matching her fingers to mine. "I couldn't leave Emma there. She's like us. I wanted a chance to be happy, and she deserves that, too. I had to try."

The water runs up the sand and kisses Imogen's toes. "Danny is carrying Emma."

The Grays stare at me. Was this the way I looked at them when we first met? But it's not that bizarre. I've seen how the Grays carry the ones who came before them, the ones who looked and felt and fell in love like us.

"So is this like the hermit all over again?" Lelia asks. "He . . . controlled you."

"No," I say. "She can't control me. She's just *with* me." It's a truth that I can feel all the way through my body.

Imogen kisses my cheek. "I'm so glad it worked," she says, and the words seem to travel deeper, all the way to Emma.

Her spirit flutters.

Rush is still holding my hand.

"Are you okay?" I ask Rush.

She nods. Slowly. Carefully.

"I wanted to tell you about Emma a long time ago," Imogen says, and now she's reaching out, one hand on Rush's shoulder. Seeing them touch doesn't have the sting I thought it would. We stand like that, all of us joined for a long, awkward minute.

I don't know how this is going to work: me and Rush and Imogen and Emma. I don't know where this will lead us, but I'm the one who finds things. Hidden things, desperately needed things, paths no one else would notice. I can find us our way.

Water rushes in fast, covering our feet, breaking the moment. Imogen gives us a smirk, and I wonder if that was her magic at work.

We head down the beach, a long thin line that follows the bottom of the cliffs. The sand is gritty, harsh, and Emma loves the way it scrapes against my toes. We all strip down to our underwear, and the rest of the Grays run straight for the water, but I stand at the exact spot where the waves can't quite reach. I sink my feet into the sand until I hit water. And then Lelia comes up behind me and shoves me into the ocean, and I'm stinging in places that I didn't know were bloody, where the sticks of the faerie ring must have bitten into me.

I feel a soft tap on the chin. It could be the wind, or it could be Emma asking me to look up at the moon. I do, falling backward until I'm floating. I let the water carry my body, the words of the Grays breaking around me.

Rush swims over, slicked with water and coated in starlight. Her drenched camisole clings to her in all the same places I want to. The flush that fills my body is only mine. It doesn't belong to Emma or the Grays or anyone else.

I kiss her, and she kisses me, her legs sliding against mine under the water, and we kick to keep ourselves afloat, spinning and grabbing on to each other, and I can feel the future coming for us like waves gathering far, far offshore.

I swim with the Grays and let Emma feel the soft hold of the water, and when I'm too cold to stand it, I head toward shore. Waves break against the backs of my legs, pushing me gently toward the beach. The Grays get out and stretch out on the beach in their underwear and bras and tank tops, soaking in the moonlight like the weirdos they are. They wave at me and shout as they get covered in sand. I run over and join them — they're *my* weirdos.

Hawthorn gets up and starts drawing something in the sand with a long stick.

"What is this?" I ask as I get closer.

It looks like a bottle.

"Lie down inside of it," June commands, and when I do, they press in around me, standing above me, their salty-wet seaweed hair dripping, their smiles crowding out the moon.

"What am I supposed to do?" I ask.

"You're supposed to pull everything about this moment in and keep it," Hawthorn says.

"That's what Grays do," Imogen informs me.

She's telling me that I'm one of them. They're all inviting me in. I breathe those words in deep and add the feeling of the sand under me and the water drying on my skin and the smell of California, balmy and soft.

"What if I don't get to stay?" I ask, thinking of Mom and her threats.

"You'll still be magical if you're in Michigan," Lelia says.

"And you'll still have us," June promises.

"But you should stay," Rush adds, in that raw voice of hers that doesn't even try to hide what she needs. I love that voice. I don't want it to be a fading memory at the other end of a long-distance phone call.

I scramble to my feet. "I'll be right back," I say, already running down the beach. I reach the small pile of my clothes, and my skirt drinks in salt water as I pull it over my legs and find the lump of a cell phone in the pocket. It feels like a guilty swallow that I started taking hours ago, one that's been stuck in my throat all night.

There's something I need to do.

I take it out, turn it on, and start dialing the only number I know by heart.

"Mom?" I say, tears streaking my voice. "I'm alive."

"Danny," she says. "Danny, Danny, Danny." And it keeps going, her voice reminding me who I am, and she doesn't stop for the longest time.

ACKNOWLEDGMENTS

When I was a teenager, I moved three thousand miles away from everything I knew to live in the redwood forest of Northern California. To everyone I knew during that wondrous time — thank you.

This book is for everyone who is finding out who they are, where they belong, and who they belong with. This book is for the different ones, especially those who live where it's very hard to be different. I see you. I think you're magic.

My heart is indebted to all the people who make LGBTQIAP folks safer and happier and help us find one another. In particular, I'd like to shout all the way back to Michigan, to Tirzah Price, who literally made me cry when she told me about a new GSA and an upcoming Pride parade.

Lily Anderson, you befriended these witches when they needed you most. Allyson Capetta, you read and gave notes when you probably should have been planning your wedding. Writers of the first Rainbow Workshop (aka Queer Pete), you are the squad I've always hoped for. Let's all be Grays together.

Sara Crowe and the Pippin team, I'm so proud to work with you.

Thanks to the Vermont College of Fine Arts community, especially Nova Ren Suma, who inspired me to embrace the ghosts when they showed up in my book, and Will Alexander, who gave me the organizing principles for a complicated story — and this quote from Charlie Jane Anders: "Every spell is a manifesto."

Big love to the Candlewick team for embracing this book with all their thoughtfulness and care. Matt Roeser, you designed the cover of my dreams, and Sherry Fatla, your interior designs are perfectly lovely. Betsy Uhrig and Hannah Mahoney, you copyedited and somehow wrestled a time line out of my manuscript, which makes you champions. Jamie Tan, working with you is a total delight. Allison Hill, and Jamie, thanks for your help with June. Christine Engels, thank you for your help with the beginning. Hilary Van Dusen, thank you for your help with everything!

Miriam Newman, you believed in this story before the first word was written. This book is deeper and weirder and even less linear because of your brilliance. I feel like we've been summoning this one together.

Cori McCarthy, I'll always remember that long night drive to the Lost Coast. We found the town that became Tempest, and the entire story spilled out from there. We found each other, and everything changed. You are what I was searching for.